❦ PRAISE FOR ❦

THE NIGHT GARDENER

★ "Lots of creepiness, memorable characters, a worthy message . . .
and touches of humor amid the horror make this cautionary tale one
readers will not soon forget." —*Kirkus Reviews*, starred review

★ "Storytelling and the secret desires of the heart wind together
in this atmospheric novel that doubles as a ghost tale."
—*School Library Journal*, starred review

★ "The eerie setting, the pacing of the plot and the cast of characters
—each of whom, in his or her own way, evolves as a storyteller—
makes this an ideal family read-aloud and a vacation pleasure."
—*Shelf Awareness*, starred review

"Auxier achieves an ideal mix of adventure and horror,
offering all of it in elegant, atmospheric language that forces the
reader to slow down a bit and revel in both the high-quality plot and
the storytelling itself." —*Bulletin of the Center for Children's Books*

"All proper scary stories require a spooky, menacing atmosphere,
and Auxier . . . delivers the goods with his precise descriptions of
the gothic setting and teasing hints of mystery and suspense."
—*The Horn Book*

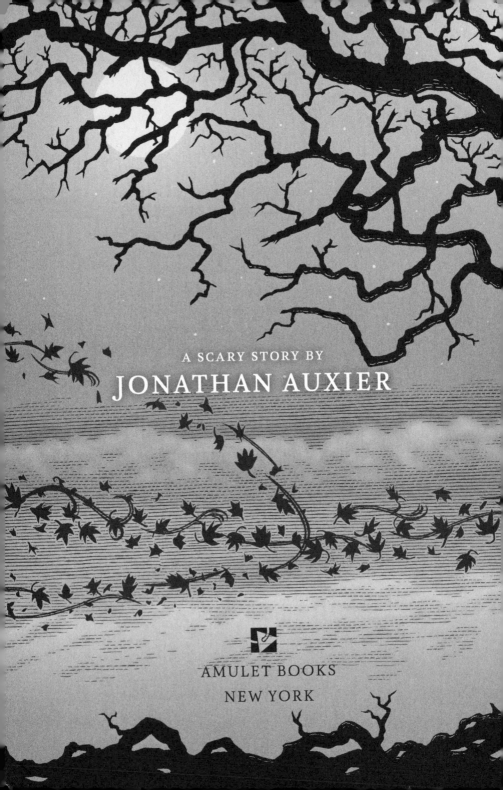

A SCARY STORY BY

JONATHAN AUXIER

AMULET BOOKS

NEW YORK

PUBLISHER'S NOTE: This is a work of fiction.
Names, characters, places, and incidents are either the
product of the author's imagination or are used fictitiously,
and any resemblance to actual persons, living or dead, business
establishments, events, or locales is entirely coincidental.

The Library of Congress has catalogued
the hardcover edition of this book as follows:

Auxier, Jonathan.
  The Night Gardener / by Jonathan Auxier.
     pages cm
  Summary: Irish orphans Molly, fourteen, and Kip, ten,
travel to England to work as servants in a crumbling
manor house where nothing is quite what it seems
to be, and soon the siblings are confronted by a
mysterious stranger and secrets of the cursed house.
  ISBN 978-1-4197-1144-2 (hardback)
  [1. Ghosts—Fiction. 2. Household employees—Fiction.
3. Brothers and sisters—Fiction. 4. Orphans—Fiction.
5. Storytelling—Fiction. 6. Blessing and cursing—
Fiction. 7. Dwellings—Fiction. 8. Horror stories.] . Title.
  PZ7.A9314Nig 2014
  [Fic]—dc23
     2013047655
  ISBN for this edition: 978-1-4197-1531-0

Text copyright copyright © 2014 Jonathan Auxier
Illustrations copyright © 2014 Patrick Arrasmith
Book design by Chad W. Beckerman

Amulet Books and
Amulet Paperbacks are
registered trademarks of
Harry N. Abrams, Inc.

Printed and bound
in U.S.A.
10 9 8 7 6 5 4 3

Amulet Books are available at
special discounts when purchased in
quantity for premiums and promotions
as well as fundraising or educational
use. Special editions can also be created
to specification. For details, contact
specialsales@abramsbooks.com or the
address below.

ABRAMS
THE ART OF BOOKS SINCE 1949
115 West 18th Street
New York, NY 10011
www.abramsbooks.com

❧ For Mary ❧
Halloo! my fancie,
whither wilt thou go?

OF MAN'S FIRST DISOBEDIENCE, AND THE
FRUIT OF THAT FORBIDDEN TREE, WHOSE
MORTAL TASTE BROUGHT DEATH INTO THE
WORLD, AND ALL OUR WOE.
— JOHN MILTON, *PARADISE LOST*, BOOK I

WE WOULD OFTEN BE SORRY IF
OUR WISHES WERE GRATIFIED.
—AESOP

CONTENTS

PART ONE
ARRIVALS

1

STORYTELLER AT THE CROSSROADS

The calendar said early March, but the smell in the air said late October. A crisp sun shone over Cellar Hollow, melting the final bits of ice from the bare trees. Steam rose from the soil like a phantom, carrying with it a whisper of autumn smoke that had been lying dormant in the frosty underground. Squinting through the trees, you could just make out the winding path that ran from the village all the way to the woods in the south. People seldom traveled in that direction, but on this March-morning-that-felt-like-October, a horse and cart rattled down the road. It was a fish cart with a broken back wheel and no fish. Riding atop the bench were two children, a girl and a boy, both with striking red hair. The girl was named Molly, and the boy, her brother, was Kip.

And they were riding to their deaths.

This, at least, was what Molly had been told by no fewer than a dozen people as they traveled from farm to farm in search of the Windsor estate. Every person they spoke to muttered something ominous about "sour woods" and then refused to tell them more.

"The *Windsors*?" said one lanky shepherd, whom Molly had stopped in the road. "I'd just as soon lead my flock to a lion's den." He propped himself against his crook, eyeing Molly from heel to head the way that men sometimes did.

"Be that as it may," Molly said in her most polite voice, "it's where we need to be. The Windsors were expectin' us last week."

"Then they can wait a little longer." The man summoned up some phlegm from his throat and spat it on the ground. "My advice: go back to whatever country you came from. The sourwoods is no place for anyone." He shuffled across the road and into the trees, a trail of bleating sheep behind him.

Molly sighed. That was the third shepherd that hour.

"What do you think they all mean by *sourwoods*?" Kip asked when the flock had passed and they were moving again.

Molly did not know, and so she made something up. "You dinna know about the sourwoods?" she said, pretending to be astonished. "Why, it's a whole forest of nothin' but lemon trees and lemon blossoms and lemon moss and lemon weeds. They say that when summer comes and the fruit is ripe, just breathin' the air will make your whole face pucker." She said things like this to let her brother know she wasn't worried.

But she *was* worried.

She and Kip had been riding almost nonstop for four days through rain and cold, led by a horse that barely tolerated them—due in part to the fact that Molly did not know the creature's name (she had told her brother it was Galileo, but the horse seemed to disagree). She had somehow imagined that English roads would be broad and level, but these roads were even worse than those back home. The mud was black and greedy, holding on to whatever touched it—including their back wheel, which had lost three spokes only the day before. What little food there had been in the back of the cart had long since been eaten, and now only a rancid, fishy odor remained.

"Are you cold?" she said, noticing her brother shiver under his coat.

He shook his head, which she could now see was damp. "I'm hot."

Molly's heart fell. Kip had been sick for weeks and showed little sign of getting better. He needed clean clothes. He needed a bed and a bath and a proper meal. He needed a home.

Kip stifled a cough against his sleeve. "Maybe all these folks is right," he said. "Maybe we should turn back to town . . . or go back home."

Molly couldn't allow herself to wish for that. She and Kip were an ocean away from the place they called home. She put a hand on his forehead, which was warm. "To hear you talk, a person'd think Ma an' Da raised a pair of quitters. We'll find the place soon enough—directions or not—and there'll be hot food and a warm bed and honest work."

They rode on, growing ever more lost, until midafternoon, when they came across someone unexpected. First they heard her song—a sonorous drone that crept around the bend, slow and seductive. The music became louder as they approached, and they could soon make out a voice singing. It was an old manikin woman, not much taller than Kip, seated in the middle of a crossroads, singing to herself. The woman was clearly some sort of vagrant, for she carried upon her shoulders a huge pack bound with twine. The pack contained a clutter of random objects—hats, blankets, and lamps—as well as more interesting things like books, birdcages, and lightning rods. It reminded Molly of a snail's shell. The woman was hunched over a strange instrument almost the size of her body. The instrument had a crank at one end, and when she turned the handle, deep notes came out that Molly thought might be what it would sound like if honeybees could sing.

Molly slowed the cart and observed the woman from a safe distance. She was singing about an old man and a tree; her voice was surprisingly sweet. Molly had seen beggars playing instruments like this before in the market at home. A "hurdy-gurdy," they called it.

"You think she's a witch?" Kip whispered to his sister.

Molly smiled. "If that's a witch, she ain't much of one . . . hardly a wart on her! Only one way to know for sure, though." She flicked the reins, and their horse moved a little closer. "Pardon me, mum?" she called out to the woman. "My brother here'd like to know if you're a witch or not."

The manikin woman continued playing, her fingers darting

along the keys. "I fear my answer will disappoint," she said, not looking up.

"So you *ain't* a witch, then?" Kip called, apparently wanting to be completely clear on this point.

The woman set down her instrument and peered at him, eyebrows raised. "Not everything old and ugly is wicked. I daresay that with enough years your lovely sister will look no better than I do . . . and it'll be *her* that's frightening children that come by!" She punctuated this with a suspiciously witchlike cackle. The woman struggled to her feet—which seemed a difficult task with so heavy a pack—and offered a neat curtsy. "The name's Hester Kettle. I'm the storyteller in these parts. I travel here and about, trading my songs for lodgings and food and odd things." She wiggled a shoulder, jangling the forks and wind chimes that hung from her pack.

Molly hadn't known there was such a job as storyteller, but it sounded like fine work. Telling stories was one of the things she herself did best. She had told stories to sneak her brother out of the orphanage. She had told stories to get a horse. And if she en-countered any questions at her new job, she would tell stories once more. Still, there was something about this woman that made her uneasy. "And pray, mum," Molly said, "what's a storyteller doin' all the way out here? On foot, no less?"

The woman shrugged, sucking something from her teeth. "I'm on foot because I've got no horse. As to why I'm here: new stories are rare in these parts. It's not every morning we get strangers come through the hollow. And two foreigner children with nary a parent between them riding due south on a stolen fish cart?" She clucked her tongue. "Why, that's a story if I ever heard one."

Molly caught her breath. It took everything in her not to look at her brother. "Wh-wh-who says the cart was stolen?"

The woman grinned at her. "That look on your face says it twice over, dearie."

"You take that back!" Kip said, surprising Molly. "We're no thieves. My sister bought the cart from a fisherman who had no use for it. He was joining the navy to fight giant squids." He beamed at his sister. "Ain't that right, Molls?"

Molly nodded vaguely. "More or less." She stared at the woman, silently pleading with her to drop the subject.

The old woman whistled. "*Giant squids*, you say? Seems the truth is more compelling than the lie." She nodded to Molly. "I apologize for accusing you in front of your brother. And let me congratulate you," she added, "for picking such a fine name for your vessel." She winked. "I've a feeling it suits you."

The woman was talking about the letters painted on their wagon. The side had once read ST. JONAH'S COD SHOPPE in gold script, but the paint had mostly worn off so that only the letters S, C, O, and P remained. "It's just a random jumble," Molly said. She didn't like this conversation. Something about the way the woman looked at her—looked *into* her—made her wary. "If you don't mind, mum, my brother and me are expected somewhere this morning."

The woman stepped near, blocking their path. "You're headed to the Windsor home, is that right?"

Molly tried not to look startled. "Do you know 'em?" she said.

"Not really. I did meet Master Windsor once, when he was no older than you. That was near thirty years back. Right before they shipped him off to live with relations in the city, poor thing." The old woman shook her head. "When he moved back here last autumn, family in tow . . . well, let's just say that surprised a few folks."

Molly didn't think there was anything strange in returning to the place where one grew up. Only a few weeks here, and she would give anything to be back home in County Donegal—famine or not. "We're a little turned around at the moment," Molly said. "We asked some farmers what roads to take, but they were a bit shy with the answer."

Hester Kettle nodded, looking out into the forest behind her. "Folks here think they're doing you a good turn by not telling you the way. None of them wants to be the one who steered two innocent babes to the sourwoods, foreigners though you may be."

"And what's so bad about the sourwoods?" Molly asked.

"Why, everyone in Cellar Hollow knows to keep clear of that place. Children are warned off by their parents, who were warned by their own parents, and so on as far back as any soul can remember."

"So you *don't* know," Molly said.

"Firsthand accounts are rare, but most folks claim to know some- one who knew someone fool enough to venture across the river into those woods." The woman hesitated for a long moment, her fingers playing at the edge of her patchwork cloak. "They say the sourwoods changes folks . . . brings out something horrible in them. And then there's *the other thing*. Tragic, really."

Kip leaned forward. "Wh-wh-what's the other thing?" he asked.

Molly clenched her jaw. The last thing she needed was this old loon filling her brother's head with frightening nonsense. She caught Hester's eye. The old woman seemed to weigh Molly's glare and then smiled at Kip. "Just rumor and hokum, luv. Why, half of it's stories I made up just to earn a meal. You'll be fine."

Molly nodded a silent thank-you. Whatever the rumors about this place were, it didn't matter. This job was their only chance to be safe and together. Who else would take in two Irish children with no guardians or references? Besides, if it were so bad, why would Master Windsor have moved his family there? "So, you'd be willin' to point us the way, then?" Molly asked.

Hester rubbed her chin as if thinking it over. "I would. But I might ask a small favor in return."

"We got no money," Molly said.

Hester waved her off. "Nothing so large as that, dearie. I only ask that you come around and tell me a story or two about what you find there. Ever since the Windsors moved back, the hollow's been all abuzz with curiosity. A woman of my trade could eat for a month on that information."

"That, I can do," Molly said.

The old woman stepped aside and pointed down a path to the

left. "Ain't three miles as the crow flies. Follow the sound of the river, and if you hit a fork, take the way that looks overgrown—sourwoods is the road less traveled by far. When you come to an old bridge, well, you're right on top of it."

Molly still wasn't sure whether the woman was being completely honest, but she decided that some directions were better than none. She thanked Hester Kettle, snapped the reins, and rode past her onto the rougher path. She and her brother descended into a gorge, and behind them she could hear the woman resume her singing. The haunting melody carried through the air, growing more and more faint. Molly wondered about what might be awaiting her and her brother at the house in the sourwoods, and what sort of story she might bring back for the strange old woman.

She wished, silently, that it would be a happy one.

2

THE SILENT TREES

Kip held tight to his bench as his sister drove them down ever-rougher roads. Despite all the old witch-lady's warnings, he still didn't know what to expect inside the sourwoods. At first the landscape remained largely unchanged—tangled forests abuzz with the life of early spring—but as they traveled deeper into the hollow, a prickling sense of dread came over him. Galileo must have felt it, too, for the horse became increasingly reluctant to go on. Kip glanced up at his sister, who watched the road with a stoic expression. "Have you noticed how quiet it's got?" he whispered.

Molly had apparently been too busy driving to notice. "And what of it?" she said, tugging the reins to keep them clear of a ravine.

"There's no birds, no insects, just the woods . . ." Kip swallowed, eyes searching the silent trees. "Like the whole forest is waitin' for us."

To this, his sister gave no answer.

Kip knew she was taking him to a house called Windsor. She had been hired by a man in some kind of office in town. But what sort of place that might be, she would not tell him. He suspected that this was because she herself did not know—though he would never say that aloud.

They pushed through the silence until they came upon a deep river that cut like a scar through the valley. They soon saw a large parcel of land right in the middle of the water. It was flat and covered with trees: an island of woods.

"That's the place!" Molly said to him. "We made it."

Kip forced a smile for his sister's benefit. To him, the sourwoods looked no more inviting than the rest of the valley. "I suppose I do like the idea of livin' on an island," he offered by way of encouragement. "Reminds me of home."

The only way across the river was an ancient bridge made from rope and wood that looked like it might collapse at the slightest provocation. Galileo took one look at it and stopped. He snorted and stomped, trying to back away from the water. After some coaxing and some more threats, Molly convinced the horse to venture onto the bridge. The structure groaned and sagged as their wagon rolled over the rotting slats, littering bits of debris into the river below. Kip held his breath the entire way.

The heart of the island had been cleared away to create an open field surrounded by dark trees. The lawn was not flat but covered in a series of miniature hills, each ranging between one and two feet in height. Wind swept across the grassy mounds to create an effect that reminded Kip of rolling ocean waves. At the far end of the lawn stood the Windsor mansion. The house had obviously been left vacant for some years, and in that time it seemed to have become one with the landscape. Weeds swallowed the base. Ivy choked the walls and windows. The roof was sagging and covered in black moss.

But strangest of all was the tree.

The tree was enormous and looked very, very old. Most trees cast an air of quiet dignity over their surroundings. This one did not. Most trees invite you to climb up into their canopy. This one did not. Most trees make you want to carve your initials into the trunk. This one did not. To stand in the shadow of this tree was to feel a chill run through your whole body.

The tree was so close to the house that they almost seemed to have grown together—its gnarled trunk running up the wall like a great black chimney stack. Palsied branches crept out in all directions like a second roof—including a few that appeared to cut straight through the walls. "It's almost a part of the house," Kip said softly.

Why any person would build a home so close to such a terrible tree was beyond him. Had it been too difficult to cut down?

His sister smiled and pulled him closer with her arm and mussed his hair with her fingers. Kip hated that. "Maybe they'll let us tie a swing to it. Or build a fort," she said.

Kip did not think building a fort in this tree would be a very good idea. He shrugged his sister's arm off and slid down from the bench, landing expertly on his good leg. His head was a bit light, probably from all that sitting still, and he had to steady himself with one hand on the sideboard. He reached under the bench and retrieved his crutch. His father had carved the crutch from the branch of a fallen wych elm on the farm back home. It was strong and thick and had just enough spring to be comfortable when he walked. His father had named it "Courage," saying that all good tools deserved a good title. Kip had always liked the idea that courage was a thing a person could hold on to and use. He fit the crutch under his left arm and tried to ignore how it was getting a bit short for him.

Kip hobbled around the back of the cart and lowered the gate. Inside was a battered wooden trunk with leather straps and no proper handle. It looked like something a pirate might use to store gold pieces, but instead of treasure, it held ratty clothes—everything they owned. "I still dinna see why we had to come all the way here," he said, struggling to pull the trunk free. "We coulda just stayed in town."

Molly hopped down and helped him. "You'd prefer the orphan-age?"

He glared at her. "No, 'cause I'm no orphan." The trunk dropped to the cold ground, nearly crushing his left foot—not that it would matter.

Something passed over his sister's face that Kip couldn't quite read. It was the same look she had been giving the old witch when they were talking in the road. It was a look that made his stomach clench up. Then Molly smiled at him, bending her knees so their faces met. "Of course you're not an orphan," she said, "but they'd have to put us somewhere until Ma an' Da came round to fetch us."

Kip swallowed his anger. He wished for the hundredth time that his parents were already with them; they would know better than to take a job in some ugly old house in the middle of some ugly old forest.

"Look here," Molly went on. "I got a present for you." She ripped the last remaining button from the flap of her coat. She cupped it in her hands like a treasure. "Do you know what this is?"

Kip tensed his jaw. He knew what his sister was doing, and he did not want to play along. "A button," he said flatly.

Molly shook her head. "Not just any button—it's a special *wishing* button. Watch close." She lifted her hands to her mouth and whispered, "Dear Button: I wish that right now my brother would give me . . . a kiss on my cheek."

Kip didn't move. Nearly eleven, he was a bit old for kisses and make-believe.

Molly shook the button. "Did you get that, Button?" she said a little louder. "All I'm askin' in the whole wide world is one teensy, wee, bitty, little—"

Kip knew from experience that she would carry on like this until he gave in. He leaned over and gave the smallest peck he could manage.

Molly gasped, staring at the button. "It worked!" She sprang to her feet, eyes aglow with awe. "Did you see that?! It really worked!"

"You shoulda picked a better wish," Kip muttered.

"Aye, perhaps." Molly took his hand and pressed the button into his palm. "I'm givin' this button to you, but only if you promise to make *really* great wishes. And also, you must promise not to cry or grouse or lose hope. I need you to be brave." She shrugged. "I dinna care neither way—but it's important for Galileo . . . He's a bit of a scaredy." Kip glanced up at the horse, who, for his part, snorted back at him. "You think you can do that for me?" she said.

Kip nodded, releasing a slow breath. He turned the button over in his hand. "But . . . maybe Gal's got reason to be scared. Horses got good sense."

"Not this horse," Molly said. "He hardly knows his own name."

She put a hand on his shoulder, and the two of them turned back to the Windsor house, which towered over them. A breeze moved past Kip, and the giant tree groaned against the siding.

Kip peered at something behind one of the branches. "Did you see that?" he said. Some movement behind one of the second-story windows had caught his eye. He stared at the heavy curtain behind the glass. It was swinging back and forth, gently—

As if someone had been hiding behind it.

As if someone had been watching.

3

MISS PENNY

hile her brother set out to find the stables for Galileo, Molly went to the house to speak with her new employers. She dragged her trunk to the front door and took a deep breath. All these days of travel—all the exhaustion and hunger and cold—had led her to this place: her only hope. Molly had resolved to keep a brave face for her brother, but now she allowed herself a moment of honesty. The house looked like something from a horrible fairy tale. It might as well have come with a drawbridge and boiling cauldron. "Be brave," she said to herself.

Molly had not been hired directly by the Windsor family—she had been hired by a solicitor in the city. The solicitor, a nervous man who licked his lips entirely too much, had apparently had some difficulty filling a position in so remote a place. Molly had been prepared to lie about references, but the man had assured her none were required. She need only make the journey and the job was hers. It was more than she could have possibly wished for. And now, at last, she had arrived.

Molly smoothed her skirt, pinched her cheeks, and tucked her hair behind her ears. Standing as tall as she could, she knocked against the door—

Creak.

It opened slightly. Molly hesitated, unsure if she was meant to enter. She peered through the crack in the door but could see nothing. "Hullo?" she called into the shadows.

"You can come in, if you'd like," said a small voice from somewhere inside. "We haven't a butler, and I'm not allowed to answer the door. But if you come in by yourself, I can't get in trouble."

Molly pushed the door open and carried her trunk inside. She shut the door behind her, blinking to let her eyes adjust to the dim light. She was standing in what once must have been a stately foyer. The air smelled stale, like an attic. Dust and dry leaves crowded the corners. Cobwebs dangled lazily from lamps and furniture. But strangest and most alarming by far was the presence of the tree, which seemed to have insinuated itself into the very architecture: crooked limbs grew straight through the plaster walls, thick roots pushed through the floorboards, and a broad, twisted branch hovered just below the high ceiling like a black chandelier. She stepped over some muddy tracks, peering into the unlit hallway.

"Up here!" shouted a voice above her. On the far side of the room was a great curved staircase that led to an upper hallway. Crouched at the top of the stairs was a pale-faced little girl with dark hair and extremely thick spectacles. The girl peered through the banister rails like a prisoner. "Who was that lame boy who kissed you outside?" she called down.

Molly raised an eyebrow. "The boy's name is Kip," she said.

The girl narrowed her eyes. "Is he your husband?"

Molly did her best not to smile. "He's my brother, miss."

The girl stood up. "Well, that's a rotten trick. Papa said someone might be coming from town, only he didn't say anything about one of them being a brother. I hate brothers—they're pests." She descended the staircase, hopping, feet together, down each step. Molly watched the girl, feeling a sense of relief. Surely a house with a child like this could not be too frightening. The girl took a giant leap from the bottom step and landed in front of Molly with an impressive *thump*. "Does your Kip have a tin cup?" she said, adjusting her glasses, which had slid down her nose.

"Pardon, miss?"

"A tin cup. I've seen boys like him back in the town where I used to live. They'd sit on the road looking cold and sad and hold out tin cups for people to put money in."

The question was innocent, and Molly tried not to let it annoy her. "The only cup he's got is for drinkin' water, same as you."

The girl nodded, as if filing this information away for future reference. "What is your name?" she demanded.

Molly bowed. It was clear enough that this little girl was a member of the Windsor family, and it would serve her well to win the child over. "Molly McConnachie. And yours, miss?"

"Penelope Eleanor Windsor, but you can call me just Penny because that's what everyone does. Or you can call me 'miss' like you already did—that's all right, too. I'm almost seven. How old are you?"

Molly demurred; she hadn't been exactly honest with the broker about her age, and she wasn't sure she wanted these people to know just how young she was. She put a hand to her chest. "Miss Penny," she said with a touch of horror, "a lady never tells her age."

The girl looked down, embarrassed. "I didn't know that . . . I suppose I shouldn't have told you my age, either. Can we pretend you guessed it all on your own?" She looked at the case at Molly's feet and then back to Molly. "Is it true you've come to live with us?"

Molly nodded. "It seems that way, miss."

"Well, I hope you do," Penny said. "You have no idea how *tedious* this place is. That's a word Alistair taught me that means no fun at all." She plopped down in front of Molly's trunk and started fiddling with the straps. "In our old home in town, we had all sorts of lovely things to play with—jewelry and silver teapots and china statues." She glared up at the house. "Here, there's nothing but cobwebs and spiders and nasty brothers." She finished with the straps and lifted the lid to expose a mess of old clothes.

"May I ask what you're doing, Miss Penny?" Molly said.

"Opening your valise. I want to see what's inside." The girl examined each item briefly before tossing it aside in search of something new. Her interest seemed to grow considerably when she discovered the unmentionables that were packed at the bottom, and she soon had a petticoat around her head like an Indian war-bonnet.

Molly looked down the hall to see if anyone might be coming. She didn't exactly relish the idea of her new employer walking into a foyer littered with her underwear, but Penny didn't strike her as the sort of child who was accustomed to hearing the word "no." Perhaps it was time for a more artful approach.

For as long as Molly could remember, she had possessed a gift with words. It was not magic, exactly. Rather, it was a way of talking that made other people believe in magic things, if only for a moment. It was a skill her parents had taught her to use carefully. "You know, Miss Penny," she said, sitting beside the girl, "where I come from, it's bad luck to wear someone else's clothes on your head."

"Where is it you come from?" asked Penny, squinting at her through a hole in the toe of some stockings.

Molly shrugged, affecting a casual tone. "Oh, an enchanted isle."

The girl dropped the stockings. "You do not!"

Molly pretended not to hear her. She hummed to herself, folding a discarded shift and replacing it in the trunk. Penny picked up the stockings and did the same. "Is it *really* enchanted?" she said, scooting closer.

Molly stopped humming. "Aye, but not in the usual ways. The whole thing's made of emeralds." She made a space for Penny on her lap. "Sit right here and I'll tell you all about it."

The girl immediately scrambled into her lap, forgetting all about the trunk. Molly reached out to either side, picking up the remaining clothes, answering the girl's questions as best she knew how: Were there fairies? (More than you'd think.) Could people fly and do tricks? (Yes, but no one likes a show-off.) Had she ever been chased by a monster? (Only a very tiny one, about the size of a toad.) With every word Molly spoke, Penny's eyes grew wider and wider—an effect made all the more pronounced by her thick glasses.

In a few short minutes, Molly's talk had utterly tamed the girl, who was now excitedly chatting about how much she might like to visit Molly's island and be chased by monsters. "We can catch fairies in a jar and then feed them to the monsters so they'll be our pets!"

The little girl turned to face Molly, her face screwed up in a way that suggested critical thought of the highest order. "Was it living on a magic isle that made your hair so orangey?" she asked.

Molly had never considered it quite that way. "I suppose it was, miss," she said, tucking a curl behind her ear.

Penny looked down at her own dark locks. "I wish *I* had magic hair," she said. "No matter how many ribbons Mummy puts in, it still looks terrible and dull."

Molly had to admit that the assessment was somewhat accurate. The girl's braids hung lifelessly from her head like a pair of black willow fronds. Still, Molly knew that no good could come of a person hating what they could not change. She put aside the last of the clothes and smiled at Penny. "Oh, but you *do* have magic hair!" She took a dark plait in her hands, examining it like a jeweler. "Have you ever heard of a lady named Queen Cleopatra?"

Penny shook her head.

Molly smiled. "Well, Cleopatra was the most beautiful woman who ever lived. Her hair was raven black . . . just . . . like . . . yours. And every man in the kingdom fell instantly in love with her. Even the great Sir Lancelot."

"Never heard of him," Penny said.

Molly tried again. "Perhaps you've heard of a man named *Robin Hood*?"

The little girl's eyes went wide. "Really? Who else?"

Molly leaned in close, her voice low. "You didn't hear it from me, miss . . . but some even say . . . the archbishop of Canterbury."

Penny gasped, both hands over her mouth. "His Grace fancies *girls*?"

"He most certainly does not," interrupted a voice behind them.

Molly turned to find a tall woman standing in the hallway. She had dark hair pulled back in a tight bun. Her skin was porcelain-white, just like Penny's, and she wore on her face a look of extreme unamusement.

"Mummy!" Penny sprang to her feet and ran for the woman, shouting, *"This-is-Molly-and-she's-from-a-magic-island-and-she's-come-to-live-with-us-and-even-though-she-has-a-brother-I-like-*

her–lots!" in a single breath. She grabbed the folds of the woman's skirt and collapsed to her knees. "I've never wanted anything so much in the whole world. Can we keep her?"

Molly stood and curtsied, eyes on the floor. "Only if it pleases you, mum."

The woman stood upright, arms folded. "Tell me," she said coldly, "do I look pleased?"

4

THE HELP

Molly stood against one wall of the Windsor kitchen. It was a large space with a walk-in pantry, brick furnace, dumbwaiter, and two service stairs. Kip, who had been called in from the yard, was leaning beside her.

Constance Windsor paced in front of them, hands clasped together, shoulders erect. "Have you and I met before?" The woman fixed her dark eyes on Molly, awaiting an answer.

"No, mum," Molly said.

The woman paused, brushing something invisible from the lace on her sleeve. Behind her were two children: Penny and an older boy, who looked extremely bored. "And when you approached this property, did I greet you and say 'Come in'?"

"No, mum," Molly said, unable to hide the tremor in her voice. She could feel her brother watching her, his eyes full of questions. She reached down and gently squeezed his hand.

"Interesting." Constance heeled around for another lap. "And yet I find you inside my home, uninvited, already unpacked, telling my daughter goodness knows what kind of nonsense about monsters and amorous clergymen." Even though she had not asked a question, the woman looked as though she expected an answer.

Molly shifted her weight, feeling the cold stone floor through the hole in her right boot. "It was just a story, mum. I didn't mean nothin' by it."

Penny, who had been listening from a safe distance on the far counter, hopped to the floor. "Mummy, you're not being fair. I was the one who let her in."

Constance gave her daughter a stern look, and the girl climbed back to her perch. The woman rubbed her temple, speaking slowly. "Surely you can appreciate how this looks from my perspective?"

Molly opened her mouth but was having trouble forming a response. At the present moment, she "appreciated" almost nothing. In the last half hour, what she knew—or thought she knew—about this house and this position had been turned on its head. "Forgive me, mum," she finally said. "I think there's been some sort of confusion. We was hired by an agency at the behest of your husband, Master Windsor."

"*Were* you?" Constance creased her lips. "I'm afraid that you, the agency, and my husband were mistaken. I have told him repeatedly, as I am telling you now, that I neither need nor want servants in my home. As you can see, I am managing just fine on my own."

Under other circumstances, Molly would have admired a woman who so boldly contradicted her husband. But now it only felt like some wicked joke. One look at the room they stood in revealed how little this woman knew about keeping house. The floors were thick with dust and grime. The walls, stained with mildew. Crumbs and spilled food covered every surface. Dirty pans and dishes spilled out over the basin. Molly had spent her whole life scrubbing and cooking alongside her mother. She knew what a well-maintained house looked like—this was not it.

"I say you have them both arrested. They're dirty and they smell like fish." The comment came from the boy leaning on the counter beside Penny. He looked about Molly's age. Like Penny and Constance, he had pale skin and dark hair. *Un*like them, however, he was exceedingly ugly: his wide face was marred with pimples, and his deep-set eyes were connected by thick eyebrows that met in the middle to create a single line. He was presently digging through a bag of toffees, apparently trying to stuff as many pieces as he could into his mouth at once.

Constance turned toward him, her face filled with some complicated emotion that Molly couldn't name. "Alistair, what have I told you about sweets before supper?" The boy rolled his eyes and spit the whole glob of chewed toffee back into his bag. It was a disgusting sight, but food was food, and it was all Molly could do not to stare.

"Lucky for the pair of you," Mistress Windsor went on, "I cannot heed my son's advice. There are no such authorities in this backward place. If you leave immediately, I shall consider the matter done with. As you can see, I have children enough to care for already. Surely you and your brother can find jobs in town."

Molly felt a hot flush of blood prickle her cheeks. Did this woman honestly think they would have come all this way if that were true? She had spent weeks knocking on doors, begging for work, then for food, then for mercy. At every turn, people had made it clear: they did not want her kind. "There are no jobs in the city," she said. "Not for us. If it's a question of money, we'll work for room and board, you don't even need to pay us—"

Constance cut her off. *"We do not need your charity."* She said this with such force that Molly stepped back. Who had said anything about *charity*?

"Mum, I gather your family lived in town before movin' out here. If ever you walked a street after dark, surely you know what kind of work falls to those in our desperate position? Please, if you knew what we've gone through these last weeks, all that's happened . . ." She could have said more, much more, but not with her brother beside her. She shook her head, eyes brimming. "My brother's health is fragile—*he's* fragile." She knew Kip would hate her for talking of him like this, but she had no choice. "We're only askin' for a chance."

The woman studied Molly for a long moment. "How old are you, child?" she said, her voice softer.

"Mummy!" Penny said, mortified. "Don't you know a lady never tells her age?"

Constance ignored the rebuke and waited for an answer.

Molly dropped her head. "Fourteen, mum." When she had applied in town, she had told the solicitor she was sixteen. "I know it's young, but I swear to you I'll work harder than ten grown-ups put together. My brother and me was brought up hard on a farm. I've kept house my whole life, and Kip can grow anythin'. He's got ten green fingers, and toes to match. Why, give him a month and he'll have these grounds lookin' like your own personal Eden."

"That and then some," Kip said, standing tall beside her. Molly smiled down at him and mussed his hair.

Constance watched, her eyes pained, perhaps understanding for the first time the weight of duty upon Molly's shoulders. "Fourteen . . . ," she said, as much to herself as anyone. "And your parents. What of them?"

Molly glanced down at Kip and then back to Constance. What could she say to make this woman understand? "Our Ma an' Da . . . they got slowed down a bit on the way over from Ireland. We're on our own."

"Goodness. I do hope it's nothing serious." If Molly didn't know better, she might have thought the woman was genuinely concerned.

"Oh, it's *very* serious," Kip said, eyes wide.

Constance raised an eyebrow at Molly, awaiting further explanation. Molly swallowed, her throat suddenly dry. "Well, mum, it seems that . . . as fate would have it . . . our folks was kidnapped . . . by pirates."

"They forced 'em to join the crew or else walk the plank!" Kip said, a proud smile on his face. "Just like young Saint Patrick!"

"How extraordinary," Constance said, her voice growing colder.

Molly wanted to say something—to explain that she wasn't mocking the woman—but she could only stare at her, eyes wide, trying to say with her face what she could not speak aloud. "Please, mum," she managed. "We've no one to turn to."

The woman blinked, shaking her head. "You do not know what you're asking, child. This house is *no place for you*." She said this without any bitterness. For a brief moment, it occurred to Molly that perhaps this woman did not want to be in this place, either. Constance kept her head down as she walked past Molly. "I suggest you leave before it gets dark." She opened the back door.

Molly stared at the wilderness waiting for her outside. Cold air rushed in from the door, cutting straight through her coat, rattling her bones. She watched Kip as he fixed his crutch under his arm and hobbled to her side, suppressing a shiver. Even in this moment, he was the picture of courage. "Not yet," Molly said, turning back to Constance. "Mum, we'll go, just like you told us. Out in the wild, not a word o' protest. But before we do, will you hear one thing?" If the woman had looked closely, she would have seen a tiny spark burning in the ring of Molly's green eyes.

"I suppose you're going to tell me I'm a wicked person," she said.

Molly shook her head. "No, mum . . . I'm gonna tell you a *story*." She swallowed, pushing away her fear and exhaustion so that she could focus on this woman in front of her—a woman who, like all people, longed to hear something that they had once known but since forgotten. "Imagine wakin' up tomorrow, like you always do," she began, "only there's somethin' a bit *different*. At first it's just a faint sound, a whistle at the back of your ear. The sound gets louder, and you realize: it's a kettle, callin' for tea." Molly spoke with a hypnotic lilt, and, behind her voice, you could almost make out the song of the kettle. "You open your eyes to a room flooded with warm sunlight. The curtains is already drawn apart, and your window's wide. You stretch and yawn—fresh air fillin' your lungs. Your clothes is already pressed and waitin' for you. And there, on the mantel, a jar of fresh-cut flowers from your very own garden." Molly saw Constance close her eyes and take a deep breath, as if smelling the phantom bouquet in the warm morning air. "You sit up, and your nose catches the delicious waft of hot sausages cracklin' in a pan and fresh rolls brownin' in the oven. And then, all of a sudden, there's a polite knock at the door, and . . ." Her voice trailed off.

"And?" Constance said after a moment.

Molly shrugged. "Afraid you'll have to hear the rest tomorrow."

The woman blinked, looking at her surroundings as if for the first time. Her eyes drifted from the dirty floor to the stained counter to the neglected pots and finally to her own children, huddled by the stove.

"You never make us sausages," Alistair muttered.

Penny slid down from the counter and rushed to Molly's side, hands clasped together. "Mummy, can't we *pleeeeeeee*"—she took a breath—"*eeeeeeaaaaase* keep them?"

Molly smiled down at Penny—this sweet little girl who wanted her when no one else did. She put an arm around her and faced Constance.

The woman shook her head and loosed a long breath. She shut the back door. "You will start this evening." She wrinkled her nose. "But first: baths."

5

Portrait of a Lady

Whatever warming effect Molly's story might have had on her new mistress, it did not last very long. The woman was as cold and impersonal as ever during her tour of the house and grounds. "Breakfast at eight. Tea at eleven. Supper at six," she said, moving briskly through the downstairs rooms. "I want new linens on the table before every meal. You shall cook from recipes I choose—you can read, can't you?"

Molly struggled to keep up. "Well enough, mum," she said, pinning back a strand of her still-damp hair. The bath had been her first in ages, and even though the water was cold, it felt wonderful to be clean. She was wearing a worn maid's uniform that was clearly meant for someone several years older (and several pounds heavier). She adjusted her apron and followed the woman into the hall.

"As you can see, I haven't had time to properly unpack our things," Constance said, passing some furniture and crates along one wall. "See that you take care of it."

"Yes, mum," Molly said. This phrase had quickly become the

girl's answer to nearly every command. Even if Molly had wanted to ask a question about one of her tasks, Mistress Windsor moved so quickly that there was scarcely time. Chamber pots cleaned by ten! *Yes, mum.* Floors scrubbed twice weekly! *Yes, mum.* Silver polished every month!

Yes, mum.
Yes, mum.
Yes, mum.

Molly repeated these words until they were burned into her mind. She felt certain she would hear *Yes, mum* in her dreams, pounding against her skull like a drum.

"And what about that room there, mum?" Molly asked, pointing to a rather smallish green door at the top of the stairs, which Constance had passed without comment. Unlike most other doors in the house, this one did not have a simple latch but instead boasted a large iron bolt—the sort used to secure safes and storehouses.

"You needn't concern yourself with that door. I don't even think we have the key." She gestured toward some muddy boot tracks in front of the bedrooms. "Do clean those up when you get a chance."

Despite her terse manner, Mistress Windsor possessed a refined quality that appealed to Molly. Molly had not had much opportunity to mix with the higher classes of society, and watching this woman was a rare glimpse into another world. Her clothes were not only well made but beautiful. The dark folds of her skirt hung from her slender frame at a perfect angle, ending just above—but never touching—the floor. From her delicate neck and wrists hung diamond jewelry the likes of which Molly had never seen before. Even her movements were elegant. *Like a picture come alive*, she thought to herself.

Mistress Windsor's fine appearance was made all the more stark by her surroundings. The woman looked completely out of place in this distressed and crumbling house, and Molly suspected that her occasional comments about their previous dwellings in town were spoken with a touch of longing. Every so often, Constance tried to engage Molly in what seemed to be her version of friendly conversation. These exchanges usually didn't go very well. "Your brother," she said, mounting the stairs, "how long has he been a cripple?"

Molly gritted her teeth. "He was born that way," she said, trying not to let her irritation creep into her reply. "Leg turned in on itself."

The woman waved a dismissive hand. "Well, whatever it is, I don't want the children catching it. He's to sleep in the stables."

Molly slowed. "The stables, mum?" Her brother's health was worsening; he needed to sleep in a warm bed—not in some drafty shack with animals.

"Or the woodshed, if he prefers."

"He's only ten, mum." Molly knew she should not speak out, but she could not help it. "There's plenty of beds in the servants' quarters—surely he can sleep in one of the rooms down there."

Constance faced her. "Out of the question. There's a reasonable fear of illness in this home. It wouldn't be the first time sickness had spread inside these walls." Molly thought instantly of what the old storyteller had mentioned out in the hollow about Master Windsor being sent off to town as a boy. "The other thing," she had called it. "And Molly," Constance said, stepping closer, "I am unaccustomed to having my orders questioned. If you so much as *think* of contradicting me again, you and your brother will find yourselves out in the cold before the words even leave your mouth. Are we clear?"

Molly stared at the woman, cheeks burning. "Yes. Mum."

Constance brightened, smiling. "Excellent. Follow me, then."

It was nearly evening by the time Mistress Windsor concluded her tour in the library on the second floor. It was a large room with furniture covered in gray tarpaulin sheets that were stiff with age. "My husband spends much of his time in town," Constance explained, "and so we have little use for a study." She pulled apart the heavy curtains to light the room. "You can see a dusting is in order."

The space looked to Molly like it had not been occupied in some time. The high walls were filled to the ceiling with old books. Molly, who had dreamed many times of being in possession of so rare a thing as a book, was overwhelmed. "Is Master Windsor a scholar, mum?" she asked.

"A scholar? Heavens, no!" She said this with the passion of someone who had just been asked if her husband were in the circus. "These books belonged to Bertrand's father. I understand he was something of an eccentric."

There was an audible gust of wind outside, and a branch from the giant tree tapped against the window behind Molly. She moved away from the glass, slightly unnerved. It seemed that wherever she turned in this house, there was the tree. "You know, mum, I could have my brother prune back some of them branches. Maybe patch the walls where it's broke through?"

"Would that we could," Constance said lightly. "Unfortunately, the tree has grown too close to the house. Disturbing it might threaten the foundations."

"Surely clipping back a few branches wouldn't—"

Constance cut her off. "Under no circumstances are you or your brother to touch the tree," she said, her voice like an icicle. "Do you understand?"

"Yes, mum." Molly could feel her cheeks flushing again. She had only meant to be helpful. Just when it seemed like her mistress was becoming kinder, the woman would lash out at her for no good reason. She scanned the room with her eyes, trying not to let Constance see her frustration.

And that was when she noticed the portrait.

It was a large painting, almost up to Molly's shoulders. It leaned against the fireplace mantel, waiting to be hung. The impressive gold frame was wrapped in protective cloth that had come undone on one side, leaving it half-dressed like a Roman emperor. Behind the cloth, Molly could make out the four members of the Windsor family: Constance, Alistair, Penny, and a man she took to be Master

Windsor. Only it wasn't the family as she knew them. Their faces were plump and healthy, with bright eyes and ruddy cheeks. Instead of dark hair, they all had chestnut curls. Molly studied the painting, unsure of what to make of the image. It was one thing for an artist to flatter his patrons, but this seemed altogether different.

"Is something the matter?" Constance said, startling her.

Molly looked at the face of the woman standing beside her. It was the same mouth, eyes, and nose—only now her skin had lost its color. Her once-blue eyes were pools of black ink. Compared to the figure in the painting, Constance looked drained and frail. "Is . . . is that you, mum?" she said, pointing to the portrait.

"Who else would it be, child? We had it painted last summer. Just before moving here, in fact." *Last summer?* Molly marveled at how the woman could have looked so different only a few months before. Constance stiffened, feeling Molly's eyes on her. She touched the back of her dark, straight hair. "Perhaps it's time you started supper," she said and walked away.

Molly remained behind a moment. A breeze wuthered through the house, and the tree outside scraped against the glass, almost as if it wanted in. She inched back a step, looking again at the painting. The four faces in the portrait smiled out at her, happy and healthy. Something sinister was changing these people, and they didn't even seem to know it. Molly covered the portrait and retreated into the hall.

6

The Figure in the Fog

T he servants' quarters were in the basement floor of the Windsor house. Molly had been allowed to pick any room she wanted, and she chose the one with the fewest spiderwebs and an actual bed— such as it was. Beyond those amenities, the space was dank and spare. She had a wardrobe and a small dresser with a mirror mounted above it. The ceiling was stained with mildew. In several places, roots from the tree had broken through the walls, creating a veiny relief pattern beneath the faded wallpaper.

Molly and her family had always slept together in one room, and the idea of having a space all of her own both thrilled and frightened her. She dressed for bed, making a mental list of all she needed to do the next morning. She took comfort in the idea that "next morning" was no longer a thing plagued by uncertainty and fear—too many nights she had gone to bed with an empty stomach and heavy heart. Upstairs in the foyer, the grandfather clock chimed twelve times. Midnight. As if awaiting the hour, a dark breeze swept across the grounds outside. Old boards groaned as the wind pushed against cracks, searching for a way inside the house. Molly's room had a window above the bed—just big enough for a person to fit through. She took her lamp and perched it on the sill. She blinked the light three times with her hand, like a mariner signaling a passing ship.

A few minutes later, she heard a rap at the glass. Molly opened the window to find Kip crouched in the mud. "Boo," he said, wind grasping at his hair.

"Boo, yourself." Molly took his crutch from outside and propped it against the bed frame. She grabbed him under the arms and helped him through the window. "Remember what we talked about: you're to be up and away by dawn—before anyone sees you." Molly knew it was dangerous to disobey her mistress, but she also knew that her brother needed some place dry and warm to sleep. "Watch your boots," she warned too late as he touched down on the mattress. "And shut that window before any leaves get in."

Kip was a little out of breath and his cheeks were flushed. He peered over his shoulder, searching the darkness outside. "Comin' over here, I coulda swore someone was followin' me." He shut the latch and carefully climbed to the floor.

Molly set to making the bed. "Well, did you tell him to stop?"

Kip sat on the floor to remove his boots and trousers. "I ain't foolin'. I was out at the stables, waitin' for your sign at the window. All of a sudden this wind comes and it gets real dark—no moon, no stars. That's when I seen your light, so I set to walkin' over here. I'm halfway to the house when the hairs on my neck stand straight up. It was like I could *feel* it, Molls, right behind me. I turned around, and there, in the fog . . ." He shook his head. "For half a heartbeat, I thought I saw someone there, watchin' me."

Molly continued with the bedding, trying not to look alarmed. It was her fault that he came up with such things. Her fault for stuffing his brain full of goblins and witches and giant squids. "I thought you said it was too dark to see," she observed.

"Well, I could see *this*," he said through the nightshirt over his head. "He was real tall, dressed all in black, with a tall black hat. I walked a few more steps toward the house and looked again . . . but he was gone."

Molly helped her brother into the freshly made bed. "He probably got a look at your face and was scared off," she said.

"It's no joke," he insisted. "Something's wrong with this whole place. You seen how pale they all are—it ain't natural."

"That's just how folks look in England." Molly suddenly felt very glad that she had not told Kip about the portrait in the library. There was no reason to add to his worry. "I'm sure we'll get used to it." She blew out the lamp and lay down beside her brother. She stared at the ceiling, letting her eyes adjust to the night. In the shadows, she could make out the place where a thick root had broken through the exposed wooden beams. After all these weeks of struggle, she and Kip had finally made it to a safe, warm bed. And yet she couldn't shake the feeling that they shouldn't be here.

"Molls?" Kip said softly. He was staring at the cracked button she had given him earlier that day. "Why'd they have to go round the world without us?"

Molly propped herself up on one arm. "You know well as I do, Kip. They didn't want us gettin' hurt."

He nodded. "Drowning."

Molly swallowed a lump in her throat. "Aye. Or that."

Kip turned toward her, his eyes shining in that little-boy way that spoke of distant adventure. "Do you think they've seen any dragons yet?" he asked.

"I'm sure of it. The ocean's full of 'em. Maybe, if we're good, they'll even catch one for us." She looked at him, very serious. "But in the meantime, we've got a job of our own."

"What's that?"

She smiled, pinching his side. "Gettin' sleep."

Kip might have protested were he not already in the middle of a yawn. Molly had observed that for children of a certain age, thought is action. No sooner had she put sleep in his mind than he was already halfway there. Molly could actually see it happen right before her eyes. His head grew heavy against the pillow, and his breathing became soft and regular. His fingers uncurled, revealing the wishing button, nested safe in his palm.

Molly turned onto her back and slowly shut her eyes. For the first time, she let herself feel the exhaustion that she had been fighting for weeks. Every part of her was worn out. Her hands, feet, legs, arms—even the tips of her hair felt tired. Molly was too tired to think about the strange pale family or the strange ugly tree or the strange portrait in the library.

She was too tired, even, to register the sound of a door opening and heavy footsteps entering the house.

PIT AND POCKETS

Kip was dressed and outside just after dawn. A good night's sleep and two hot meals had done wonders for his spirit. Even his left leg, which usually ached in the mornings, felt better. Molly had said that Master Windsor was returning at the end of the week, and Kip thought if he worked hard, he might be able to tame the front lawn by then.

He started with the overgrown ivy at the base of the mansion. He trimmed around the back and sides of the house. He would have continued around front by the tree, but it appeared as though someone had already cleared the growth on that side. When the ivy was finished, he chopped some firewood, repaired the stable door, and swept Galileo's stall.

Kip enjoyed working outside. It reminded him of hours spent with his father, tending their farm on the shore. It was a small farm—just a few animals, a vegetable garden, and a potato patch—but it had been more than Da could handle by himself. Kip had always secretly wondered, if he had been stronger, if he had been able to work as much as a healthy boy, whether their farm might have thrived. Then maybe his family wouldn't have needed to leave Ireland for work, and they would all still be together.

It was early afternoon, and Kip was drawing water for Galileo at the well when he heard a pained voice in the direction of the house. "But Alistair, I'll ruin my favorite dress!" It was the little girl, Penny. She was speaking to her brother, who was leaning against the big tree out front.

"You should have thought about that before you agreed to play," Alistair said matter-of-factly. "Now get in there, or it'll be a double penalty."

Kip had known bullies in his life, and he could tell at one glance that Alistair was a bully of the highest order—the sort who took a special delight in torturing things smaller than himself. Show him a spider's web and he would tear it. Show him a bird's nest and he would kick it. Show him a lame boy? Kip preferred not to find out what he would do. He had thus far managed to avoid Alistair, which was not difficult, as both the Windsor children seemed to prefer playing indoors, and even when they were outside, the low hills covering the lawn created a sort of natural barrier between any two points.

Now, however, Kip found himself with an opportunity to study the children, unobserved. He watched the little girl lower herself into a hole near the base of the tree. He had not noticed this hole before because it had been covered with leaves. Kip made a note to himself that he should rake them clear when he got the chance. It was not a deep hole, for when Penny touched bottom, her chin was still aboveground. As soon as she was in, Alistair pushed leaves around her body with his foot until she was properly buried.

"Alistair, I don't think I want to play this game," Penny said. Her glasses had slipped down from her nose, and she was trying unsuccessfully to fix them without the use of her arms.

"Today's game is entirely new." The boy paced in front of the tree, hands behind his back like a captain of the guard. "It's something I call 'Pit and Pockets.' You've likely already figured out the 'pit' part. Now for the next bit: I've got something in each of my pockets. In one pocket is a bag of sweets; in the other is . . ." He spun around dramatically. *"Certain doom!"*

Penny made a small, terrified sound. She blinked up at her brother. "I pick the sweets," she said in a tone more befitting a question.

Alistair stood back. "No, stupid. You have to choose: Right or left? And whatever you pick, you have to eat."

Kip could not say for certain, but something in Alistair's voice made him suspect that no matter which pocket the girl selected, she would lose. He watched as Penny screwed up her face, concentrating all her mental energy on determining which pocket was the winner. "I . . . I think it's the left one," she ventured after a moment.

"Left, she says!" Alistair reached a hand into his left pocket and pulled out a fistful of something dark and stringy. The prize hung limp between his fingers, squirming slowly.

Kip had spent enough years working in soil to know what Alistair was holding. "Earthworms," he said under his breath. Penny gave a shriek that confirmed his suspicion.

Alistair held the creatures over his sister's head. "Let's see which one reaches you first." With a great flourish, he sprinkled the worms around the edge of the hole.

Penny, who up until this point had been a commendable sport, broke down. "Alistair, pull me out of here." She spun her head about, trying to keep clear of the worms blindly inching toward her. Suddenly she gave a sharp scream that surprised Kip for its sincerity. Even Alistair looked a bit taken aback. "Help!" she shrieked. "They're getting my feet! I can feel them!"

"You're just being hysterical," Alistair protested. "I can see for myself the worms have barely made it past the first layer of leaves." He crouched down and took one of the worms between his two fingers. "Look here, all you have to do is eat one worm, and then you're done."

Penny did not hear him, as she was too busy screaming about how she could feel the worms moving around her ankles. Seizing a perfect opportunity, Alistair raised the worm over her open mouth.

Kip had seen enough. He took up his crutch, Courage, and hobbled out from behind the well. "You leave her alone!" he called, moving toward them as fast as he could.

Alistair turned around slowly. A look of pure pleasure crept across his face. "If it isn't our new groundskeeper!" he said. "I thought I smelled something foul."

Kip ignored the comment and hopped closer. Alistair took a lazy step to one side, planting himself between Kip and Penny. The two boys were now only a few feet from each other. At this range, Alistair looked even bigger. Kip swallowed, steeling himself. "She ain't done nothin' to deserve that. Let her go."

"Or else what?" Alistair said, tossing the worm aside. "One word to Mother, and you'll be turned out—two fishy orphans, alone in the cold."

"I ain't no orphan," Kip snapped. "And you're a bully." His face was flushed, his free hand clenched tight in a fist. He knew talking was useless; this was going to be a fight.

Kip was by no means a good fighter, but he had been in enough scraps to know a few tricks. The first trick was to always strike first— to guarantee he got in at least one good blow before things went bad. The second trick was to bite his tongue, as hard as he could, right before things got started. That way, when he was hit, the pain wouldn't surprise him. The last thing, and this was important, was to level the field as quickly as possible by getting the other boy onto the ground. Down there, having only one good leg was not as much of a problem. None of these tricks had ever helped him win a fight, of course, but they usually helped him lose a little less badly.

Kip dropped his crutch and sprang across the grass, tackling Alistair at the knees. The boy shouted out as they both came crash- ing down onto the wet lawn. Kip concentrated on hitting the places he knew hurt most: the kidneys, just below the ribs, the back of the leg. It quickly became clear to him that, for all his posturing, Alistair knew next to nothing about proper fighting. The boy landed a few ineffectual blows upon Kip's shoulder blades and elbows before resorting to a campaign of hair pulling and ear biting.

While Penny screamed from her hole, the two boys rolled back and forth across the lawn, fighting with everything in them. Kip heard a satisfying *crack* as his forehead struck Alistair square in the nose. Blood clouded his vision, and his head throbbed horribly. But from the way Alistair was howling and clutching his face, Kip knew he had scored a direct hit. He grinned as the significance of this fact dawned on him: he was actually winning.

The next moment, Kip felt someone grab his arm from behind. "Get off him!" Molly shouted as she pulled them apart. "What're you thinkin'?" It took Kip a moment to realize that she was talking not to Alistair but to him.

He saw her cast a panicked glance toward the open front door. Mistress Windsor was rushing out to meet them. She crouched down and helped Penny out of the hole. The little girl clung to her neck like a barnacle. "Just what is going on here?" the woman demanded.

Alistair scrambled to his feet and ran to his mother's side. "It was the cripple who started it! He came at me like a murderer!"

Constance looked between the two boys. They both had grass stains and mud on their clothes. They were breathing heavily, and Alistair had blood on his face. "Is this true?" she said to Kip.

Kip, still on the ground, stared up at her, unable to deny the charge.

Molly stepped in front of him. "Forgive me, mum, but your son's lying. I saw the whole thing. My brother was only defendin' himself as any person would."

Kip stared up at Molly, confused; if she had really seen them, then she would have known that Kip had struck first.

"Don't listen to her, Mother!" Alistair said, clutching his nose. "She's just trying to protect him! Ask Penny—she was there."

Unfortunately, Penny was too busy sobbing about the worms eating her toes to give any kind of testimony. Constance gave her son a weary look. "Tormenting little girls and crippled boys? Don't think your father won't hear of this."

Alistair sneered. He fished a crumpled bag of sweets from his pocket and opened his mouth. "And then what? He'll *puh-puh-punish* me?" He said this with an exaggerated stutter.

Constance snatched the bag from his hands. Her eyes were wide, dangerous. Every muscle in her body looked tense. "You will respect your father," she said in a constricted tone. "Go to your room immediately." For a moment, Kip thought she might strike the boy.

Alistair turned from her, his face burning. He gave Kip a special threatening look before marching back into the house.

The woman turned to face Kip. He thought for a moment she was going to apologize for her son, but she did not. "See that you fill that hole at once. Heaven forbid someone falls in and gets injured." She looked at Molly. "Shouldn't you be in the kitchen?" Then she turned and carried Penny into the house without another word.

Molly picked up Kip's discarded crutch and offered it to him. "You fight with the young master on our first week? That's a sure way to promise there won't be a second. What were you thinkin'?"

What was *he* thinking? All Kip had done was the thing she had taught him. For as long as he could remember, Molly had defended him against other children. Not a week went by when she didn't get into a fight on his behalf. Kip had just been doing the same for Penny—only now his sister was outraged.

Kip did not accept the offered crutch. Instead, he rose on his one good leg, which was sore and threatening to buckle. "You shouldn't 'a lied about seein' the fight," he said, his breathing raspy.

"Better that than tellin' the mistress her son got walloped by a boy half his size." Molly made a silly face, but Kip refused to smile. She sighed. "Kip, I said that to protect us. It was just a story."

"Was it?" He fixed her with as hard a gaze as he could. "Do they count as stories when the other person thinks they're true?" He took his crutch from her and started toward the stables. Suddenly he felt exhausted and sore from the fight—and shaky. The exhilaration of his victory had been replaced by a cold gloom.

8

MASTER OF THE HOUSE

Though Molly had perhaps stretched the truth about her domestic prowess, she was determined to make good on the claim. She spent the first week at Windsor Manor scrubbing, scouring, and dusting every surface she could find. She made a sort of game for herself out of anticipating her mistress's every wish so that she could fulfill it before being asked. (Penny helped in this matter, often acting as a spy who would come back with reports of half-filled wineglasses or drafty windows.) By the end of the week, Molly had succeeded in her efforts, as evidenced by not one but *three* separate instances of her mistress uttering "thank you" after being served.

It was mid-Friday before Molly finally met Master Windsor. When she heard his carriage rolling up the drive, she put aside her wash and fetched her brother in the yard. The two of them rushed to the front stoop so they might greet him at the door. Molly had enough sense to know the importance of winning her master's approval—and if he was anything like his wife, she knew it would be a difficult thing to gain.

Molly and Kip both stood at attention, straight as candlesticks, like proper servants. They were wearing clean (if oversized) clothes and shined shoes. Molly had even gotten her brother to wash his face, though he hadn't done a very good job around the ears, and his neck still had some red marks from where Alistair had bitten him. Molly wasn't sure whether she should be furious with her brother or proud of him for getting into that fight. She imagined her parents would have shared her ambivalence—Ma, impressed with his courage; Da, disappointed in his hotheadedness. This thought made her smile. Then it made her sad.

When the carriage rattled to a stop in front of the house, Molly was surprised by the man who climbed down from the driver's seat. His shoulders may have once been broad, but they were now severely sloped. He had a weak chin and round face. Even his mustache was halfhearted. Like the rest of his family, he had pale skin and dark eyes, which he blinked incessantly—as though he were afraid that someone might strike him. Looking at the man, Molly understood at once why Alistair had not been afraid of his mother's threats: to put it plainly, Bertrand Windsor was a milksop.

"We expected you some hours ago," said Constance, who had rushed to meet him. She had been increasingly anxious for his arrival all afternoon. "Have you any news?"

"F-f-forgive me, darling," he said with a distinct stutter. "I was a bit late getting out of town." Master Windsor knocked some mud from his shoes. "It didn't help that the roads have turned to marsh since Monday—I daresay at this rate, the whole valley will be a bog by Easter!" He looked up at his wife, perhaps expecting a laugh, but none was forthcoming.

"And your meetings?" she pressed. "Were they productive?"

He apparently did not hear her and turned to Molly and Kip. "H-h-heavens!" he exclaimed. "How my two children have changed! One would h-h-hardly recognize you for Windsors."

Molly took this to be a joke and obliged him with a polite smile. "Alistair and Penny are upstairs, readyin' for supper. I'm Molly, and this here's my brother, Kip."

"We're the help!" Kip said, bowing as best as his crutch allowed.

Molly took the man's hat and cloak. She couldn't help but notice the sour odor of tobacco and ale on his clothes. "I've nearly got food on the table, sir."

"Ah, victuals!" Master Windsor clapped his hands, rubbing them together. "There's nothing I prefer to a hot meal at the end of a long ride . . . Well, perhaps a hot meal at the end of a *short* ride!" He turned toward his wife, offering a low bow. "After you, my dear."

Mistress Windsor rolled her eyes and walked into the house, closing the door behind her. It shut right in his face.

Bertrand gave Molly a somewhat embarrassed smile and then trotted inside after his wife, calling out some joke about the tortoise and the hare.

Molly exchanged a look with her brother. "He seems . . . friendly," she said.

Kip snorted. "Friendly like a housefly. I'd 'a shook his hand if I didn't think it'd frighten him to death." He hobbled to the carriage and climbed onto the driver's seat. "It's a mixed-up world where *he's* the one bein' called Master." He snapped the reins and drove into the yard.

Molly spent the next half hour finishing supper. She stewed alongside her food, thinking about how unfair Kip's comment about Master Windsor had been. Her brother, of all people, should know what it meant to be disregarded.

The evening menu was mostly burned pork roast with a side of mostly bland vegetables—the best Molly could do in light of all the extra housework. Penny spent the bulk of her mealtime trying to see how many individual peas she could spear onto her fork tongs, Alistair busied himself with smuggling what looked to be peppermints from his pocket into his mouth without his parents noticing, Constance seemed more interested in her wineglass than her plate, and Bertrand Windsor was too busy talking to eat much of anything. "Ah! Your native cuisine!" he exclaimed as Molly spooned some boiled potatoes onto his plate. She smiled and resisted the urge to tell him that the potatoes she grew up on had been black and slimy—sick with blight.

Bertrand appeared to be the sort for whom silence was uncomfortable, and he made it his mission to furnish the meal with conversation—mostly by telling jokes he had learned in town. "Th-th-the one gentleman says to the other: 'My wife's always after me for money. When I wake up, she says, *Give me five pounds!* And then when I come home that night, it's the same thing, *Give me five pounds!*' The other fellow asked what she does with all her money. And the first one says: 'I don't know, I haven't given her any!'" He chuckled, shaking his head.

Penny looked up from her peas, pointing at Molly. "I like her stories better."

Molly smiled modestly. "I thought it was very funny, sir," she said.

And so it went for the rest of the meal. Master Windsor stumbled through a series of bons mots and "corkers" (a word he had picked up in town). The less interested his family acted, the more eager he became to please. No one appeared more irritated with his performance than Constance, who made repeated attempts to change the subject to something more sensible. "I should like to hear a bit more about the men from the bank, darling," she interjected at one point. "Did they seem receptive?"

"Ah! That reminds me," he declared, "I overheard the most amusing story about two bankers trapped in a nunnery. How does it go? Let me see . . ."

"Let us *not*." Constance dropped her silverware against her plate, rose from her seat, and marched from the room.

Master Windsor smiled weakly at his children, who were now watching him. "Indigestion, p-p-perhaps?" he said.

Constance's abrupt departure shattered any illusion of this being a happy family reunion, and the children soon excused themselves, leaving Master Windsor to eat alone. The sight was too much for Molly to bear, and she waited in the kitchen as he finished eating before returning to clear the dishes.

It wasn't until later that evening that Molly got a clearer idea of why her mistress had been so upset. She had just dried and hung the pots in the kitchen when she heard two voices echoing faintly beside her. They were coming from the dumbwaiter, which connected to one of the rooms upstairs—

"Is that how your new business associates spend their days?" Constance said. "Telling rude jokes in public houses?"

"Wh-wh-why, of course not all day, darling. B-b-but these gentlemen . . . you must understand they're cut from a different cloth. They're earthy blokes. Still! They're top-notch speculators. They know their way around markets and—and speculation, and . . . you must believe me when I tell you that these men are the fastest way out of our trouble—perhaps the only way . . ."

At this point they must have moved away from their spot, because Molly could no longer hear their conversation. She felt an overwhelming desire to learn more about the nature of their disagreement, which she thought might shine some light on the reasons for their moving to this old house in the first place. She filled a pitcher with water and rushed from the kitchen up the main stairway. The pitcher was her excuse, in case she was discovered eavesdropping. She had already learned that, so long as she was doing housework, the members of the family treated her like she was invisible—which suited her just fine. She quietly walked to the sideboard at the far end of the hall and began watering some wildflowers Kip had brought in from the woods. Beside her was the drawing room, and through the gap where the door hinged, she could see the Windsors close to each other, deep in conversation.

Constance had her arms folded tight across her chest. "I feel as though I'm not even part of this marriage. I tell you I want nothing to do with this house, and you ignore me. I say I don't want servants here, and what do you do? You send me a pair of children. *Children*, Bertie."

"Well, they're working for free," he said brightly. "That's something." Bertrand rested a hand on her shoulder. "P-p-please trust me. This will work, but it will take time."

"You told me there was no time."

"You're right. You're right." He moved closer, lowering his voice. "But there is, of course, a way to *buy* time." He held out his hand.

Constance stiffened. Molly leaned close to the jamb, trying to read the expression on her face. The woman sighed and removed something from her dress pocket. "Promise me this will end," she said.

Master Windsor did not answer but snatched the object, which was long and seemed to be made of metal, from her grasp. He clutched it in his fingers like a treasure. He turned around and marched into the hallway. Molly pressed herself against the wall, hoping the half-opened door might hide her. He walked right past her, and she caught a glimpse of the object gripped in his pale hand—

It was a key.

9

THE ROOM AT THE TOP OF THE STAIRS

All right. Into bed with you."

Molly stood in Penny's room, a battlefield littered with the corpses of dollies and wooden toys and stuffed animals. With all the additional work to prepare the house for Master Windsor's return, Molly had not had time to clean it. Tomorrow, perhaps. The bed was covered in lace pillows and had a muslin canopy overhead. How was it fair that this family should have so much when she and her brother had so little? She pulled back the thick covers, and Penny—hair brushed and wearing a fresh nightgown—scrambled onto the feather mattress. She climbed to her knees. "What else can you tell me about Cleopatra?" she asked.

In the week since Molly's arrival, bedtime stories had developed into something of a sacred ritual. Unlike most six-year-olds, Penny eagerly awaited the hour when she might run upstairs, put on her nightgown, and snuggle under the covers—because that meant she was about to hear another of Molly's thrilling tales. (On Wednesday, she had been so keen to hear a story that she'd tried advancing the hands of the grandfather clock so that she might convince Molly to tuck her in just after tea.) Molly removed the girl's glasses and set them on the nightstand. "Well," she said, buying herself a moment, "some folks say she was actually a fallen angel."

"I bet that's why the archbishop fancied her," Penny said. "Did she have real angel wings?"

Molly nodded. "But she had to give 'em up when she got here. You could see the stitches from where they cut off her wings"—she ran a finger along Penny's shoulder blades—"right here." The girl squirmed and collapsed onto the mattress. Molly pulled the covers over her. "I'll tell you somethin' else about Cleopatra. When she sang, her voice was so pretty that the whole world stopped what it was doin' just to listen. Wherever you were, you could hear her, like a choir of bells."

"Can you sing?" Penny asked.

Molly shook her head. "Not like that, I can't."

The girl sighed. "Mummy used to sing to me. She'd sing about Princess Penny—that was me. And afterward she'd hold my hand the whole way while I fell asleep."

This surprised Molly, who had trouble imagining her mistress being anything but stern. Just thinking of the way she had treated poor Master Windsor at supper left Molly feeling a chill. "Your mother don't tuck you in no more?" she said.

Penny sighed. "Not since we moved to this ugly house. Now she's only cross with me. I hate this place. There's no one to play with."

"You've got your brother, miss. And mine."

The girl sat up, her face a picture of scandal. "I can't play with *boys*." She flopped back down. "Besides, Alistair won't let me play with him. He just bullies me."

Molly pulled the covers right up to Penny's chin. "I promise that whenever I'm around I'll not let him bully you. Fair?" She crossed her heart to show she was serious.

Molly glanced at the girl's bed stand. She noticed a stack of books hidden behind a lamp. They were square and thin—the sort of books that contained more pictures than words. Each one was brightly colored and had gilded lettering along the spine. They seemed to be part of a series:

Princess Penny and the Beast
Princess Penny Eats a Whole Cake
Princess Penny Visits the Moon
Princess Penny Stays Up Late

Molly reached for the closest one, which had a picture of a girl with glasses fighting a sea dragon. "Princess Penny . . . just like your mum's tales!"

Penny sat up. "Don't!" She reached out to intercept Molly's arm. "You're not supposed to see those."

Molly thought she was making a joke, but the girl looked very serious. "Fair enough, miss. We're all entitled to our secret things." She winked. "Only you might want to look for a better hidin' place."

Penny sat back, apparently satisfied that the issue had been settled. "Why did you and your brother leave Ireland?" she said.

Molly knew that these questions were a way of tricking her into another story, but she found it hard not to oblige. "The truth is, I came here because I had a dream."

The girl gave a small gasp, sitting up. "Was it a very bad dream?" She spoke with the tone of someone who knew the subject all too well.

Molly shook her head. "Far from it, miss. I dreamed about a little girl named Penny who needed a maid." She stroked Penny's dark hair. "And she was so pretty and well behaved that I decided to come right over and do the job myself."

Penny shrank from her touch. "That's not true," she said.

"True as time, miss."

Penny tugged at a knot in her hair. "I used to have dreams like that. But here, everyone has horrid dreams. Every night. Mummy, Papa, even Alistair. I hear them in their rooms."

Molly thought of her own dreams, which had lately been terrible and haunting. She looked into Penny's dark eyes and wondered if this was the reason the girl had become so dependent on bedtime stories: they were a candle to light her to bed. "Of course, you know bad dreams is only that," she said. "They're none of 'em real. They canna hurt you or anyone else."

Penny shook her head. "It's not the dreams that frighten me." She peered about the room, as if the walls might be listening. "It's that sometimes, when I can't sleep, I hear something else . . . I hear *him*."

Molly caught her breath. "Him, who?" she asked.

Penny leaned close, her voice barely a whisper. "The night man."

Molly stared at the little girl, trying to discern if she was making a joke. Penny went on. "He walks through the whole house, room to room, and then he's gone. I asked Mummy about him, and she said I just made him up. But I'm sure I didn't, because some mornings I see the footprints he's left behind. They're muddy and shaped wrong and I don't like them."

Molly's heart was beating very quickly. She thought of the footprints she'd been scrubbing throughout the house, and she thought of the story her brother had told their first night, about a figure in the fog—had he told the same story to Penny, who had added some details of her own? "Well, the next time you hear this night fellow, could you tell him to wipe his boots before comin' inside? I dinna break my back scrubbin' these floors just to have him ruin it all while I sleep." She stood up.

"Don't go," Penny protested through a yawn.

"You've a lifetime of tuck-ins ahead of you." She silently hoped this was true. But even in the orange lamplight, the girl's complexion was as white as a headstone. Dark shadows flickered and danced across her face, clinging to the wells beneath her eyes. Molly put on a smile. "And until then—

"You sleep soft, you sleep sound,
You sleep the snow in Dublin town."

This was a rhyme her own mother had sung to her when she was little. When Molly sang the words now, she could almost hear Ma's voice echoing in the air, distant and faint, calling to her from someplace far away. Molly hid her face from Penny's view and slipped from the room.

The grandfather clock struck nine as Molly walked down the hall. Penny's tuck-in had taken longer than she'd planned, and she knew her brother would be waiting at the window. When she turned the corner toward the stairs, however, she stopped. In the last week, she had been inside every room of Windsor Manor—every room, that is, but for the one with the green door at the top of the stairs. Mistress Windsor had given Molly the impression that the key had been lost, and Molly had believed her. But what she had witnessed that night between Bertrand and Constance in the drawing room after supper had changed her mind.

And now, the green door was unlocked.

It was not completely open, but Molly could see a sliver of light shining out from the side that should have been closed tight. She glanced at the bank of windows above the foyer. Kip was waiting outside, probably catching cold at this very moment. Still, perhaps there was time for a quick peek. She dimmed her lamp and crept toward the door. She could hear sounds of someone moving on the other side—scraping, clinking, shuffling, grunting. The noises would have been frightening if they were not so obviously comical.

Molly was about to reach for the handle when the door swung open to reveal the folds of a man's nightgown. It was Master Windsor.

He was bent away from her, trying to drag a large canvas sack into the hall. The bag was half-full and seemed quite heavy; whatever was inside rattled and clinked as he pulled it across the floorboards. Molly watched him struggle, unsure whether she should interrupt him. "Pardon, sir?" she said softly.

Bertrand let out a startled noise and spun around. The moment he saw Molly, he lunged for the door and pulled it shut behind him. There was a look of panic on his pale face. "M–M–Molly!" he said, doing a bad job at sounding happy to see her. "I thought you had turned in for the night."

"Just puttin' Miss Penny to bed, sir." She craned her neck to get a better look inside the bag, but he had tied the end shut. "It looks heavy," she said. "Can I help you with it?"

"N-n-no! I'm p-p-perfectly fine. Wouldn't want you to, er . . . strain yourself . . ." He fumbled with his key, dropping it twice before he managed to fit it into the lock. He secured the green door and mopped his brow with the end of his nightcap. "Goodness!" He covered his mouth, giving a theatrical yawn. "It certainly has been a long day—for you as well, I'd imagine! Perhaps it's time we turn in." He said this in a way that led her to understand that "we" really meant "you."

Much as Molly wanted to see what was inside the bag, she knew it would not happen tonight. "Good night to you, sir," she said, bowing. She turned and walked down the stairs, her small lamp lighting the darkness.

Molly reached her room to find her brother waiting at the window, looking half-frozen and exhausted. When he asked what had taken her so long, she muttered something about chores and promised to make it up to him with an extra big breakfast the next morning. The two of them undressed and went to bed with scarcely another word—slipping into the rare, comfortable silence of those who know each other even better than they know themselves.

As Kip nestled beside her, Molly kept going over her encounter with Master Windsor in the hall. The man had been so startled to find her outside the door. *More than startled*, she thought to herself as she drifted to sleep—

He had looked afraid.

FOOTSTEPS

Molly jolted awake in the middle of the night. Her hands were shaking and she was cold with sweat. She swallowed her dry throat, calming herself. She had been having a bad dream, that was all. It was not a new dream; it was the same one she had been having every night since coming to the house. Her mother and father holding her, letting her down into the churning water; Molly scream-ing for them as they disappeared in the darkness. But every night, the dream got a little worse. Tonight, the swells were as steep as valleys, the lightning was black and gnarled like roots, and her parents' faces were pale and ghastly.

Molly sat up, letting her eyes adjust to the moonlight. Kip tossed beside her, caught, it seemed, in a bad dream of his own. He let out a frail whimper, recoiling from some unseen horror. Molly thought of waking him, but she knew that bad rest was better than none at all. "Brave now, love," she whispered to him, brushing the hair from his damp brow.

Molly heard a creaking sound and saw that her bedroom door

had somehow come open in the night. She peeled back the covers and tiptoed across the cold floor. She gently shut the door and leaned back against it—steadying herself against the dark waves still churning inside her. She tucked a loose curl behind one ear. Her fingers found something dry caught in the tangles of her hair—

It was a dead leaf.

Molly held it up against the window, letting the moonlight shine through its brittle skin. Tiny twisted veins branched out from the center stem—a tree inside a tree. Molly noticed other leaves in her room, scattered across the floor. Blown in through the open door, perhaps?

She was about to return to bed when she felt something at her feet. This was not a leaf. It was wet and cold. *Mud,* she thought. She knelt down, looking at the mark. It was a heavy footprint, similar to the ones Molly had cleaned from the stairs earlier that day. She could tell at once that this print was too large to belong to her brother. She looked across the stone floor and saw more tracks. They went right to the side of her bed. Molly stood, a shiver passing through her body.

Someone else had been inside her room!

At that very moment, a prickling sensation filled her ears. She remained still, listening to the silent house. Somewhere above her she could hear a heavy sound—

THUMP!

THUMP!

THUMP!

Footsteps.

Hearing this sound, Molly wanted nothing more than to bury her head under the covers and plug her ears. But her parents had raised her differently: Ma and Da believed that if you suspected a monster was hiding under your bed, you should get down on your hands and knees and find out for certain. And if you were lucky enough to discover one down there—fangs dripping, eyes glowing red—you should be quick to offer him a blanket and a bowl of warm milk so he wouldn't catch a chill. It was with this difference in mind that Molly put on a shawl and went upstairs in pursuit of the phantom footstepper.

The first thing she noticed was the wind in the halls. Large houses were often drafty, but this was something different altogether—more like a quiet storm. Molly thought she had latched all the doors and windows before bed, but perhaps she had forgotten. She held her hand over the lamp glass to protect its flame and continued up the narrow service stairs.

When she reached the main floor, Molly found the front door wide open, creaking back and forth in the wind. Dry leaves danced all around her. More swirled across the floorboards. She could see wet footprints glistening in the silver moonlight. "H–h–hullo?" she called into the shadows.

The shadows did not answer.

Molly cleared her throat to call again, but her words were cut off by the sound of more footsteps—

THUMP!

THUMP!

THUMP!

They were coming from upstairs.

Molly left the door as it was. She could not help but think of her brother's story from earlier in the week about the man in the fog. Perhaps Kip really had seen someone. Perhaps it was a prowler, come to rob the Windsors. Molly wondered whether her lamp might draw attention. She set it on the sideboard and picked up the heaviest candlestick she could find, just to be safe.

She crept up the staircase, weapon clenched in both hands. Gusts of wind swept past her, pulling at her nightgown and hair. She reached the top of the stairs and heard a faint creaking sound. The little green door was open again, moving slightly in the wind. Molly felt a prickle of excitement. She walked toward the door, but then another sound stopped her—

Somewhere in the back of the house, she could hear voices.

Molly left the green door and went to investigate. She rounded the upstairs hall to find all the bedroom doors open, and from inside each room she could hear the family members tossing and moaning in their sleep—a gallery of bad dreams.

Mistress Windsor's bedroom was at the end of the hall. Molly could hear the woman murmuring, caught in her own nightmare. She could hear the footsteps again—heavy and slow. Through the crack around the door, she saw a tall shadow move inside, a shadow the size of a man. "Master Windsor, is that you?" she said as bravely as she could.

The footsteps stopped.

The wind stopped.

Her heart stopped.

Molly wiped the perspiration from her palm and adjusted her grip on the candlestick. She took a deep breath and inched toward the door. A howl split the darkness, and she felt a great burst of wind. The gust knocked her to the floor and swept along the upstairs hall. She covered her face as dry leaves skittered over her like bats from a cavern.

She heard a loud *slam* behind her, and the next moment, everything was still and dark. Molly climbed to her feet, trembling with fright. She felt her way along the wall until she reached the main stairs. She could hear no footsteps. The wind and leaves were all gone. The bedrooms were silent, and the front door was safely shut. The house was completely still. By the time she reached the bottom of the stairs, it almost seemed as if she had dreamed the whole thing.

Molly was about to turn into the service hall when a shadow caught her eye. There, lying in the middle of the floor, was something that hadn't been there before. It was an old top hat, tipped on its side. Molly remembered Kip's words. "A tall black hat," he had said. Molly knelt down and picked it up. It was as real as anything she'd ever touched, its brim damp with mildew and age. She slowly turned the hat over in her hand—dead leaves spilled from the crown, forming a pile at her feet.

Molly stared at the silent house, which only moments before had been filled with these leaves. It wasn't a dream. Kip, Penny—they had both been telling the truth.

The night man was real.

II

CHAMBER POTS

The morning after Master Windsor's arrival, Kip sat on the bridge, repairing a rotting plank. Molly had come out to visit and to tell him something of what had happened to her the night before. "And you're sure you wasn't dreamin'?" he said. "Sometimes folks have dreams where they think they wake up, but really, they're still inside the dream."

"It wasn't no dream," Molly answered. She tossed the contents of a porcelain chamber pot over the edge of the bridge into the river below. There were three more pots sitting in Galileo's cart, all of them full to the brim with urine and night soil. Kip wrinkled his nose. The smell was enough to make a person wish for rotting fish again. "I didn't see him, exactly," she clarified. "But I heard him plain enough."

Kip's bad leg dangled carelessly over the edge of the bridge, braving the river below. He stared at the churning current, his own mind churning at the thought of a stranger being inside their room. "Ears are trickier'n eyes," he said. "It coulda been anythin' that made them sounds."

"Maybe this'll change your mind." She went to the cart and re- turned with an old black top hat. "That's his hat. He musta dropped it at the door."

She held the hat out for Kip, but he did not touch it. He looked up at his sister, wondering whether this might be a trick. Molly some- times teased him like that—bringing him a dragonfly wing and saying it came off a fairy, or placing moss and a handkerchief inside his shoe and claiming it must have been where an elf made its bed—but when he looked up into her face now, it was clear she was telling the truth. "You told me the front door was open," he said. "Maybe the wind just knocked it off the hat stand."

"Wind don't leave footprints," she said.

Kip gave a noncommittal nod. He had noticed some dry mud smeared across the floor when he had gotten up early in the morning to return to the stables. But it was hardly what he would have called a footprint. "What makes you so sure it ain't the master's old hat?"

Molly shook her head. "I checked. All his hats got round tops, and they're bigger in the crown." She knelt beside him, looking him sharp in the eye. "Kip, remember when you said you saw that man in the fog?" Kip nodded. At the time, his sister hadn't believed him. It seemed that she had changed her mind. "You told me he was all in black. I need to know: Was he wearin' a hat like this?"

Kip picked up the hat and ran his fingers along the brim. It was ragged and torn and smelled like it had been buried underground for a long time. "Can't say for certain." He gave it back to her. "It was pretty dark." It was, in fact, the exact same kind of hat Kip had seen, but he wasn't sure whether he wanted to admit it. A part of him felt as if saying the words aloud would somehow make them true. He looked up at her. "If there really was a man, what do you think he was after?"

Molly shrugged. "I dunno. Money or jewels maybe? Only . . ." She hesitated. "There was somethin' else. When I went upstairs, all the bedroom doors was open, and I could hear the family inside their rooms. They was all tossin' about, caught in these terrible dreams." She looked straight at him. "I heard you, too."

Kip steadied a nail between his fingers and hammered it down into the new plank. He had in fact spent the entire night trapped inside a nightmare that refused to end. Usually in Kip's dreams he was a hero—saving people from rushing rivers and burning houses. But since coming to Windsor Manor, his dreams had been different. "I was dreamin' that some gang of older boys was kickin' a lost dog," he said. "I pushed 'em away, to save the dog, but when I came close, the dog attacked me—chomped down, right on my left leg." He glanced at his bad leg, hanging like a dead weight over the water. "The dog wouldn't let go. I screamed for help, but the boys around me just laughed and jeered, cheerin' as it bit my whole limb clean off." Even now, he could still hear their taunting voices, and it made him shiver.

He hammered down another nail, accidentally bending it. "What about you?" he said, pulling the nail out and starting over. "Did you have bad dreams?"

Molly's eyes were on the river rushing below them. "Aye," she said.

He watched her face, searching for clues. "About what?"

"About nothin'." She said this in a way that let him know he should stop prying.

Kip looked past her to the house. There were so many things about this place that didn't add up—none of them good: the silent forest, the pale faces, the mysterious prowler, that giant tree out front. If there really was somebody walking the halls at night, maybe he would be better off sleeping in the stables like the mistress wanted.

He took his crutch and pulled himself to his feet. "I know you're doin' your best to take care of us, Molls. But if there really is danger, shouldn't we leave?"

"And go where? Back to town? We were homeless and halfway to starved."

Kip looked at her and knew she was right. "Ma an' Da would know what to do," he said, collecting his tools. "I wish they was here."

His sister tensed her jaw, still staring at the water. "Well, they're not. And it's no use wishin' otherwise."

"You think I dinna know that?" He picked up his toolbox and hobbled toward the wagon. He knew it hadn't been fair to bring up their parents that way. Molly wanted to see them again just as much as he did. But they were gone for now, and there was nothing either of them could do about it. "Forget I said anythin'."

"Don't be sore," Molly called out behind him.

"I ain't sore," he said, hefting his tools into the wagon bed.

He felt her hand on his shoulder. "You're right to miss 'em, Kip." Ma an' Da aren't here to tell us what to do . . . but maybe . . . maybe we could ask 'em?"

Kip turned around. He could tell from her face that she was being serious.

"Ask 'em how?" he said.

Molly looked down at the hat, which was still in her hands. She screwed up her mouth as if she didn't want to say what she was about to say. "We could write 'em a message." She smiled weakly. "Well, *I'll* write it—your letters ain't so good."

Kip steadied himself against the back of the wagon. Again he had that feeling inside like he was being tricked. "But they're at sea. And we dinna even know where."

Molly shrugged. "We can send it to the navy postmaster. He'd be able to deliver it easy enough. Or we could put it in a bottle and toss it out in the river like that Robinson Crusoe fellow I told you about." She moved toward him, taking his hands in hers. "Think of it, Kip. We could tell 'em everything in our hearts. We could tell 'em how we miss 'em."

Kip did think of it, and just doing so made him feel less alone. A letter was not the same as being with them, of course, but it was something. "And that way they'd know where to look for us when they reach land," he said.

Molly beamed. "Exactly!"

Molly's smiles always had a way of catching, and before Kip knew it, he was smiling, too. "I've got just the thing to help." He fished through his trousers pocket and removed a folded sheet of paper. It was an advert with a picture of a metal leg brace some doctor had invented. "We can use this paper I found in town. There's words all on one side, but the back is plain enough." He shrugged. "I'd been savin' it to teach myself letters, but maybe this'd be a better use."

Molly took the sheet from him and read it. "Kip, this . . ." She looked up at him, her eyes full of something he couldn't quite understand. "This'll never do for a letter." Before Kip could react, she tore the paper in two and tossed it over the edge of the bridge. "I tell you what: meet me at the stables at sundown. I'll bring us somethin' hot to eat, and we'll do it proper."

Kip nodded, and Molly seized him in an enormous hug. "Get your chamber-pot hands off me!" he said, squirming.

Molly kissed him on the cheek and sprinted back to the house. Kip took Galileo's bit and limped toward the stables, his heart swelling. They were going to talk to Ma and Da. And everything was going to be all right.

12

The Stationery Box

Sundown couldn't come quickly enough for Kip. He spent the rest of the afternoon pulling weeds in the garden and imagining what he might say to his parents in the letter. He was so absorbed in his thoughts that he hardly noticed his work, and when he finally stood up, he was surprised to discover that he had completely weeded half the beds. He used Galileo's cart to haul the weeds to the edge of the property, where they made a pile nearly as tall as himself. The stems were still wick, and so Kip had to bait the fire with a bit of lamp oil. The pile burned wet and smoky in the damp spring air, and the smell reminded Kip of peat fires back home. He imagined his parents somewhere on the other side of the world, making a fire of their own. (He wasn't certain that ships had fireplaces aboard, but he figured the crew needed some way to keep warm.) Kip stood over the blaze, petting Galileo's side, watching until the last bit had burned away, leaving only a black patch on the ground.

When Kip reached the stables, he found them empty. "Molls?" he called.

"Up here!" sounded a voice from above. He hobbled back outside to find his sister sitting atop the roof, legs dangling over the edge. She waved down at him. "There's no better place for writing than a rooftop—the fresh air makes your words come out like songs."

Kip hopped around to the back wall where the gutter connected to an old rain barrel. He laid down Courage and climbed onto the barrel. With the help of the windowsill, drainpipe, and Molly's hand, he pulled himself to the eaves.

"Tell me this isn't better," Molly said.

Kip had to agree. From up here, he felt like king of the forest. He stared out over the glowing treetops and then looked to his sister, lit golden against the red sky. He smiled. She always knew just the right thing to do to make him feel better.

Molly untied a cloth bag she had brought up with her. "I know you've already had supper, but I thought you could do with a snack." Inside were warm biscuits with butter. She had also snuck a half jug of fresh cream, which was Kip's favorite.

"Careful you dinna drown yourself," she said as he drained the cream in just two breaths. Kip set the jug down and started on the biscuits. "I brought you more than just food—look what I found in the study." She pulled a polished wooden box from the cloth. "It's a stationery desk—for writin' letters," she said before he could ask.

Kip wiped the cream and crumbs from his face and opened the lid of the box. Inside he found a stack of ivory paper. He picked up the topmost sheet. It was thicker than normal paper and had a rough surface. "It feels expensive." He resisted the urge to put the paper against his cheek.

"I think it belonged to Master Windsor's father," Molly said. "I saw it last week when I was cleanin' the bureau. Mistress Windsor says nobody hardly goes in there, so I figure they won't miss it."

Kip put the paper down. "You took this without asking?"

She shrugged. "If the Windsors object, they can dock it from our pay."

Kip knew that they were not being paid, and so he took his sister's words to mean that they were somehow allowed to take things—but of course they weren't. Kip looked at the paper. He imagined how impressed Ma and Da would be to see a letter so fine. And surely one sheet wouldn't be missed, would it? "Maybe we could figure out some other ways to pay 'em back for what we take," he said.

Molly snapped her fingers. "That's just what we'll do! I'll work some extra chores, and you collect a few more bunches of flowers—all the paper in the world ain't worth one of your blossoms, and that's a fact."

Kip smiled. He knew she was just being nice, but he liked hearing it nonetheless. "All right," he said. "Let's write a letter."

"Perfect!" Molly took the paper from him and laid it on the lid of the box. She produced an inkwell and pen from her cloth and wet the nib. "How do we start it?"

"*Dear Ma and Da,*" Kip said, leaning closer. He watched as she wrote the words down. When she had finished, she looked to him for further dictation. Kip thought a moment. "*We,* um, *me and Molly . . .*" He sighed, scratching the back of his neck. He had never written a real letter before, and he wanted it to be very official.

Molly tapped the end of the pen against her bottom lip, thinking. "How about: *We hope this finds you in good health*?" she said.

"That's perfect! Fancy, just like a real letter!" Kip leaned over his sister and watched her write. "Next, tell 'em: *We're in ugly England. Where are you?*" After that, the words came more naturally. He told their parents all about the orphanage, and leaving the city, and the scary old witch Hester, and the sourwoods, and the pale family, and the house, and the big tree, and the man in the fog, and most of all he told their parents that they loved them and missed them and wanted them to come back right away.

When the letter was finished, Molly signed her name and then helped Kip sign his. They carefully folded the paper and put it into the envelope and sealed the flap with wax from a candle Molly had swiped from the pantry.

Kip sat back on his hands, staring out across the lawn. The sun was fully hidden now, and stars were starting to show in the night sky. He took his sister's hand. "I hope they find it soon," he said, imagining what grand adventures the little envelope was about to sail out on.

His sister stared out at the house, which was dark but for one light at a small window on the second floor. "Aye," she said softly. "Me, too."

13

A VISIT FROM FIG AND STUBBS

Mistress Windsor fit a glove over her porcelain fingers. "I should be back within the half hour, at which time I would like tea."

Molly held open the kitchen door, which led to the garden. "Of course, mum," she said, bowing. As soon as the woman was outside, Molly closed the door and listened to the house. She could hear Alistair and Penny playing up in their bedrooms. Master Windsor was working in the study. Molly took the kettle off the stove and went downstairs to the servants' quarters. She slipped into her bedroom and shut the door behind her. A moment alone. She slid a hand into her apron pocket and removed the envelope addressed with her parents' names. She stared at the made-up address, written in her own clumsy hand. The letter inside did not weigh much, and yet it felt very, very heavy.

In a brief moment of weakness, she had shared her fears with Kip, which had led to the pair of them writing a letter that, for a variety of reasons, could not be delivered. The logical thing would

have been to destroy the letter, but every time she'd had an opportunity to burn it or throw it away, she'd hesitated. Kip had poured
his very heart into its composition, and to ignore that seemed cruel,
like setting fire to a prayer.

Molly removed her old trunk from the wardrobe and opened the
lid. This was where she hid the things she did not want to think about.
Inside lay the rags she and Kip had worn before coming to the house.
Beside them sat the old top hat she had found in the foyer. Molly had
done her best to put the night man out of her mind. This was not hard
to do, for with the sunlight comes a sort of boldness that takes the scare
right out of things. But now, even in daylight, the sight of the hat sent
a shiver through her body, and she could not help but remember the
heavy sound of footsteps in the hall—

THUMP!

THUMP!

THUMP!

A violent knocking startled Molly out of her thoughts. The racket
was coming from outside. It was not footsteps but the sound of someone banging on the front door. Molly buried the envelope inside the
trunk, shut the lid, and rushed upstairs.

The person outside was knocking with such force that it shook the
whole house. By the time Molly reached the foyer, half the paintings
on the wall were askew. She opened the door to find two men standing

on the stoop. One of them towered over Molly; the other barely met her chin. Both of them were unshaven and emanated a sweet, some-what garbagey odor. Molly could tell from their clothes that they weren't from the hollow but from the city.

"Well, lookee there, Fig," said the shorter one, lowering his cane, which he had apparently been using on the door. "Somebody *is* home." The man seemed to fancy himself a gentleman. He wore a too-small suit that was covered with greasy stains and the occasional patch. Pinched in his right eye was a cracked monocle. He adjusted the lens, eyeing Molly up and down. "Dear me. Ain't you a pretty thing?"

Molly cringed. "Can I help you, sirs?"

The man tipped his hat. "I reckon so. I'm Mister Stubbs, and this here's my associate, Mister Fig." He gestured grandly to the man beside him, who gave her a dirty wink. Stubbs went on, "We've come to see the man o' the house, as it were."

Molly looked between the two men. She had run into more than a few of these types back in town. "Cockney," people called them. "I'm afraid he's unavailable," she said. Molly tried to shut them out, but the man Fig had positioned his foot so as to prevent the front door from moving.

"Can't be rid of us so easy, pet." Stubbs wagged a thick finger. "Not when we gone to such trouble to come all the way out here."

"I understand, sirs. But, the thing is, um . . ." Molly hesitated, struggling to come up with some kind of story that might drive this ugly pair from her door. For perhaps the first time in her life, her imagination seemed to be failing her.

"It's all right, M–M–Molly," said a voice behind her. "I know these men." She turned to see Master Windsor standing in the hall. If possible, he looked even paler than usual.

Stubbs beamed. "Ah! Speak o' the devil!" He and Fig approached Master Windsor like old friends, their arms spread wide.

"That's close enough!" Bertrand said sharply. He swallowed. "I'll ask you to st–st–stay outside of my house."

The two visitors exchanged a look of mock chagrin and then took a tandem step backward. Stubbs bowed with a flourish. "Right, then. Now that we've obliged you—we'd like it if you'd kindly oblige us." He held out his hand, rubbing his fingers together in a way that led Molly to understand he was asking for money.

"H–h–has it been a month already, then?" Master Windsor sighed, shaking his head. "I have it upstairs." He crossed to Molly's side and took her arm. "See that they remain *outside*." He gave a nervous glance toward the back of the hall. "And if, er, Constance happens to return early from her morning constitutional, perhaps . . ."

Molly understood what he was asking. "I should keep her occupied, sir?"

He nodded and then crossed to the staircase, taking the steps two at a time.

Molly remained at her post, cheeks burning, trying to ignore the men on the stoop. She could feel them both staring at her, and it made her flesh crawl. Stubbs propped himself against the door frame. "Let this be a lesson to you, pet," he said. "Don't fall into arrears unless you want blokes like us stoppin' by."

Fig leaned toward her, his head nearly grazing the lintel. "'Less, of course, you *want* blokes like us stoppin' by." He smiled, revealing a row of rotting teeth.

Molly wilted under the man's putrid breath. What possible connection these two had to the Windsor family she could not fathom, but she had the feeling it could lead to no good. She glanced upstairs, wishing that her master would be a little faster in returning.

After a few very long minutes, Master Windsor appeared at the top of the staircase. He was pulling behind him a large canvas sack similar to the one Molly had seen him with the week before. He grunted and groaned as he dragged the load inch by inch down the stairs.

"Seems you're havin' a touch o' trouble," Stubbs hollered from the stoop. "Perhaps you'd like the little girl to give you a hand." The two men chuckled.

"I'm p-p-perfectly capable, thank you!" Master Windsor called back, gasping for breath. He braced himself against the railing and resumed his task. The bag hit each step with a sharp—

Clink!

Clink!

Clink!

"Now, that's my kind of music!" Stubbs nudged his accomplice. "Sounds like he's got the crown jewels in there!" Molly thought to herself that it sounded more like a bag of chains.

Master Windsor eventually made it to the front door. He straight-ened up, gasping for breath. "Thank you . . . Molly . . ." More gasping. "I can handle things from here."

But Molly didn't move. Her eyes were fixed on the canvas bag at his feet—she was certain it was the very same bag she had seen him carrying before. "You sure you dinna want me to stay, master?" she asked.

"Quite," he said firmly.

Still, Molly didn't move. This was her one chance to learn what was inside that bag, and she wasn't going to give up so easily. "I thought maybe you would want me to keep an eye on the hall for your wife's return, sir."

"I see, well . . ." Embarrassment flushed his pale cheeks. "Perhaps that might be wise."

Molly bowed and stepped to the back of the hall. Enough distance to give the illusion of privacy but not so much that she couldn't over-hear the conversation between them.

Master Windsor turned back to the door. "There you are." He eyed the bag with something like disgust. "Take it and leave."

"Now, that's a hefty parcel!" Stubbs rubbed his hands together. "You even gift wrapped it!" The men squatted down, untied the bag, and peeked inside. Molly could not see, but she heard a faint clinking noise. Stubbs looked up, disgust on his face. "What in bloody hell is this?"

Fig plunged a hand into the open bag and came up with a pile of dark coins. "It's ha'pence, that's what it is!" He bit a coin just to be sure. "A whole ruddy bag of 'em."

It was more money than Molly had ever seen in her life. The men, however, seemed far less impressed. Stubbs stood, scratching his chin in mock rumination. "Well, Fig. This here's a real enigma. First he comes to us with banknotes. Then it's pounds. Then sovereigns. Then shillings. And now this." He kicked the bag with his muddy boot. "If I didn't know better, I'd say the gentleman was mocking us."

Master Windsor set his jaw. "I assure you that if anyone is being mocked in this scenario, it is not you." He stood tall, an imitation of resolve. "Whatever the denomination, it's what I owe."

Stubbs eyed the bag as if making a visual count. "It still ain't enough."

"There's an entire sackful!"

"But full o' what? That's the question. If we wanted to buy some lollies, this might pinch it." He poked a fat finger into Master Windsor's chest. "But you owe us a lot more than lollies."

The conversation was interrupted by the sound of a door opening somewhere in the back of the house. Mistress Windsor had returned from her morning walk in the gardens. "Bertie?" Her voice rang out from the kitchen. "I thought I saw someone at the drive."

Bertrand turned back to the men, his face flushed with panic.

"P-p-please," he whispered. "My wife is coming. Just take the bag. It's all I have."

As it turned out, this was exactly the wrong thing to say. Fig and Stubbs looked at each other and then back at him. "It's *all you have*?" Stubbs repeated slowly.

In a flash, Fig snatched his lapels in both fists. He lifted Master Windsor clean off his feet and slammed him against the foyer wall. Paintings fell to the floor. A vase on the sideboard rocked over the edge and shattered. Bertrand sputtered and struggled, beating uselessly against the man's mighty forearms.

Molly watched, frozen, her hand clasped over her mouth. She knew she was meant to intercept Mistress Windsor, but she could not look away from the assault.

Stubbs wandered across the threshold, polishing his monocle with a handkerchief. He replaced the handkerchief, and as he did so, Molly glimpsed a long knife sticking out from under his coat. She took a trembling breath, fearing how that blade might play into negotiations. "You know the reason we do business with stuffed-ups like you?" Stubbs fit the monocle back into his eye. "Abundant collateral. I don't mean money or furniture or houses. I mean a desperate man with a wife and two children that he would do *anything* to protect from harm." His voice was so low that Molly could barely make it out. "Do you understand my meaning, *Bertie*?"

"P-p-please!" Master Windsor had stopped struggling. He spoke with naked desperation. "You must listen to me. There *is* more money, family money—*all you could wish for*! It will just take *time*." He stared between the men, his dark eyes pleading.

Stubbs considered this for a long moment. "You got a month to deliver the balance—no more games, no more interest. We want every last pip." He nodded to Fig, who released his grip.

Master Windsor collapsed to a heap on the floor. "Y-y-yes! Thank you!" He was up on his knees now, practically groveling.

Fig marched over to the sack of coins and slung it over his shoulder with surprising ease. He carried it outside and threw it in the back of their cart. Stubbs remained in the doorway. "If we have to come back 'ere, it won't end well for the Windsors. That's a promise." He tipped his hat and shut the door behind him.

Molly rushed to Master Windsor and helped him to his feet. Whatever manly pride may have been left in him before this encounter, now it was completely gone, and he accepted her aid without comment. She stared at his trembling face, her fear replaced by pity.

"Bertie, who were those men?" said a voice behind her.

Molly turned to see Constance in the hall. It was unclear how long she had been there or how much she had seen.

Bertrand rushed to meet her, smiling a weak smile. "Wh-wh-why, it's nothing, my love! Just some, er, fellows who were, well, um . . ."

Molly intervened before he could do further damage. "They were evangelists, mum," she said. Both Windsors looked at her, their faces marked with two different kinds of surprise. "They came by to see if we had any heathens or sinners they could baptize or burn—I told 'em to try the village a few miles on."

Bertrand clapped his hands together. "Yes, exactly! Evangelists! As I said, nothing to worry about . . . unless you're a heathen." He chuckled.

Constance looked between them, her fingers playing at the diamonds draped around her neck. It was unclear whether she believed the story or not. She looked at Molly. "Next time, see that you don't leave the door open so long. You'll give us all a chill." She turned and walked into the hall. Master Windsor followed after her, trying out a few more heathen jokes as they both disappeared into the parlor.

Molly stood alone in the foyer, thinking about what she had just witnessed. Master Windsor was in debt, that much was clear. But there was more going on. She thought about his trip to the room at the top of the stairs, emerging with a sackful of coins. She remembered his words to those men, how he'd told them that with time he could get more coins—

All you could wish for.

Molly's eyes drifted upstairs. Through the banister, she could just make out the edge of the little green door.

14

CATCH AS CATCH CAN

Molly spun beneath the prickly afternoon sun, both hands clasped over her eyes. *"Arghh!"* she shouted in her most frightening giant voice (which, Kip had told her more than once, was not very frightening). *"There's pitch in me eyes!"* She could hear the sound of children running in the grass around her. Running for dear life.

Molly spun around one final time and pulled her hands from her face with a great roar. She was standing in the middle of the lawn, legs bent, shoulders hunched, hands spread like claws. "The giant realized that he'd been *tricked*," she called out, continuing her story. "But by the time he scraped the pitch from his eyes, it was too late—for the children had hid themselves in the mountains, shouting: *Catch as catch can!*"

The "mountains" were the little hillocks covering the Windsor lawn. Each mound was about as high as Molly's knees and perhaps seven feet long—roughly the size of a canoe—and they were perfect for hiding. Not only could you disappear behind them, but you could crawl between them without being seen by flesh-eating giants. *"I'll gobble you up!"* she bellowed, storming over the grass, her every foot-step an earthquake.

Molly spotted something dark behind a hill and leapt toward it. It was Kip's cap, hanging from the end of his abandoned crutch. *"Arghh! Fooled again by these clever chiddlers!"* She threw down the hat and turned around. "But the giant did not lose hope," she called out. "For he knew that children had a particular sweet smell to 'em. And so he sniffed at the air, sayin'—

> *"'Fee! Fum! Foe! Fie!*
> *I smell the blood of an English child!'"*

Molly heard a small giggle just behind her. She turned and saw a pair of small shoes with ribbons on top poking out from behind a hill. She crept closer, lowering her voice—

> *"'Fie! Fiddle! Fum! Furl!*
> *I smell the blood . . .'"*

Molly leapt over the hill and grabbed hold of Penny—

> *"'Of an English girl!!!'"*

Penny screamed with equal parts glee and terror as Molly de-scended, tickling her to death.

Penny's capture marked the end of the round, at which point the other fugitives emerged from their hiding places. "It's not fair," Alistair said, appearing behind a largish hill near the stables. "Just when I've found a perfect hiding spot, she goes and gets captured—on purpose, no doubt!"

"It *was not* on purpose!" Penny sat up. "It's my sweet smell!"

"Leave her alone," Kip called from behind the well. "Besides, your spot ain't so great."

"Says you!" Alistair shot back.

It was during this dispute that Molly noticed activity by the front door. Master Windsor had on his riding cloak and hat and was readying his carriage, which he had apparently fetched himself from the stables. He had a leather case under one arm that looked quite heavy. Mistress Windsor stood in the open doorway, arms folded tight across her body. Molly stood and watched them. She could not hear what they were saying, but it sounded like they were having yet another disagreement.

It had been four days since Fig and Stubbs had visited the house, and in that time, Molly had noted a distinct change in the interactions between her employers. Gone were Bertrand's lighthearted jokes and good-natured smiles. Constance, for her part, simply pretended she had no husband. Every room they occupied was filled with a quiet tension, which put Molly in mind of a powder keg waiting to explode. She thought of how different this was from her own parents, who disagreed plenty, but always out in the open and with half smirks and teasing jabs—like a pair of actors in a play. Molly preferred the out-in-the-open way, for it meant that neither parent would ever say something they couldn't bear for their children to hear. It meant there were no secrets.

Penny rolled over. "What are you doing?" she demanded. "You haven't even gobbled me up yet!"

It is a difficult thing to look away from a private conflict taking place in public—like trying to ignore an open button on someone's clothes. Molly had the feeling that she should be distracting the children, but her eyes were fixed to the spot.

The other children soon joined her side, watching the unfolding scene with similar interest. "Are the master and mistress plannin' a trip?" Kip said. "I coulda fetched the horse for 'em." He did not especially like it when other people did his job for him.

"I dinna think they're goin' together," Molly said.

Alistair spoke up. "That would be Father rushing off to town to meet some 'business associates.'" He snorted. "The *pawnshop* is more like it. I saw him pilfering the dining room this afternoon—stuffing that bag full of candlesticks and flatware . . . He even took my silver pocketknife with the mother-of-pearl handle that I got for Christmas last year. It's a lucky thing I hid my sweets, or he'd have gotten them, too." So saying, he pulled a crumpled bag of caramels from his trouser pocket.

Molly didn't understand why Master Windsor would need to pawn his possessions when he had a room full of money upstairs. "He's sellin' your things?" she said.

"What's left of them, anyhow." Alistair popped a caramel in his mouth, chewing loudly. "He did the same thing before we moved away from town—trying to pay off creditors. When we came here, he gave his word that those days were over and done with. Shows what his word is worth."

Penny hit him on the arm. "Alistair, you shouldn't say bad things about Papa."

"Why not?" he shot back. "It's the truth."

Molly looked at the boy and felt a pang of sympathy: it could not be easy to see one's father in such dire straits. Da had never been rich, but he had always been someone she could admire.

Alistair rocked back on his heels, pointing. "Oh, look! Now he's promising it's the very last time. Until next time, of course."

Master Windsor still had the bag in his hands, and it was now open. He stepped close to his wife—at first, Molly thought it was to kiss her cheek—and unclasped the diamond chain from around her neck. He likewise removed her bracelet and earrings, dropping them all into the open bag. Finally he reached for the ring on her left hand. At this, Constance stepped back. She shook her head, clutching the ring to her breast. The ring, it seemed, was special. Molly had noticed the ring before. It had a dark band and a small, pale blue diamond. There was more arguing, and finally Mistress Windsor relented. She pulled the ring from her finger and threw it at her husband, who dropped down to retrieve it from the gravel.

Molly felt a tug at her apron. "Can we play now?" Penny said. "It's my turn to be giant."

"You can't be giant," Alistair said. "Last winner gets to be giant, and I was winning!"

"You were not," said Kip.

"That's right!" Penny said. "Kip was! He wasn't even caught once!"

"Well, I was about to *start* winning!" Alistair shot back. "Besides, you can't be giant because you're not even a little bit frightening."

"Well, I say we give Miss Penny a chance," Molly declared. She knelt down in front of the girl. "You sure you're up to the job?"

Penny roared and showed her claws. *"I'll pop out yer eyeballs and eat 'em like grapes!"* she snarled.

Molly nodded, impressed. "All right, then, count o' thirty." Penny smiled and clasped both hands over her eyes and started counting aloud. Alistair and Kip disappeared behind two hills. Molly stood and glanced back toward the house. She noticed some movement behind a small window on the second floor, half-hidden by thick branches. She shielded her eyes from the sun, staring at the figure on the other side of the glass.

By the time Penny finished counting, Molly was already at the house. She closed the front door behind her, careful not to let it make any noise that might alert anyone to her presence. She climbed the stairs as quietly as her shoes would allow. Just as she reached the top step, the green door opened and Mistress Windsor emerged from within.

"Molly!" she cried, obviously alarmed to find someone lurking nearby. "I . . . I thought you were outside." She pulled the door shut behind her.

Molly gave a contrite bow, keeping her eyes on the floor. "We was playin' hide-and-go-seek, mum. I thought one of 'em might've snuck in the house and . . ." She looked up and her voice trailed off. On Mistress Windsor's left hand was a small ring with a dark band and an icy blue stone.

"And . . . ?" the woman said.

Molly stared at the jewel, unable to speak. "That . . . that's a very pretty ring, mum," she said.

"Isn't it?" Constance examined the stone on her delicate finger, watching it sparkle in the dim light. "Bertie gave it to me long ago . . ."

Molly looked at the woman looking at the ring. The very same ring she had seen cast off on the driveway only moments before. She swallowed. "Forgive me, mum . . . but didn't I see Master Windsor take a ring very much like that?"

The woman looked up, her face suddenly hard. "You are quite mistaken." She took a key from her pocket and locked the green door, pulling on the handle to make sure it was secure. "I think I heard the children by the stables. Perhaps you should bring them inside." She gave a humorless smile. "We wouldn't want them falling prey to any *rogue evangelists*, would we?"

Molly looked down, cheeks burning. "Yes, mum." She bowed and went back downstairs to join the others. When she stepped outside, the world had changed in some minute but indescribable way. The blue sky suddenly looked less blue. The cool air was less cool. Even the sun looked dim. And when it was her turn to be giant and Molly covered her eyes, she saw only one thing—

A ring, shining on a pale finger.

15

The Other Thing

Cellar Hollow burned in the red-orange light of the setting sun. Kip sat at his post atop one of the old stone pillars at the far end of the bridge. The pillar was too slick to climb, but he had found that the old ropes lashed around it made a serviceable ladder. The top of the rightmost pillar had a flat spot that was perfect for long sitting. Kip kept his eyes trained on the road, staring in the direction of the nearest village. He was watching for the same thing he had been watching for every night: a letter from Ma and Da.

When he and Molly had sent their letter off, she had warned him it might take weeks—maybe even months—for it to reach its destination. Kip knew it was foolish to expect a response so soon. Still, he didn't want to run the risk of missing the letter because the postman was too scared to approach the Windsor house and ring the bell. And so, every day after his work was done and he had eaten dinner, he sat and watched.

Kip shivered in the early evening. Even though the sky was ablaze, the air was cold. He stuffed both hands into his coat pockets, balling his fists up to make them warm. He could feel the wishing button in his right pocket where he always kept it. He knew the button wasn't really magic, but it was nice to pretend. He closed his eyes and made a secret wish that he could see what his parents were doing right at this moment. For all he knew, they were on the bottom of the world where up was down and night shone bright as day.

Kip kept his eyes closed and listened to the river flowing under the bridge and along the road. He liked being near the road because it reminded him of the last time they had all been together as a family, the four of them leaving the farm to board a boat that would carry them across the sea to a new life. Kip had been too sick to remember much of the voyage. He hadn't even been able to give Ma and Da a proper good-bye. He had awakened in an orphanage, where Molly had explained how their parents and the rest of the grown-up folks had been carried off by pirates. Kip suspected it wasn't actually pirates—that was just the sort of detail Molly would make up—but he did know his parents would come back soon. They had to.

When Kip opened his eyes, he saw a figure approaching from the eastern road. It was not the postman but the old witch they had met their first day in the valley. He remembered her name was Hester Kettle, which had struck him as a little bit funny and a little bit frightening.

The woman was walking straight toward Kip. There were no other homes for miles, and so it was pretty clear she meant to call upon the Windsors. Kip considered running off before she reached him but then thought better of it—if she really was a witch, he didn't want to provoke her.

He watched her shuffle nearer, her pack of junk clattering with each step. She wasn't playing her instrument, but she was humming something to herself. It took Kip a moment to realize that she was singing in the same key as the water flowing alongside the road. "Why, look who it is!" she called when she was near enough to speak. "The little brother, come to bid me welcome."

"I'm waitin' for the postman," Kip said.

"You'll be waitin' a long time, I wager. Post comes but once a month, and rarer still in this direction. You don't mind if I rest my bones, do you?" She untied a three-legged stool from her pack and set it on the ground. She sat upon it with an unsteady plop that left the stool groaning. She grinned at Kip. "Not so grand as your throne, but it'll do."

His eyes drifted to a pair of long, rusted garden shears hanging from the side of her pack. "I thought you never came near these woods," he said.

"You thought correctly," she said, gracefully tucking the shears out of view. "But when I spied Master Windsor racin' toward the city on that carriage of his, I figured it was worth the risk to check on my investment." She smiled in a way that let Kip know she was talking about him. "You may recall promising me a story."

"That was my sister who promised it, not me," Kip said. "I dinna tell stories. Molly's fixin' supper in the house, if you care to call on her."

The woman glanced toward the house but quickly looked away again. "Here's close enough for me, luv." Kip could tell she was nervous—for all her jokes and stories, she was just as scared of the sourwoods as everyone else. "No need to interrupt your work. I only come to put a niggle in your ear. And to make sure you two lambs weren't"—she hummed, as if searching for the right word— "indisposed."

Kip did not know that word, but he understood her meaning. "You thought we was dead," he said.

The woman laughed, which was no kind of answer. "You got a keen eye for what's what. It's not like me to be so dramatic, but when two whelps disappear into a place such as this"—she gestured to the wooded isle—"you can't help but fear the worst."

Kip looked hard at the woman, trying to disentangle her teasing from her truth. What did she really know about this place? "Back when we was on the road, you said there was somethin' tragic about these woods. You called it 'the other thing.'"

The woman gave a cryptic smile. "I'm not sure your sister would appreciate me frightening you."

"I ain't afraid," Kip said. "Well, I *am* afraid . . . but I'm not afraid of *being* afraid. If that makes sense. True is still true, even if it's bad. That means I want to hear it."

"That's a rare thing, in a boy or a man," she said. "Your sister raised you up right." Kip wanted to tell her that Molly didn't raise him—that he was raised by Ma and Da—but he held his tongue. The old woman drew a churchwarden pipe from her pack and stuffed it with tobacco from a pouch around her waist. She lit the bowl and began smoking like a man. The smell reminded Kip of autumn leaves. "You know by now that Master Windsor grew up in that house," she said.

"He moved away when he was a boy," Kip said. "They told my sister it was some kind of bad fever that took his whole family—left him an orphan."

The woman nodded. "He is an orphan . . . though I'm not so sure about the rest of your story." She drew a deep breath and released it. "I remember the night it happened—it's the sort of night you don't quickly forget. 'Twas a terrible storm, howlin' winds, cold rain. Some- time in the wee hours, there's a wailing sound come down the village road—the kind of scream that sets your every hair on end. Folks rush out of doors to find young Master Windsor—no older than you—in his nightclothes, soaked to the bone, not even shoes on his feet. He's pale as a ghost and thin, too. We hardly recognize him. He's frantic with fear and keeps saying something evil's come for him—come for his parents."

Kip suddenly wished very much that he were not having this con- versation. He wanted to be at the stables, in the house—anywhere but on the bridge, talking to this old woman. Still, he had to know. "Did they find out what it was?" he said. "The evil thing that was after him?"

"We may be superstitious around these parts, but we aren't

heartless. A few of the men got together rifles and dogs and lanterns and rode out here. The house was wrecked twice over from the storm. Furniture tossed, doors ripped open, windows smashed . . . and nothing else."

Kip swallowed. "What about his ma and da?"

"Gone." She pointed the long stem of her pipe at him. "So tell me this: What kind of fever turns a house inside out and makes flesh-and-blood people vanish into thin air?"

Kip had no answer. He tried not to think of that screaming boy in the stormy road. He tried not to think of what evil might have taken the boy's family. He looked at the woman and saw she was watching him carefully—probably waiting to see what effect her story had made upon him. "I dinna believe you," he said sharply. "If any of that stuff had happened to Master Windsor when he was a boy, there's not a thing in the whole world that would bring him back here."

The woman nodded, puffing. "You'd be surprised. Windsors aren't the first to try and lay claim to these here woods—I'll wager they won't be the last." Her eyes lingered on the house, looming large in the dusky shadows. "There's somethin' about this land that draws folks in, even when every bone in their bodies is telling them to run far, far away . . ." Her voice trailed off, and she was silent for a long while.

Kip was beginning to wonder whether she had forgotten about him altogether when she turned to him with a wooden smile. "Now, if you'll forgive me, I'd like to get clear of these parts before the moon's out." She stood up and tied her stool to her pack with a bit of loose rope. She jabbed a finger in Kip's direction. "Maybe don't tell that sister of yours what I said about Master Windsor. We wouldn't want to frighten her."

"I won't," he said. But he crossed his fingers as he said it.

The old woman curtsied and faced the road to the west—the opposite direction from where she had come. She adjusted her pack. "Always walk in a straight line, I say. Don't ever turn back." So saying, she started down the path, humming and jangling as she went.

Kip watched her disappear around the darkening bend, his hand clenched tight around the button.

16

The Garden in the Woods

When Molly arrived at her room that night, she found a gift on the bed. It was a long dark dress, carelessly folded. Atop the dress was a note:

> *Molly—*
> *This is an old frock for which I no longer have*
> *any use. I thought you might want it to wear on*
> *your errands. It may want hemming.*

It was written in Mistress Windsor's hand. Molly wondered what might have prompted this sudden show of generosity. Constance did not strike her as the sort of person to give gifts with no strings attached. Was this a peace offering or was it a bribe? Molly thought back to their conversation at the top of the stairs. The woman had been so flustered, so unlike herself. She had not wanted Molly to see the ring. Was she buying her silence?

Whatever the motive, a new dress was a new dress, and Molly was only mortal. She set down the note and picked up the garment. It was well worn but well made—certainly finer than anything she had ever owned. She ran her fingers over the thick fabric, which she thought might be called "velvet." The color was almost black but for the edges, which glowed green when caught by the light. Molly loved wearing green because of the way it made her red hair even redder.

She shed her food-spattered uniform and knickers. The night air was cold against her bare skin. She shivered, quickly pulling the dress over her body. The fabric was as soft as down. The dress was clearly intended for someone who had servants, and it took some struggle for Molly to lace up the back without help. She eventually managed, though, and stood straight like Mistress Windsor, wishing she owned a piece of jewelry to place at her neck. She turned her hips and felt the long skirt swish from side to side at her feet.

Molly walked to the mirror above her dresser and looked at herself. She had hoped that the dress might make her appear transformed, statuesque even, but it did not. The gown was loose around the bodice, and the skirt hung limp around her legs. She looked exactly as she was: a fourteen-year-old servant wearing a rich woman's cast-off clothes.

Molly wondered if she might be helped with a little "propping up"—a phrase her mother used to utter. She dragged her battered trunk from the wardrobe and opened the lid. She knelt and rummaged through the rags in search of a petticoat that might fill out the skirt. Molly's old clothes were even more ragged than she remembered—all of them threadbare and stained. She reached the bottom of the trunk, where she found the letter to her parents, right where she had hidden it. She expected to feel the top hat but found only more clothes. Molly frowned. She leaned over the trunk and pulled out clothes with both hands, heaping them onto the floor. She stared into the now-empty trunk . . .

The top hat was gone.

Molly sat back, her eyes searching the walls. Someone had gone through her private things, and they had taken the hat. She thought about who in the family might have done it. Penny? Alistair? Master Windsor? Mistress Windsor? Her eyes fell on the clothes scattered at her feet. She reached out and removed a dry leaf from the pile. Or was it someone else?

Molly was startled by a rapping at her window.

She turned around to see Kip, crouched on the grass. Molly was not expecting him that night. Ever since the weather had turned, he had insisted on sleeping outside in the stables with Galileo. Molly glanced at the leaf and wondered whether he had made the smarter decision. Still, there was no sense in alarming him with news of the missing hat. She quickly stuffed everything back into the trunk—including the unsent letter—and stood up.

She smoothed out her velvety dress and opened the window. "Too cold for you?" she said.

Kip didn't bother to climb inside. "Galileo's gone missin'."

"The little sneak!"

"That's exactly what I said." He hopped back from the open window. "C'mon on, then."

Molly gave an irritated sigh. She pulled a coat over her dress, slipped on some boots, and climbed atop her bed. She cast a final glance back at her room before crawling through the window and into the darkness.

The air surrounding the house was damp and cold. Already a dewy fog had descended on the entire valley, making it feel twice as dark as it should. "You sure this canna wait for tomorrow?" Molly said, lighting her lantern on the third try. She clutched the hem of her skirt, trying to keep it above the wet grass.

"I've already circled the yard twice," Kip said, ignoring her question. "We'll have to try the woods."

Molly raised her lamp, trying to see the edge of the forest through the fog. Even though it was spring, the air was winter-cold. She silently chided herself for not taking time to change into warmer clothes. "It's on your head if I catch fever and die," she said, walking with Kip toward the trees.

"You shouldn't joke about that." He hobbled between two low hills. "Besides, I ain't the one who decided to go outside wearin' nothing but . . . whatever that is you're wearin'."

"It's one of Mistress Windsor's old dresses. She let me have it."

Kip slowed and looked at her sideways. "They're givin' you gifts now?" His tone was unusually serious, and Molly couldn't tell whether he was speaking with concern or jealousy.

"I can get you one, too, if you'd like," she said, mussing his hair.

Kip pulled away and reaffixed his cap. "It's my fault Gal's out here. I was late bringin' his oats. He musta got hungry and went off to find his own supper."

Molly did not need to ask why her brother had been late. She knew that every day at sundown he watched the main road—sitting later and later into the night. Sometimes, through the upstairs window, she would see him alone at his post. Perched atop the bridge, waiting for a letter that would never come. "Still no postman?" she said, trying to keep the guilt from her voice.

"Not yet," Kip said. "But it wasn't the post that kept me late. That old witch Hester came by. She was askin' for you."

It took Molly a moment to realize he was talking about the story-teller they had met in the road. The realization was not a pleasant one. The woman had a way of seeing right through Molly, and the idea of her being alone with Kip seemed dangerous. "What did she want?"

"You gave her your word you'd come around the village and tell her about the Windsors," he said. "Or don't you remember?"

Molly didn't like the tone with which he said this; it felt like an accusation. "I remember just fine. Only I'm not sure the master an' mistress would like me tellin' tales to nosy old hags."

"Then maybe you shouldn't 'a promised you would," he said and continued on toward the trees.

Usually Molly had to slow down to let Kip keep up, but tonight he was moving fast; it was all she could do to keep apace of him without running. For this reason, she was grateful when they reached the woods and he was forced to slow down. The floor of the forest was just as uneven as the lawn, and the canopy of branches hid the moon, leaving only Molly's lamp to guide them. She walked alongside her brother, calling out Galileo's name, shining her light at their feet so they could look for hoofprints. Kip didn't like to carry a lamp. He claimed he could see in the dark, but Molly knew it was really because he already had one hand on his crutch and didn't want to lose use of the other.

"Shine your lamp here," he said, pointing ahead. Molly's light found a hoofprint in the black mud. There were more prints leading through a bramble. Kip pulled himself up on his crutch and continued in the direction of the trail.

Molly cupped a hand to her mouth and sang out into the fog:

"Oh, where did you go, dear Gal-i-le-o?
Your oats are a-ready, an' we miss you so!"

It was a simple tune she and Kip used when they were making up songs. One of them would start a verse, and then the other would finish it with a silly rhyme—the sillier the better. Kip, however, did not seem to be in a mood for singing.

"Ain't you the gloomy one," she said.

"Just thinkin' is all," Kip said as he hopped around a rock. "The old woman told me what really happened to Master Windsor's family when he was a boy."

"They died of fever," Molly said, repeating what she had been told by Mistress Windsor. "Nothin' too strange in that."

Kip shook his head. "That old witch says it wasn't no fever. She says they was all killed—all at once—by somethin' wicked. And their bodies were never found." He kept walking.

A cold wind swept through the woods, shivering the branches. Molly shivered, too. She pulled her coat tight over her dress, the bottom of which was now certainly muddy. She could have throttled that old woman for filling her brother's head with such nonsense. "She was just tryin' to frighten you," she said, catching up.

"Frighten? Or warn off?"

"And now you're tryin' to frighten me. Shame on you both."

Their conversation was interrupted by the welcome sight of Galileo. The horse stood in the middle of a clearing, struggling against something at his feet. "He's caught his leg in some kinda snare," Kip said, rushing to his side. "Bring your lamp here." Molly knelt at her brother's side to help him. The "snare" was actually a root that had somehow coiled itself several times around Galileo's ankle. "His leg's hurt, but I dinna think it's broken."

Kip carefully pulled the root away. The moment Galileo was free, he reared up, knocking them both backward. Molly's lamp fell to the ground and the flame went out, leaving them in complete darkness. "Perfect," she muttered, feeling out in front of her for the lantern. She found it and set it upright. She fished a match from her coat pocket and raised the storm glass.

Kip stilled her hand. "Don't," he said softly.

Molly followed his gaze toward the surrounding darkness—

Only it wasn't dark.

She stood, eyeing the forest floor, which seemed to be glowing softly in the moonlight. As her eyes adjusted, she could make out flowers of different shapes and sizes poking up through the rocks and brush. She knelt down and touched a large blossom at her feet; the petals were silver–white. *Like slices of the moon*, she thought. "You ever heard of flowers that bloom at night?"

Kip shook his head. "I walked these woods a hundred times in the daylight and never once saw so much as a bud. Now look at 'em. They're like something from one of your stories." He glanced over at Galileo, who had wandered to a cluster of shimmering teardrop–shaped blossoms and was happily munching away. "I'll bet that's what got him so far from the house. Gal's crazy for honeysuckle and bluebells—it's all I can do to keep him from eatin' up the mistress's whole flower bed." He stood, wiping his hands on his trousers. "Makes you wonder who planted 'em."

"*Planted* 'em?" Molly said. "They're wild."

"They're wild enough now, but look at how they're sorted. All in groups. Those lily–shaped ones, the big old spiny fellows, them little hangin' things—each of a kind." He shook his head, adjusting his cap. "Someone had to plant 'em like that, one by one. Wouldn't that have been a thing? To see a whole garden like this, all silver and shadow?"

Molly could now see that Kip was right: the flowers were indeed in some sort of pattern. But it felt less like a garden than the memory of one. Weeds and time had choked it. "Even if there was someone who planted 'em, he's long gone." She picked up Galileo's rope. "We should be, too, for that matter." She took one last look at the glowing flowers, relit her lantern, and started back for the house.

The stillness of the garden remained with Molly and Kip as they wandered through the dark woods. After a few false starts, they found some of their own tracks, which they were able to follow to the edge of the trees. Galileo, for his part, was acting more mule than horse; as they neared the lawn, he became increasingly reluctant to go on. He nickered and snorted and pulled against his bit with all his might. By the time they got him to the stables and inside his stall, Molly's new dress was covered in mud and torn in three places. "Stupid animal," she muttered, retying his rope with a special double knot her father had taught her.

"Don't be sore at Gal," Kip said, holding open the door. "C'mon. I'll walk you back to the house."

Molly knew Kip must have been just as exhausted as she was, and it meant something that he would keep her company. The two of them walked across the lawn in quiet. As she walked, Molly's mind kept turning back to the image of those pale flowers. Kip's mind was apparently on the same subject. "You don't need no fancy dress to look nice," he said to her as they approached the drive. "Just like them flowers in the woods don't need no vase."

Molly put an arm on his shoulder. No gift in the world was worth more than a kind word from Kip. She looked back up at the house, wondering if she had remembered to put out her bedroom light, and stopped short.

"Molls?" Kip said.

Molly did not answer. She remained still, eyes fixed on the front door of the house—

"It's open," she said.

Ever since her first night with the top hat, Molly had made a careful point of locking the Windsors' front door before bed. She did this every night, and tonight had been no exception. And yet, here she was, staring at an open door. Wind swept in and out of the house like a tide, pushing the door back and forth as it moved.

Kip inched closer to her. "Maybe . . . the wind pushed it loose."

She nodded, taking his hand. "Maybe so." They were both whispering.

It could have been a trick of the light, but it looked like something was moving just inside the door frame. Something dark. Something tall. Something she did not want to be there.

A sharp gust of wind swept across the lawn, and the door swung wide. Molly caught her breath. A figure stepped onto the stoop. Dry leaves swirled all around him. His face and hands were pale in the moonlight. He was wearing a long black cloak and a black hat that looked horribly, horribly familiar. Molly swallowed, barely able to form the words.

"The night man," she whispered. "He's back."

17

THE NIGHT MAN

Molly grabbed Kip and pulled him to the ground. She pressed her body flat against the grass, hiding herself behind one of the small hills. Not a hundred feet away was the man her brother had seen in the fog. The man she had heard stalking the hallways. The man she had told herself a hundred times over didn't exist.

Molly listened to his footsteps, slow and heavy on the gravel drive. She closed both eyes—her mind reeling. Where had he come from? What did he *want*?

The footsteps stopped somewhere near the front of the house. Molly peered over the top of the hill, but her view was blocked by fog and shadow. She dropped back down. "I canna see him," she whispered to Kip. "You stay here."

Molly crept between the hills, her stomach flat against the ground. She tried not to think about whether the man could see her through the fog—it was all she could do to keep her head down and keep moving. She had less than fifty feet to go, but it felt much, much farther.

Molly finally reached the old well beside the drive. From there she thought she might be able to watch the man unobserved. She sat up and poked her head around the edge of the well. The man was working at the foot of the big tree. His clothes were tattered and worn, but his skin was as white as soap. Looking at his hands, Molly couldn't help but think of the blossoms she and Kip had found in the woods. The man's gaunt face was half-hidden behind a long, unkempt beard. The wells of his eyes were darker than pitch—like a shadow's shadow.

The man carried with him a collection of old gardening tools. Molly saw a rake and shovel as well as pruning shears and a hand spade.

"What's he doin'?" said a voice in her ear.

Molly spun around to find Kip crouched beside her. "I told you to stay put!" she hissed.

"And let you get snatched up?" He shook his head. "Scoot over."

A scolding would have to wait. Molly inched to one side to make room for him behind the well. "Keep your voice down," she said and clamped her fist around his collar—just in case he got the idea to sneak any closer. Together, they peered at the house.

The man was kneeling before the giant tree, holding a rusted pair of shears. He carefully trimmed back any moss and ivy that had encroached around its base. "Are those your tools?" Molly whispered.

Kip shook his head no.

Molly watched as the man leaned close to the tree, tenderly running his fingers along the bark, whispering softly. As he spoke, Molly thought she could hear voices echoing and hissing in the wind—she did not understand what the voices said, but they sounded beautiful. And sad.

The man finished his words and stepped back from the tree. He picked up a large metal watering can. Molly felt a surge of panic. "He's comin' to the well!"

"No he ain't," Kip whispered. "See how he's holdin' the can—it's already filled to the brim." Molly looked again and saw that her brother was right. The man brought the can to the tree. He moved carefully, as though he were carrying something much more precious than water. He gently tipped the can, wetting the roots and soil around the tree. It could have been a trick of the moonlight, but the water looked un-natural as it fell—reflecting a silvery light all its own.

The man shook the can, expelling every last drop. He stood again and held his hand out over the ground. A gust of wind blew past Molly and circled around the man, scattering the leaves at his feet. He took his old shovel and thrust the blade into the exposed ground. He dug into the earth, heaping scoops of dark soil onto the grass beside him.

Molly felt Kip nudge her arm. "That's right where I filled the hole before—the one Penny fell into." He scooted closer. "But why do you think he's diggin' another one?"

The man looked up, seemingly alarmed.

Molly dropped behind the well, pulling Kip down with her. The night man had looked straight at her. Had he heard them? Had he *seen* them? A cold wind was now wuthering around her. The house groaned. The tree creaked. Leaves shuffled. She could almost see the icy currents sliding between the hills like living things, feeling every twig, every pebble, every blade of grass—searching for prey.

A shiver licked up her spine as the wind moved over her body, grasping at her legs, her arms, the back of her neck, as if trying to identify her. Molly clenched her eyes shut, holding her brother tight, trying not to breathe. *If I don't breathe*, she thought, *he might not find me*.

Suddenly the wind died. Leaves fell softly to the grass, and all was silent but for one sound—

The slow *crunch* of footsteps on gravel.

The night man was heading straight toward the well. Molly gripped Kip even tighter. She didn't dare turn her head, didn't dare look at the man who was twenty, now ten, now five feet away. Molly felt a chill that might have been his shadow, and the footsteps stopped right beside her. From the corner of her eye, she could see the night man standing next to her, nearly on top of her, facing away toward the woods. Molly stared at his boots. They were caked in mud, worn with decay, and did not match. Molly knew those boots. They were the boots whose tracks she cleaned from the halls every morning—each time telling herself they meant nothing. But, of course, they did mean something. Something wicked.

The man whispered into the air, his fingers moving slightly like he was reading the currents with his hands. Molly knew that the wind would tell him where she was. Tell him that all he needed to do was turn around, and he would find them. She closed her eyes and uttered a silent prayer. *Don't turn around,* she thought. *Don't turn around. Don't turn around. Don't—*

Neighhhhhh!

A high-pitched whinny broke the silence. It came from across the lawn and nearly made Molly gasp. She opened her eyes to see the man facing the stables. The door was open, and through it Molly could see Galileo inside, kicking, snorting, straining against his rope. The horse whinnied again, knocking the walls of his stall, fighting to get free. Molly smiled. She would have kissed that stupid horse if she could.

The man waved his hand, and a sharp gust of wind hit the stable door, slamming it shut with a violent clatter. He lowered his hand and turned back toward the house. Molly listened as his footsteps receded into the darkness. She wanted desperately to run, but she knew there was no place to run to. They were trapped.

She felt Kip stir at her side. He was staring up at her, his eyes wide and pleading. "What do we do?" His voice was less than a whisper.

Molly stared back, and for the first time in her life, she had no story or smile for him. "You were right, Kip." Her voice was shaking. "Right all along. We never shoulda come here. Tomorrow we run."

Tomorrow, however, was a long way off. She held her brother close against her chest, shivering in the darkness, listening to the sharp crunch of the man's spade as it cut the soil over and over again.

Digging . . .

Digging . . .

Digging . . .

18

A Rude Awakening

Kip heard two voices in the darkness.

"It's like I told you," the first voice said. "They're dead."

"They're not dead, dummy," said the second voice. "Look, you can see their breath."

"Are, too! That breath is just their ghosts leaving the bodies. I think we should play funeral. You'll be pallbearer, and I can give the homily!"

"They're just sleeping. Look here, I'll prove it."

Kip heard a deep hawking sound, and he caught a faint aroma of licorice. He opened his eyes to find a long glob of black spit dangling just above his nose. Alistair and Penny hovered over him, blocking out the blue sky.

"Get offa me!" Kip shouted, shoving Alistair back with both arms.

Alistair fell onto the grass and the spit landed on his own shirt, a sight that made Penny burst into laughter. "Wait until Mummy sees what you've done to your clothes," she said. "Then it'll be *you* who needs the funeral."

Kip pulled himself up, blinking against the morning sun. He had been asleep on the lawn; his back and sides were wet with dew, and he could feel the imprint of grass against one cheek. His left leg was stiff with cold. Molly was beside him, curled up against the well. He touched her arm—

"No!" She jolted awake, eyes wild with terror.

"It's just me." Kip knelt in front of her, taking her shoulders in his hands. "We're all right, Molls." He tried to make his voice calm, the way his father used to when Kip got frightened by storms. "We fell asleep outside, but *we're all right*."

Molly blinked her eyes, still breathing heavily. "And . . . *him*?" she said.

Kip knew exactly what *him* she was speaking of. He grabbed his crutch and stood up, ignoring the pain shooting into his hip. He gripped the well for support as he and Molly looked toward the house. In the daylight, everything appeared normal, peaceful even. The new hole around the base of the tree was now hidden under a bed of leaves.

Penny forced her head between them. "Why were you two sleeping out here?"

Kip exchanged a look with his sister, who smiled at Penny.

"You never slept under the stars, miss? Why, there's no softer blanket than an evenin' fog." She stretched her arms in an exaggerated manner and yawned. "One night out here, and I'm as rested as a rock."

Alistair glared at her dress, now visible under her open coat.

The green velvet was ruined beyond repair. "Is that one of Mother's dresses? Did you steal it?"

Kip hopped toward him. "The mistress made it a present. And if I hear you accuse my sister again, it'll be more than just spit on that shirt of yours."

Molly stood and put a hand on his shoulder. "I'm fine, Kip." She pulled her coat closed and looked back to the house. "What time is it?"

"Nearly ten," Penny answered. "We missed breakfast and there's no hot water *and* I had to dress myself." Kip thought this last bit might explain why her frock was on backward. "Mummy's having a proper fit. She's gone twice through the house looking for you."

"She'll probably fire you both," Alistair said.

"Wouldn't matter if she did," Kip shot back. He remembered what Molly had told him the night before. They were leaving this place. Leaving and never coming back. He looked back at his sister. "Tell 'em, Molls."

Molly leaned toward him. "Not like this." She lowered her voice. "We canna up and leave like bandits. Let me square things with the mistress first. I owe her that."

Kip stared at her, uncertain. He had thought they would run at first light. Now she wanted to wait. Still, he knew it was the honorable thing to do. And it would take him at least until noon to prepare the wagon. So long as they got away before nightfall, they would surely be fine. "Tonight," he said.

Molly nodded. "Tonight."

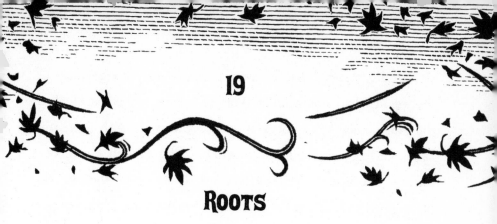

19

Roots

C'mon, Gal." Kip pulled open the heavy stable door. "We got some gardening to do." A plan was forming in his mind. If he had one day left in this place, he might as well make use of the time by learning what he could about the tree. He splashed water on his face and changed into some dry clothes. He loaded the wagon with everything he might need for his tests: a hand spade, two feed bags, some rope, a wooden rake, a watering can, and several flowers in clay pots.

Galileo was reluctant to approach the tree, and so when Kip got the wagon close enough, he unhooked the horse, who trotted gratefully back to his stall. Kip unloaded his tools and laid them carefully on the grass. Now he was ready.

He picked up one of the dry leaves around the base of the tree. It was brittle and had a starlike shape that he didn't recognize. A breeze swept past, pulling the leaf from his grasp. He stared at the blanket of orange and brown leaves surrounding the trunk. Everything else in the valley was lush and green, but this tree was bare. "Why would you be shedding in the middle o' spring?" he asked.

Kip had noticed that no grass or weeds grew near the base of the tree. He had assumed that this was because the house blocked the sun, but now he suspected it was something more. Using a hand spade, he dug a hole about the size of his fist in the soil. He unpotted one of Mistress Windsor's flowers and planted it in the hole. He pressed the soil around the roots and stem, packing it firm but not too firm.

Kip pulled himself up with his crutch and went to retrieve his watering can. When he turned back around, he caught his breath. "You little sneak!" The flower he had planted just moments before was now slumped over, its red petals turned brown. He dropped the can and hobbled closer. He knelt down, feeling the limp stem and withered leaves. There was no question: the flower was dead.

Kip spent the rest of the morning repeating his experiment, with similar results. He planted more than a dozen blossoms of all different kinds. No matter how deeply he planted them or how carefully he packed the earth or how much he watered them, every one of the flowers expired. By early afternoon the tree was surrounded by a garden of decay. The strangest thing was that Kip never actually *saw* it happen. He would get up to fetch a tool or glance away for a moment, and when he looked back, the flower would be dead.

"It ain't natural," he said after discovering that his thirteenth and final plant had shriveled away. He peered up at the tree towering over him. Everything in its shadow seemed to die. But why?

Kip hobbled to the trunk, studying its rough black hide. He

touched the bark, and a sharp wind rushed past him. He took his hand away from the tree, and the wind stopped. He shivered; it had felt like a warning.

He had noticed a number of low branches around the base of the trunk, which he thought might provide a boost to reach the higher limbs. He reached for a branch but stopped short of touching it. The branch was dark and smooth and slightly curved. It wasn't a branch at all—

It was the handle of an axe.

The handle looked very old and had become a part of the tree. Kip could see the swollen knot of bark where the tree had swallowed the axe head. He stared at the other "branches" sticking out from the base: a crude hatchet, the stub of a hunting knife, a rusted bucksaw, even what looked like the hilt of a broadsword. Some of the handles looked centuries old, others looked more recent—but every one of them had failed in its purpose. "It's like a regular battlefield," he said, his voice a whisper.

Kip hobbled back from the tree. He had no idea what stories might be behind these different handles. It was clear that many people had tried to cut down the tree, and something—or *someone*—had stopped them.

There was just one more place to look for answers, a place Kip had been avoiding all morning. Even now, he could feel it at his heels, calling to him, taunting him. He swallowed, turning around to face the pit.

He and Molly had spent half the night listening to the night man dig into the earth—his movements slow and steady, like the rhythm of a keen. Why was the man digging holes? Was he planting something? Searching for something? Hiding something?

Kip raked the area until he found the spot where the night man had been digging. Just as on that first afternoon, it was filled to the brim with dry leaves. He stared at the leaves, imagining what might be waiting beneath them. He adjusted his grip on the rake and started the slow work of clearing the leaves from the hole.

By the time Kip finished, he had created a pile of leaves as big as he was. The hole was actually more of a trench, twice as long as it was wide. He put down his rake and peered over the edge. It looked ordinary enough—he could have dug one just like it with a good shovel and enough time. Still, as he peered into its shadows, something made him uncomfortable.

Kip sat on the ground and swung his legs into the hole. He hesitated, knowing what he had to do next. The hole was not too deep. He could get down there if he wanted. But he did not want to. He took his crutch and tossed it over the edge. His precious Courage, the one thing he had from his father, lay at the bottom of the hole. "Now I *have* to go down there," he said.

Kip closed his eyes and shoved off the edge. He hit the bottom hard and fell to one side. Dirt crumbled around him. He picked up his crutch and stood. The hole was about as deep as he was tall. If he stood on his strong toes, he could peer over the top at the lawn. From this vantage, the little hills surrounding the grounds really did seem like mountains, and Kip suddenly felt very small.

He crouched down to examine the dirt floor, which was covered with the night man's boot prints. The same prints he had seen in his sister's room. He ran his hand along the dirt wall. Cold earth crumbled down, releasing a musty, rich smell that reminded him of the farm back home. He saw something nestled in the dirt. It was a root from the tree. Kip brushed away more dirt to get a better look at it. The root was black and gnarled and very, very thin. It almost looked sick. He took the end between his fingers, but when he touched the root, the most surprising thing happened—

It moved.

Kip leapt back, startled. He shook the nerves from his hand and touched the root again. Again it moved. The tiny fibers at the end came alive, reaching for him, twining around his fingertip. He looked around the hole, and he could now see tiny roots everywhere, pushing gently through the soil. The tree was *growing* right before his eyes. "You're alive," he whispered.

Just then, he felt a sharp pain. The root had tightened, choking the tip of his finger. Kip jerked his hand back, trying to pull himself free—but the root would not let go. He pulled harder. "Ow!" he cried out as his hand finally came away.

A gust of wind howled overhead. Kip looked up and saw leaves and loose dirt blowing into the hole, piling up around his feet. He tried to pull himself out of the hole, but a strong gust knocked him backward.

Dirt and leaves poured down over his body, burying him. "Help!" Kip shouted, but he knew no one could hear him. Molly and the family were inside the house. Even Galileo was gone. More and more tiny roots came out of the soil, grasping at his legs, his arms, his neck.

Kip screamed again, straining against the roots. His voice came back to him, muffled and small. He could barely move beneath the weight of dirt and leaves—a rustling, choking darkness.

Kip twisted his body and felt something hard against his face—

It was his crutch.

It was Courage.

With all his strength, he ripped his right arm free of the roots and took hold of his crutch. He pushed against it, lifting his body up and freeing his other arm. Using the crutch he pulled himself up, hand over hand, until he was standing.

His head broke through the leaves, and he gasped for air. Wind beat against his face, stinging his eyes, trying to push him back down. Kip fought the wind, raising Courage over his head. He stretched the crutch across the width of the hole and, bracing his good leg against the wall, pulled himself up to the grass.

Kip rolled onto his back, panting, shaking. The wind had died down, and everything was silent. His arms and legs and neck tingled, as though he had rolled through a bed of nettles. He sat up and examined his throbbing finger. He squeezed the tip, and a tiny red pinprick appeared—

A single drop of blood.

Kip sucked the blood away. He stared at the giant tree towering over him, its branches spread across the sky like a black web. He shook his head, his heart still pounding. "Why on earth would a person build a house next to *you*?"

20

Behind the Door

When Molly reached the house that morning, she was surprised by the woman who greeted her. Constance Windsor was indeed upset, but she was not angry. "Molly!" the woman cried, very nearly *hugging* her. "We couldn't find you anywhere. I feared that you and your brother were . . ." She stepped back, giving an unconvincing smile. "That you had left us." Molly had the distinct feeling that Constance had feared more than that.

"They were sleeping under the stars!" Penny exclaimed. "Why can't we do that?"

Molly knelt down. "That would ruin your pretty hair, miss."

"Indeed," Constance said, looking pointedly at Molly. "That was incredibly reckless. These woods are no place for a young girl after dark." The words recalled to Molly's mind something she had been told on her first day:

This house is no place for you.

Molly stared at the woman, wondering just how much she knew about the spectre that haunted her halls. Was *this* why Mistress Windsor had been so reluctant to hire them?

If Constance noticed Molly's dirty hair and ruined dress, she chose not to mention it. Instead, she told her to take the remainder of the day off and rest. Though exhausted, Molly did not want to rest. She feared that if she closed her eyes, the nightmares about Ma and Da might come back—or worse, she might dream of *him*.

So Molly decided to give the house one last cleaning before she gave her final notice. She did not know where she and Kip would go. She did not care. She just knew they had to leave.

Molly rinsed her hair and put on some clean clothes and set to scrubbing the foyer for the very last time. She pushed her soapy brush back and forth over the floorboards, thinking of the hat, the footprints, and the night man. She forced those thoughts from her mind, focusing on happier things—Kip, Ma and Da, home . . .

"Aren't you going to move?" said a voice above her. Molly looked up to see Penny hanging from the banister like a bored *ourang-outang*. "You've been at that spot for eleven whole minutes. I checked on the clock in the foyer."

Molly sat back, tucking a loose strand of hair behind her ear. "Musta been daydreamin', miss."

Penny let go of the banister and hopped down the stairs in her usual manner. "Why are you scrubbing the floors at all?" she said. "Mummy said you could have the day off to play."

Molly shrugged. "I'd prefer to scrub floors, if it's all the same to you."

"Well, it's *not* all the same to me." Penny planted her hands on her hips. "I want you to play with me and tell me stories."

Molly let out a tired breath. She tossed her brush back into the bucket and dried her hands on her apron. "All right," she said, patting her knee. "I'll tell you a story."

Penny clapped and ran toward Molly. "Is it about the good rooster Chanticleer?" She settled into Molly's lap. "Make it about Chanticleer!"

Molly wrapped both arms around the girl and rocked her gently. "This story is about two children, a brother and a sister, who had bright red hair. They lived in a big house with a little girl who was secretly a princess."

"Those are the best kind of princesses!" Penny declared. "Except, are you sure the house wasn't actually a tower guarded by ogres? Make it that instead!"

"Nay, this was just a house." Molly rested her chin on Penny's head. "The brother and sister cared for the princess, and they grew to love her very much. But one day . . ." She took a deep breath. "One day, the red-haired children had to leave the house behind. And it was very sad, and they were heartbroken, but it was the way things had to be." She held Penny tighter. "And after that, every night, no matter where they were, the girl and her brother would look up at the moon, and they knew that same moon was shinin' over the princess in her house, and it was like they were never really apart."

Penny craned her neck to look at Molly. "That's a horrid story!"

Molly lowered her eyes. "It's just a story, miss."

"Of course it's not!" Penny broke from Molly's grip and stood up. "It's about you and Kip, and how you're going to leave!"

Molly looked down the hall. She didn't want the house learning of her plan before she told Mistress Windsor. "I didn't say we were leavin'—"

"Yes, you did, right there in the story! You're going to leave me all alone in this big, ugly house!" And then, with new horror, "Who will tell me bedtime stories if you're gone?"

Molly stared at the girl, unable to answer. "Maybe you're gettin' a bit old for stories."

"That's ridiculous! Nobody's too old for stories—not even God himself. You told me that!" Penny glared at her. "Promise me you won't ever leave."

"Now, Miss Penny—"

She stomped her foot. "Promise it!" The girl's jaw was clenched tight. It was clear she was about to cry.

The sight nearly broke Molly's heart. She would have loved to promise the girl that she would never leave, that they would always be together. But Molly of all people knew that those sorts of promises could not be kept. She lowered her head. "I canna promise you," she said softly.

The girl's mouth went as small as a pinprick. "Fine!" she shrieked.

"I'll get my own stories!" She kicked over Molly's bucket, and dirty water sloshed across the hall.

"Penny, wait!"

But the little girl had already stormed off. Molly righted her bucket and set to mopping up the water. She hated the thought of parting with Penny on bad terms and told herself that the girl would return within the hour, the argument forgotten, and the two of them could then spend the rest of their last day together chatting about ogres and princesses. But even as Molly thought of this, her spirits fell. She knew no amount of stories would change the fact that Penny was stuck in this horrible place. Molly pushed the thought from her mind, telling herself that the girl would be fine. She had family. She had a home. She had a life filled with storybooks and sweets and jewelry and bags of money.

Hours passed, and Penny did not return to make peace. Molly continued with her chores, occasionally looking in some of the girl's favorite hiding places. She checked the kitchen pantry, the stairs closet, the space under Alistair's bed, even the dumbwaiter. Penny, however, was nowhere to be found.

Molly was dusting off books in the study when she finally heard the muffled trill of laughter. "Miss Penny?" she called, expecting a reply.

Penny did not answer, but a moment later Molly heard what sounded like a gasp of horror. She got down from the ladder and went into the hall. "Miss Penny?" she called, crossing the foyer. "I know it's you."

She heard someone clapping. The girl was hiding somwhere on

the second floor. Molly crept up the stairs. "Come out, come out, wherever you are," she sang. Molly reached the top of the staircase and listened for another clue.

A burst of laughter sounded directly behind her. Molly was so startled that she nearly tumbled back down the stairs.

The sound was coming from behind the green door.

Molly saw now that the door was not completely shut. Through it, she could hear the sound of Penny giggling. Molly moved toward the door, one hand still on the banister. She had waited so long to see inside this room. But now, for some reason, she felt afraid.

"Hooray!" cried Penny's voice from the other side.

Molly could take it no longer. She grabbed the handle and pushed the door open.

Penny was sitting on the floor of a small, empty room, facing away from Molly. In her lap was a large book, decorated with a giant colored picture that spread across both pages. Penny turned the final page to find it blank. "That can't be the end!" she said, casting the book aside. "I still don't know what happens!"

Molly watched as the girl jumped to her feet and marched to the far wall of the room. Only, it wasn't an ordinary wall: part of it consisted of the tree, whose massive trunk ran from the floor to the ceiling. In the center of the trunk was a big knothole, about the size of a pumpkin. Penny put both hands on her hips. "I want another story!" she said, looking up at the knothole. Molly listened, confused; it almost seemed like the girl was talking to the tree.

Penny made an exasperated sound. She rose to her tiptoes and peered into the knothole. "Hulloooo?" she called into the darkness.

Molly crouched down, picking up the book that Penny had discarded. The title read *Princess Penny and the Tower Guarded by Ogres*. The book looked like part of the same set that Molly had seen in Penny's bedroom on one of her first nights. At the time, Penny had behaved as though the books were a secret.

Molly opened the book, looking at the colorful pictures, which showed a little girl with dark braids and glasses battling a monster-filled tower. Fighting alongside the little princess were two other people, a boy and a girl, both of them with striking red hair. Molly caught her breath. She was looking at *herself*.

"Miss Penny?" she said.

The girl spun around. The moment she saw Molly, her face went white with panic. "I—I—I didn't mean it!" she cried, backing away from the tree.

Molly took a careful step closer. She pointed to herself in one of the drawings. "Where did you get this book?"

Penny lowered her head. "I only wanted to hear a story—and it's your fault because you're leaving and then I'll have no one but Alistair!" She scuffed the floor. "It's not fair. Everyone else uses this room, so why shouldn't I?"

Molly knelt down in front of the girl and spoke as calmly as she could. "I swear I'm not angry. But I need you to tell me: What is this room?"

The girl sighed. *"Not for children."* She said this as if she had been told as much many times. "Please don't tell Mummy or Papa."

Clearly the girl was far too frightened of punishment to give any plain answers. Still, there was one thing Molly could get from her. She held out her hand. "Give me the key," she said.

Penny took the key from her pocket. "I was going to put it back in Mummy's dresser—honest I was." She handed it to Molly. Molly stared at the key. It weighed like an anchor in her palm.

Penny blinked at Molly with wide, bespectacled eyes. "Am . . . am I punished?"

Molly put the book in the girl's arms. "Not this time. Just you run along." She held out a finger. "But don't speak of it to no one."

Penny seemed too relieved to question the order. She sprinted out the door and down the hall without another word.

Molly was left alone in the strange room. How many times had she imagined what lay behind the green door—and now here she was. The room was small indeed, only about the size of a broom closet. But for a small, cracked window, its walls were completely bare. And then there was the tree.

Molly stared at the knothole, which seemed to stare back at her like a giant black eye. It looked like Penny had been talking into it. Molly took a step closer and pressed her hand against the cool bark around the edge. Nothing happened. She peered into the knothole. It was dark and empty and smelled like a cellar. "H–h–hullo?" she called.

The tree did not answer.

Molly stepped back, feeling a bit silly. What had she expected? As for the book with Molly's picture—that simply had to be a coincidence. Red hair wasn't all that uncommon, especially in storybooks.

Molly stepped back from the tree and walked to the door. She would have to return the key before Mistress Windsor noticed it was missing. She was about to step into the hall when a faint sound caught her ears—

It was a gentle lapping of waves.

Molly let go of the door handle and slowly turned around. The knothole, which moments before had been empty, was now filled with dark water. She moved closer. A few foamy drops sloshed over the edge of the knothole, wetting the floorboards at her feet. As Molly came nearer, she caught a briny odor that smelled like home. "Seawater," she whispered.

She stared into the little pool: an ocean inside a tree. She noticed something white moving beneath the water. It floated up and bobbed quietly on the surface. It was an envelope. There was one word written across the front in elegant, water-stained script:

Molly

Molly's heart was galloping. She furtively looked around her and then turned back to the knothole. The envelope was still there, waiting for her, calling to her. She reached out a trembling hand and pulled it from the water, which silently drained away until the knothole was once again empty. Molly stared at the envelope in her hands—the envelope *addressed to her*. It was wet and flat and very much real. She turned it over and opened the flap. Inside was a piece of ivory paper, folded two times. A letter.

Molly unfolded it and gasped. She stared at the words written in that same familiar, cramped hand across the top of the page:

> *To Our Dearest Molly & Darling Kip . . .*

Molly clutched the paper tight, afraid to look away, afraid the words might disappear.

She knew that handwriting.

The letter was from her mother.

PART TWO
PURSUITS

21

SPECIAL DELIVERY

Kip flipped his wishing button high into the air and caught it. "Can you read it again?"

"I think three times is enough," Molly answered. "I'm already hoarser than Galileo!"

Kip grinned. Even Molly's bad jokes couldn't spoil his mood. He stared at the letter in his sister's hands. It was written on heavy paper that was stained with water and salt air. It had come from the top of the world. It had come from Ma and Da.

Kip and Molly were both sitting on the roof of the stables, legs dangling from the eaves. The valley around them was painted gold by the falling sun. At first, Kip had been afraid that the letter was a trick—something his sister had written to make him feel better. But the moment he saw the writing, he knew it was real. He could not read it, of course, but he could tell a thing written by Ma's pen just as plain as he could tell a bowl of her stew or a sock darned by her needle. The words were in watery blue ink, and they went like this:

To Our Dearest Molly & Darling Kip,

Your da and me received your letter with great joy—it surely sounds like you two have had a grand adventure! We've had some adventures of our own. After getting shipwrecked, Da made a tiny raft from an old rum barrel. We used an oar for a mast, and I wove a blanket of seaweed for a sail. We named her the "Kip 'n' Molly," and she kept us safe through still and storm till we reached the snowy north, where we met a band of Eskimo merchants in a whale-drawn skiff! The Eskimos were so pleased to find we spoke English that they invited us aboard for a steaming bowl of kraken soup, which your da and me agreed was the loveliest thing we ever did taste. We even got the recipe so's that we can make a pot when we're all together once more. Until that day, you remember to take good care of each other in your new home and keep out of trouble (that means you, Kip!). We'll write again soon, so stay put no matter what.

Be good, be brave,

Ma & Da

If Kip closed his eyes, he could almost hear Ma speaking the words as she wrote them. He could picture Da standing behind her, laughing as she said the bit about getting into trouble. Kip laughed, too. He opened his eyes and let out a deep breath—a breath he had been holding on to for a very long time.

He watched as Molly carefully folded the letter and put it back inside the envelope. "When did it come?" he said. "I been watchin' the road for weeks, but never saw any postman."

"It's hard to explain . . ." She was silent for a moment. "Let's just say, it came by *special delivery*."

Kip didn't like that she was being so mysterious, but did it really matter? His parents were out there. The letter was proof. They were coming for him and Molly. He turned the wishing button over in his fingers. "Now that I know they're all right," he said, "I dinna think I need to stay out on the bridge so much."

Molly smiled, mussing his hair. "I'm glad to hear it."

But then Kip remembered something. He had been so caught up in the letter from Ma and Da that he had almost completely forgotten about the tree. "While you were doin' chores," he said, "I did some snoopin' around that hole the night man was diggin'."

"You did *what*?" The alarm was plain on Molly's face.

"Don't worry, I was careful." He stared across the lawn. "I saw the tree's roots . . . They were *alive*. They started movin' right in front of my eyes. Like little black worms pushin' through the soil. They were so hungry, but not for water." He showed her the red spot at the end of his finger where the roots had grabbed hold of him.

"Why, it's only a scratch," Molly said, hardly even looking. "You probably just nicked it on a rock."

Kip pulled his hand back. He remembered how they had found Galileo in the woods, a black root coiled around his foot. "I dinna think there is a sourwoods," he said. "I think there's just that tree with its black roots creepin' all the way to the river. I tried plantin' some flowers right under it. They're all dead now—I think those roots killed 'em." He looked at her meaningfully. "Those same roots are in the house. In your room."

"Kip, it's *just a tree*." Molly's voice was sharp. "If you don't like it, then stay away from it. Mistress Windsor told us as much when we came here."

He sat up. "You dinna think she knows somethin', do you?"

"Here's what I think: if she found out you'd been sniffin' around her tree with spades and rakes like that—you'd have a lot more than a sore finger." She looked flustered, as if she were trying to form words that wouldn't come together. "Just 'cause the tree's ugly don't make it evil," she said.

"But it ain't just ugly—or have you forgotten about what we saw last night?" He looked back over the ground. "Because *I* remember. I remember the wind. And the man. And the waterin' can. And most of all, I remember you, hunched next to me, scared outta your mind. Just like I was." Even though it wasn't cold, Kip shivered. "The Windsors can do as they like. But we have to get outta here—the sooner the better."

When he said this, Molly looked away.

"We *are* leavin', aren't we?" he said. "We agreed to it."

Molly stared at him for a long moment, some unknown worry playing behind her eyes. "I know what I said, but that was before this." She held up the letter. "If we leave . . . we might never hear from Ma an' Da again."

"Of course we will," Kip said. "We'll just write and let 'em know where we go."

"It don't work that way . . . They might not *get* our letter. It could get lost or—who knows? Ma an' Da said as much themselves." She pulled the letter from the envelope and pointed to some words at the bottom. *"Stay put no matter what."*

Kip stared at the words. "I know they said that, but they didn't know—"

"They did too know!" Molly cut him off. "Remember? We told 'em all about the night man in our first letter. They read that letter and then wrote back and told us to *stay put*, and that's what we'll do."

Kip turned away, his cheeks burning. "You dinna sound like you're asking."

He felt a hand touch his shoulder. "Kip, I know you're frightened. I am, too, but you have to trust me. Trust Ma an' Da." Molly's voice was softer now. "The only hope we have of ever hearin' from them again is by stayin' right here."

Kip breathed a deep sigh, trying to expel the tightness from his chest. He knew it was dangerous to stay in this place, but for some reason he couldn't make Molly understand. He stared at the woods lining the ridge of the valley. They were lit with golds and reds and deep purples—the warm palate of a setting sun. He blinked, thinking again of his parents, who were somewhere far, far away, looking at the same sun. "I suppose we could stay a bit longer," he said. "Just to see if another letter comes."

"Thank you, Kip." Molly hugged him, and he hugged her back, clinging to her with everything in him. He felt her body shake, letting out silent tears. Molly had tried so hard to protect him, but now it suddenly felt like she was the one who needed protecting. "Do you want to read it again?" he said.

Molly pulled back, wiping her eyes. She nodded. "Maybe just once more."

22

SWEETS

Molly spent the next two weeks in a haze of excitement and expectation. What had started as one letter had soon grown to four, and not an hour passed that she didn't find herself wondering when the next special delivery might come. After all this time thinking she and Kip were alone, the letters had given her hope.

"Master Alistair?" Molly called, a stack of sheets under her arm. "I'm here with the linens."

She heard no response and pushed the door open with her shoulder. Alistair's bedroom was a place Molly generally tried to avoid, going in only to change linens and the pots. The air in the room was thick with the foul odor of armpits and unwashed feet. Molly opened the window, briefly pausing to watch her brother load a wheelbarrow outside the stables. She went to the bed and pulled back Alistair's quilt to reveal a mess of toffee wrappers and powdered sugar and chocolate crumbs and dead leaves. She rolled her eyes, knowing it would take twice as long to wash the stains from these sheets.

Molly stripped and remade the bed, wishing very much that she could take a short rest upon its feathery surface. She sat on the corner, yawning. Lately the chores had been catching up to her, and she was often tired. She needed something to take her mind off work and worries. She slid a hand into her apron pocket and removed a stack of worn envelopes: letters from Ma and Da.

Apparently her parents had been caught in a typhoon, whose whirlpool had sucked them straight through the center of the world and launched them out of a volcano in the South Seas. She smiled at the volcano detail—no doubt an embellishment by her father. He was the sort of man who stepped out for a box of matches and came back with a story of how he'd snatched it from the devil's own pocket.

Molly still hadn't sorted out what she believed about the letters. She had initially been afraid that they were some sort of prank. But with each new letter, writ in Ma's hand, Molly had become more and more convinced that they were real. Certainly they were *unusual*—but unusual was different from untrue. Kip was afraid of the tree; that was why Molly hadn't told him about the knothole. But she knew the truth: the tree was magic—not storybook magic, but the real thing. And why shouldn't real magic be a little frightening?

How the tree worked was still a mystery. When she had tried sending a letter of her own through the knothole, a gust of wind had knocked it back. The tree seemed to grant one specific wish to each person: Master Windsor got money, his wife got jewels, Penny got her storybooks, and Alistair got lots and lots of sweets. Molly glanced toward the boy's open closet, the floor of which was filled with caramel drops and chocolate bars and licorice wheels and peppermint sticks, all sorted into neat little piles. She stared at them, wondering what they might taste like.

The door opened behind her. It was Alistair, a new paper sack clutched in his hand. Molly stood, stuffing the letters back into her pocket. "I was just changin' the bed."

Alistair looked from her to the closet. "Did you take any?" He rushed to his pile of sweets, sitting down cross-legged like a child. "Because I count it every morning."

"I'm surprised you can count that high," she muttered, collecting the dirty sheets.

Alistair was too busy checking for signs of theft to respond. He opened the brown bag and dumped out what looked to be peanut brittle, which he added to the store. Molly watched him sort through the piles. His face had taken on a fat, flabby quality in recent weeks. The rest of him had followed suit, and Molly knew it was only a matter of time before one of her chores would include letting out the seams of his clothes. She had not yet spoken to anyone about the tree and thought it might be time. "Can I ask you somethin'?" she said, folding her arms. "I know where you're gettin' all those sweets from . . . But why sweets?"

Alistair narrowed his eyes, perhaps trying to discern whether he was being mocked. He shrugged. "They were just waiting for me."

Molly nodded. Somehow the tree had known that he longed for sweets. Just as it knew that she longed to hear from Ma and Da.

Alistair dug into his pocket and removed a red gumdrop. He stood and held it out to her. "Would you like a piece?"

She had never once tasted a gumdrop in her life. It looked sticky and soft and delicious in his pale palm. "Are you offering?" she said.

"No!" he said brightly. He popped it into his mouth, chomping loudly. "If you deserved sweets, then the tree would give them to you."

Molly shook her head. "I canna help but feel sorry for you."

He snorted. "*You?* Sorry for *me?*"

"Any wish in the whole world, and all you can think of is your stomach." She turned toward the door, but Alistair blocked her way.

"It's not like that," he said.

Molly cocked her head to one side. "Really? What's it like, then?"

He shoved his hands into his pockets. "When I was little, before Penny even, Father used to take me round to the sweets shop in town. 'Get whatever you want,' he'd tell me. And together we'd look at all the different kinds. I used to agonize over what to pick. I didn't want to seem greedy, and I wanted him to be proud of me, so in the end I'd just get one small thing—a lolly, maybe, or a square of fudge—even though I wanted more. I'd take that sweet home and have to make it last the whole week, sometimes even longer." He drew another gumdrop from his pocket, this one yellow, and rolled it between his fingers. "When we sold our things and had to move away from town, I realized what a fool I'd been as a little boy. I should have grabbed all the sweets I could. Father never took me to a sweets shop again." He shoved the gumdrop into his mouth, chewing violently.

Molly felt a sting of sympathy but only a slight one. Even if Alistair's desire for sweets had come from some deeper loss, that loss had transformed itself into plain gluttony. "There's lots worse that can happen to children than losing their sweets," she said quietly.

Alistair shifted his weight, his mouth tightening. "You think you're so much better than the rest of us? You and your secret letters?" Molly gasped, which seemed to please him. "I know all about them. I've seen you reading them to Kip out my window."

Molly put a protective hand over her apron pocket. "The letters are none o' your business, and you're not to speak of 'em again." Her voice was shaking.

A grin of discovery crept across his face. "Your brother doesn't know where they come from, does he?" He took a step closer, close enough that she could hear the crackle of his spittle as he chewed. "Suppose someone told him? Would that bother you?"

Molly clenched the dirty sheets to her body. Her heart was pounding in her ears. She took a slow breath and then forced herself to smile. "Do whatever you please, master." She took a step closer, meeting his dark stare with her own. "Though, I should warn you: it's a dangerous game to cross the person who cleans your chamber pot. I might just *accidentally* spill it all over your precious sweets."

Alistair's face froze. "You wouldn't dare!"

Molly shrugged. "Who knows? Maybe I already did and forgot to tell you." She leaned close, whispering, "How's that gumdrop tasting?"

His mouth fell open as horror washed over him. Molly had done nothing to his sweets, of course, but the idea had planted itself into his mind, and that, it seemed, was enough to keep him in check.

"Back to work." Molly hefted the sheets in her arms. "Lovely talkin' with you."

She turned around and left the room before he could see her smile.

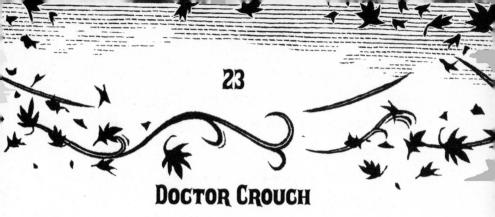

23

DOCTOR CROUCH

On Tuesday the postman finally came to Windsor Manor. Kip spotted the man on the road and ran to meet him at the bridge. "Any more special deliveries?" he said, out of breath.

"Ain't heard of no special deliveries. Give this here to your mistress." The postman handed Kip an envelope and rode on without another word.

The letter inside was not special, and it was not from Ma and Da. It was from Master Windsor, who had written from town to say that he had hired a doctor to check up on his family while he was away. Kip was to pick him up in the village the following morning. The Windsor children took this as bad news, complaining that they felt fine and didn't need a doctor. Kip, however, was excited. He had never met a real doctor before.

Kip met the man in the village just after breakfast. "Master Windsor's still in town with the carriage," he said, scooting to one side. "You'll have to ride up front with me."

"It offends me not," said the corpulent doctor, climbing onto the wagon. "The better to observe the local flora and fauna—I have something of a passion for the natural world." He produced a hand-kerchief from his pocket. Inside was a leaf. "Observe this specimen I found while riding out from town this morning. Look at the size of this petiole. Why, it's positively prehistoric!"

Kip looked at the leaf, which seemed ordinary enough to him. "Very impressive, sir." He snapped the reins, pulling out into the road.

"Impressive . . . and perhaps *unnamed.*" He tucked the specimen back into his pocket. "Who knows what medicinal value such an herb might possess? The next time I visit, I shall have to bring along some equipment from my laboratory for testing." The doctor wore a dark blue coat, white gloves, and a tall black hat. Kip eyed the black leather bag sitting on the man's lap. Some letters were painted across the side in expensive gold script—

EZEKIEL CROUCH

M.D., PH.D., ESQ., ETC.

Kip could identify letters but struggled with whole words. He suspected these letters spelled out the doctor's full name. It seemed an awfully long name for just one person. "Sorry for the bumps," Kip muttered. "These roads is less traveled by far." This was something Hester Kettle had said to him once before, and he liked the way it sounded.

The doctor raised a finger. "The roads *are* less traveled." Kip's embarrassment must have been plain because the doctor gave a conciliatory smile. "Chin up. I wouldn't expect an Irishman to know grammar any more than I would expect a baboon to know table manners." He chuckled. "Better minds than mine have tried to civilize your species—to little effect, I might add."

Kip felt his cheeks go hot. English folks, especially the rich ones, often said things like this. If Molly had been in the cart, she would have given the man an earful. But Kip couldn't afford to say anything. Not to this man. Instead, he bit his tongue and watched the road.

Kip had always imagined doctors to be like wizards—able to stay the hand of death with their instruments and books. Doctor Crouch looked the right age for a wizard, but instead of a long beard, he had bushy white whiskers that sprang from either side of his face like wedges of cheese. "It must be hard bein' a doctor," Kip said by way of conversation. "Seein' all them sick folks."

"Hmm?" Doctor Crouch looked up from a book he had been reading. "Oh, yes . . . I suppose it could be difficult for a more sentimental sort—women and children and such—but to me it is chiefly invigorating." He snapped his book shut, turning toward Kip. His weight made the wagon veer to one side, and Kip had to jerk the reins to keep it on course. "We are living in an age of medical wonders. Not a day goes by that doesn't see the discovery of some exciting new disease or malady—and I aim to be one of the men doing the discovering!"

"Disease," Kip said. "That why the master's brought you here?" He thought of the pale faces of the Windsors, all of them bloodless and thin. Since arriving at the house, he had seen them go from pale to stony. He thought of his sister, in there with them—would she fare any better?

"Oh, nothing that severe—just a touch of fever, I'm sure. Old Bertie always was a bit prone to overreaction—but you didn't hear that from me." Kip was beginning to glean that this doctor had been acquainted with the Windsors back when they lived in town. This theory was confirmed when they reached the estate.

"Gracious," the man whispered, peering at the house and lawn. "I'd heard that Bertrand had fallen on hard times, but this . . ."

"It ain't bad as all that," Kip mumbled. He had spent weeks taming the grounds, and it hurt his pride to think that the place still looked a shambles to this stranger. Kip flicked the reins and they rolled over the bridge. His hands were sweating, and he could feel a knot form-ing in the pit of his stomach. The house was fast approaching, which meant Kip would lose his chance to speak to the doctor in confidence. *Just ask him*, he told himself. But by the time Kip had mustered up the courage, they were already at the house.

Doctor Crouch consulted his pocket watch. "Oh, drat—it looks like I'll have to work through tea." He put his book into his case and clam-bered somewhat clumsily down the side of the wagon. "Don't bother stabling the horse. I'll be done within the hour." He patted his pockets. "Er, here's something for your trouble." He held out a tuppence.

Kip eyed the coin but did not take it. *Just ask him.* "That's kind o' you, sir." His stomach clenched up. "But I'd rather a question than a coin."

The man lowered his hand, peering over the top of his spectacles. "And this question . . . would it by any chance have something to do with your left leg?"

Kip looked at him, amazed. "How did you know?"

"There is very little that escapes my eye." He tapped the eye in question. "I first suspected it in the village when you did not offer to take my bag. And later I observed how you kept it tucked under the seat for the entire duration of our ride, never once adjusting. And then, of course, there's the matter of that crutch."

Kip drew Courage from its spot behind the bench. "I was born lame," he said, and even though he knew it wasn't his fault, he felt a gnawing sense of shame.

"Very well." The doctor gave an impatient sigh, removing his gloves. "Let's have a look at it."

"Yes, sir! Thank you, sir." Kip grabbed his crutch and climbed down the side of the wagon. He hobbled over to the man.

"Sit here," the doctor said, indicating the front steps of the house.

Kip eased himself down and extended his bad leg. He rolled up his trousers, exposing the limb beneath. There was almost no muscle on the calf and thigh. The bone was curved inward, and the kneecap fell to one side, as if someone had let it melt in the sun. His skin was white and shiny but for a series of ugly red scars from countless falls.

"Oh, my," said the doctor, taking the leg in both hands.

Kip looked away, feeling a surge of disgust. He could not stand the sight of his leg, and the idea of someone *else* looking at it was almost too much to bear. "I seen this advertisement in town," he said, wincing as the doctor prodded him. "There's a doctor. He has a special steel cage you can put around bad legs to heal 'em. Do you think one o' them cages would work for me?"

The doctor let go of Kip's leg, a pained smile on his face. The moment Kip saw the smile, he knew what the answer would be. "I'm afraid not. There are men out there who prey on the hopes of the weak-minded. They promise miracles that are simply outside the bounds of science. A steel cage could no more mend your crippled leg than grow you wings."

Kip pushed the leg of his trousers back down. He felt his throat close tight. "Forget I said anythin' . . ."

"Oh, chin up!" The doctor puffed to his feet, bag in hand. "We all have our crosses to bear. Why, I have a bunion on my right toe that swells up in the heat—come summer, I can hardly wear my own shoes—but you don't hear me complaining." He tipped his hat. "Thank you again." He rang the doorbell.

Kip adjusted the crutch under his arm and hobbled back to work, one word echoing in his mind.

Crippled.

24

Cold Hands, Warm Heart

Molly stood over the sideboard in the dining room, ladling weak stew into three bowls. Master Windsor had yet to return from his business trip, which meant she had not been given grocery money for the village market, which meant she was serving vegetable stew for the third night in a row—each pot a bit thinner than the last. Constance sat at the foot of the table, absently playing with the ring on the end of her finger, looking at her husband's empty chair. Alistair and Penny sat on either side of her, engaged in some argument, the subject of which eluded Molly.

"More wine, mum?" Molly grabbed the carafe from the sideboard to fill her mistress's empty glass. The woman reached to take it, and her hand brushed the back of Molly's arm. "Oh!" Molly shrieked, leaping back.

The glass had fallen, spreading red wine across the tablecloth. "What on earth has gotten into you?" Constance snapped, scooting back to avoid it spilling onto her dress.

"Forgive me, mum." Molly rushed to mop up the mess. "Nerves, I guess." She snuck a glance at the woman's pale hand. Her skin had been as cold as a corpse. Molly resolved to ask Kip to chop some extra wood that night so she could keep a fire in Mistress Windsor's room. Most folks wouldn't dream of a fire so late into the season, but she suspected the woman would allow it.

A door opened in the foyer. "Connie? Children?" It was Master Windsor. "I'm home!"

"We're in here, sir!" Molly called, rushing to get another place setting. The Windsors no longer had a tureen, which meant she had to cradle the iron pot against her hip as she hastily ladled soup into his bowl. She placed the bowl and a spoon at the head of the table.

"Ah, victuals!" Bertrand Windsor appeared in the hallway, coat over his arm, hat in hand. Molly was surprised by the look of him. His time in town had apparently had an invigorating effect. His cheeks were flushed with color, and his black hair was now streaked with auburn. He looked ten years younger.

He turned to Penny and Alistair, arms spread wide. "My beloved brood! How I've missed you!" If he was expecting them to rush forward, he was disappointed.

"Did you bring us anything?" Alistair said.

Bertrand's face fell as he made a great show of searching all his pockets. "Oh, heavens. I'm afraid I forgot . . ." His face lit up. "Ah! But what's this?" With a great flourish he produced two packages from beneath his coat. The children sprang from their seats and seized their gifts. Bertrand watched fondly as they raced from the dining room, not even asking to be dismissed.

Molly took the man's hat and coat. "Welcome home, master."

Bertrand turned to his wife, who had yet to acknowledge him. "I had a promising trip to town, my love. Nothing's set in stone, of course, but if the markets rally, I really think we have a chance this time."

"How very familiar that sounds," she said into her wineglass.

He stepped closer, almost touching her shoulder. "I brought something for you as well." He reached into his vest pocket and removed a small bottle with a sort of bulb at the top. "It came all the way from *Cologne*. It hardly makes up for things, but—" He stopped short when his wife turned to face him. "Oh, Connie. You didn't . . ." His eyes were fixed on the ring on her finger.

Molly watched from the sideboard, trying to read his expression. It was unclear whether seeing the ring made him worried or sad or both.

Constance examined the gift in her husband's hand. "*Perfume*? Something to cover up unpleasant stenches that we'd prefer to ignore." She gave him a pointed look. "How appropriate."

"I only m-m-meant to . . ." He stuffed the bottle back into his pocket. "I know it doesn't make up for what you've lost."

"What on earth do you mean, darling?" Her gaze flicked down to the ring around her pale finger. "As you can see, I haven't lost anything." Molly all at once thought she understood why Constance had wanted that ring from the tree: it held some significance between them, and she had *wanted* her husband to see it on her finger.

If her aim had been spite, it seemed to have worked. Bertrand sighed and took his seat at the head of the table. The man seemed to deflate before Molly's very eyes: his shoulders sloped, his cheeks caved, even his hair went limp. Constance watched him, too, a look of icy satisfaction on her face. She finished her wine and signaled Molly for more.

Molly took the carafe and set it hard it on the table. She looked pointedly at Master Windsor. "I thought it was a lovely gift, sir," she said and rushed into the kitchen.

She had expected Mistress Windsor to follow her and scold her, but the woman did not. This was probably for the best, as Molly wasn't sure she would be able to bite her tongue. She scoured the pots and dishes, imagining all the nasty things she wished she could say to the woman. Nasty but true.

Molly's mother had a phrase she would utter from time to time: "Cold hands, warm heart." It meant that seemingly cruel people could sometimes be kind. Molly was fairly certain that this did not apply to Mistress Windsor, whose hands were not just cold but downright *frigid*. Master Windsor had clearly been upset to see the ring on his wife's finger—and why shouldn't he be? While he was toiling away to provide for his family, she was focused on pretty jewels and petty jabs.

Still, even as Molly thought this, she knew it wasn't entirely fair. Sometimes she would come upon Constance standing at a window or sitting in the garden, just staring at the icy blue stone, her face torn with longing. But if the ring was valuable, it was clearly not valuable enough—for Molly had also seen her mistress return to the tree several times—no doubt hoping for a necklace and earrings to match. Thus far, however, no other jewels had appeared.

Molly touched the stack of envelopes in her pocket, wondering if a new letter might finally have arrived from Ma and Da. With so many people in the house, it was often difficult to get into the tree's room. For that reason, she rarely missed an opportunity when it presented itself. Right now, Penny and Alistair were playing in the garden out back. Molly heard voices from the dumbwaiter, which meant that Bertrand and Constance were in the drawing room—arguing, no doubt. She wiped her hands dry and rushed out of the kitchen.

The first trick was getting hold of the key, which was kept in a drawer in Mistress Windsor's vanity. Molly went to the bedroom, not even bothering to shut the door behind her. She opened the top drawer of the table. Inside lay a jumble of silk scarves along with a black lacquered jewelry box. The ornate box had once held a place of privilege atop Mistress Windsor's dresser. But apparently, now divested of its jewels, the woman preferred not to look at it. Behind the box, hidden safely beneath the drawer lining, was the key.

Molly grabbed the key, careful not to disturb anything else in the drawer. She was about to slide it back, when her hand brushed against the jewelry box. The box, which had been lying on a scarf, fell to one side with a rattling sound.

Molly paused, looking at the box. She had assumed it was empty, but now she was unsure. Perhaps Mistress Windsor *had* been getting more jewelry and wanted to keep it secret. Molly reached out and gently lifted the lid. The box contained several rings, all of them identical to the one Constance wore. Molly stared at the rings, each adorned with a pale blue stone.

"You can imagine how it looks," said a voice behind her, "to find a servant rooting through one's private things."

Molly slammed the lid shut and spun around. Mistress Windsor stood in the doorway. The woman's eyes were red—either from wine or crying or both.

"I'm sorry!" Molly said, dropping the key into her pocket. "I was only . . . I thought the box might need dusting." Then, "It was curiosity, nothin' more."

The woman raised her eyebrows. "Go on, then." She took a step closer. "Satisfy your curiosity."

It felt like a trap, but Molly did as she was told. She lifted the lid of the box and looked at the rings—a half dozen of them—all with identical pale blue stones. "They're all the same, mum?"

"Very nearly. Each band is a little smaller than the last." She felt Constance step behind her. "They're beautiful, no?"

Molly stared at the pale stones twinkling in the shadows. "I suppose, but—" She stopped herself from speaking before she said something she would regret.

"Speak your mind," Constance said. "I'd prefer it to your glowering."

Molly sighed. She fixed her eyes on the woman, unable to hold back. "Your family has no money for food or coal or clothes, and here you are hoardin' up diamonds like King Solomon."

"Diamonds?" A smile played on the edge of her lips. "Is that what you think those are?" She held out her hand, showing the ring on her finger. "Is that what you think *this* is?"

Molly set her jaw, her cheeks flushing. How was she supposed to know about kinds of jewels?

"You think me a terrible, vain woman, don't you?" She examined the stone on her finger. "This *diamond* is quartz. The band is more nickel than silver. Most women in my position would be mortified at the thought of wearing such a thing in public."

"But not you?" Molly said.

"But not me." Constance smiled, her eyes still on the jewel. She sighed or shivered; Molly couldn't quite tell. "When I met Bertrand—when I met Master Windsor—he had nothing. He was a clerk with no family or title or prospects. Not the sort of match my family approved of."

Molly folded her arms. "So you grew up rich."

"I'm not asking for sympathy," Constance said. "But I should think you might appreciate what it means to lose one's home." She gave Molly a meaningful look. "I married Master Windsor against my family's wishes. When they learned of it, they cast me out, revoked my inheritance, and never spoke to me again. On the day of our ceremony, Master Windsor gave me this ring—it was all he could afford. But for me, it was more than I could have hoped for." The woman rotated the ring, which was loose on her thin finger. "And to this day, every time I put it on my finger, I can remember him—both of us—the way we used to be."

The woman loosed a trembling breath. "It's obvious that you have some idea of this house." She eyed the walls as if they might collapse in on her. "But please don't presume to have any idea of our lives."

Molly stared at the woman. She thought of what she had seen weeks before on the driveway. Master Windsor had taken the ring off his wife's finger to pawn it for money—money to pay off debts he had incurred. She felt a chilling sense of guilt. "But why do you need so many of 'em?" she said, indicating the box.

Constance took a deep breath and exhaled. Molly almost thought she could see her breath against the light from the hall. "Much as I might wish to hold on to the past—I find it ever slipping away." She held up her hand, thin fingers outstretched. The ring slipped over her knuckle and fell to the floor with a dead *clink*.

"It don't fit no more?" Molly looked from the ring to the woman, who appeared so much frailer than when she had first met her. Like a thing wasting away.

"So it seems." Constance gave a bitter smile. "I suppose I shall have to get another." She held out her bony white hand. "I'll have that key now."

25

THE PALLOR

Molly stood in the middle of Penny's bedroom. "Miss Penny?" she said, her voice rising.

"I won't drink it!" the girl shouted. "You can't make me!" The girl was presently on her bed—not *in* her bed but standing atop it, each foot planted on a pillow, her back pressed against the wall.

Molly sighed. In her hand was a spoon filled with some blackish liquid that smelled bitter like alcohol. It had been supplied by a doctor who had come to check up on the family earlier that week. Molly had learned only that morning, when she saw the bottle untouched, that Penny had been lying about taking it. "Doctor Crouch said you have to drink this every night before bed." She took a step closer. "It's just a little spoonful."

"I won't! I won't! I won't!" Penny leapt to the floor, keeping the bed between herself and the spoon. "Alistair said it's made from rat's blood."

"Rat's blood?" Molly rolled her eyes. "And how would Alistair know that?"

The girl threw her arms out. "He's *older* than me . . . Older people know all sorts of things!"

Molly nodded, conceding the point. "I'm older than your brother, and I say it's *not* rat's blood. And the doctor—why, he's older than all of us put together." She sat down on the edge of the bed, catching a glimpse of herself in the dark window. She tucked a loose strand of hair under her cap. "Now, why don't you tell me what's really troublin' you?"

The girl worked her lips together, making her face very small. "I don't want us to be sick," she said, her voice low.

Molly looked at the girl's face, so pale in the lamplight. She thought of the portrait downstairs—how many times she had seen it and wondered at how the family was changing. "Miss Penny, just 'cause you don't want to believe a thing doesn't mean it's not true. If you're sick, this medicine is the way to get better. Besides, I was in the room when the doctor looked at you. He said it was just a touch of fever—"

"He said he didn't know *what kind* of fever. That means it could be anything!" She climbed back onto the bed, approaching Molly. "It could be black death or scurvy or cholera or even exploding eyeball disease . . . Alistair told me about that one."

Molly nodded gravely. "Well, if you think your eyeballs are gonna explode, please do it outside. I dinna want to clean up your sheets." She smiled to show she wasn't serious. Her gaze drifted to the small bookshelf along Penny's wall, where she noticed a number of new *Princess Penny* books lining the bottom. She turned back to the girl. "Now, what do you think Princess Penny would do if she was faced with a great, big, horrible spoon o' medicine? You think she'd run away scared? Or would she take it all down with a hearty laugh and ask for more?"

Penny tugged at the end of her braid. "A hearty laugh," she said. "But no seconds!"

Molly smiled. "Fair enough." She slid the spoon into Penny's mouth and removed it. "How was it?"

"It tastes . . ." The girl smacked her lips together. Her eyes went wide. "Like raspberry cordial!"

"Imagine that!" Molly stood and walked to the dresser. "Now, this bottle's meant to last till the doctor comes back—so don't you go stealin' sips when I'm not lookin'."

Penny sat up. "Aren't you going to have any?"

"Oh, I dinna think the doctor'd like that, miss." She set the spoon on a tray and replaced the cap on the bottle.

"Why not?" Penny said. "You're sick, too."

Molly put her hands on her hips, turning around. "So you're a doctor now?"

"But you *are*," Penny said. "Look there—in the window."

Molly turned toward the glass, which was black against the night sky. She studied her reflection, and a chill skittered through her. She took an unsteady step backward, one hand at her neck. "Let's get you tucked in . . ."

Molly barely remembered leaving Penny's room. The next thing she knew, she was racing down the staircase, breathing fast.

Molly rushed into her bedroom and shut the door behind her. She wished she had a lock. With shaking hands, she took three candles from her nightstand and lit them. She needed light. She needed to be certain.

Molly slowly walked to her dresser, which had a cracked mirror mounted on its top. She didn't want to look. But she knew she had to. She raised her eyes and stared at her reflection. "It canna be."

The girl in the mirror looked like Molly, only *different*. Her skin was smooth. The freckles that Molly had inherited from her mother had all but faded away. She pinched her cheeks hard to make them blush, but they refused to change. She carefully unfastened her cap, letting her hair fall around her neck—

It was almost black.

She lifted a curl from her cheek, and the strands of hair broke away from her head, falling limp between her fingers like dead weeds. She flung them away, horrified. "No, no, no, no . . ." She braced herself against the dresser. Her whole body felt weak, like she might pass out.

Molly knew the change couldn't have happened all at once. When had it started? Lately she had been so caught up with chores and let-ters from the tree that she could scarcely think of anything else. She thought of Kip and felt her stomach drop. He paid attention to things. He must have noticed the change—he probably saw it the moment it began. But if he had, why hadn't he said anything?

Molly put on her coat, blew out the candles, and slipped out of her room. She would not be sleeping in her bed that night.

26

HORSE APPLES

Kip lay wide awake on his creaky cot. Wind shivered past the stable walls and through his thin blanket. He had been sleeping out here ever since Molly first showed him the night man's top hat, but moving away from the house had not helped him sleep any better. His thoughts were continually haunted by the knowledge that his sister was still inside there—fast asleep—while the night man stalked the halls. Kip stared up through the windows at the moonlit heavens. He tried to draw constellations in the sky, connecting stars to each other so that they resembled good things from his life. But just when he could almost see his parents or the farm, the little stars would flicker and fade and appear anew in the shape of the tree.

A scraping in the shadows startled him. "Who's there!" he said, scrambling for Courage.

The door swung open to reveal Molly. She was still in her clothes and was clutching a lantern. "Scoot over," she said. "I'm bunking with you tonight."

Kip slid his crutch back under the cot. He peered at his sister, who looked tired and tense. Had something happened to her? "Thought you said the stables was too drafty."

"They *are* drafty." She flashed a fake smile. "But I thought you could use some company."

"I got Gal for company." He nodded toward the horse, who was standing in the stall, ears twitching, asleep. He looked back at Molly, searching her face in the lamplight. "You sure there ain't some *other* reason?"

Molly rolled her eyes. "Are you gonna make me beg?"

"Of course not, I just want..." Kip sighed. What *did* he want? For Molly to be honest with him. To tell him the fears that crowded her heart. To tell him that she, too, was scared of this place. He stared up at his sister, at her dark hair and darker eyes. "Molly, look at your-self..." He shook his head, knowing that this wasn't the time. "You're standin' in horse apples." He pointed to her feet.

Molly leapt back and hurriedly scraped the wet dung from her heel. Kip rolled to the edge of the cot, making a space for her. "Boots off," he said. He listened as she removed her boots, put out her lamp, and climbed into bed beside him.

"Thank you," she whispered, an arm around him.

"It's not like I was sleepin' anyway," Kip said. He closed his eyes, trying to quiet his restless mind. He concentrated on the sounds of life around him. Molly's breathing rose and fell in his ear. Galileo snorted softly behind him. Water dripped from the edge of the roof into the rain barrel. Crickets sang in the grass. Wind rattled in the trees.

"Molls?"

He heard Molly stir behind him. "What is it?"

Kip stared out the window. "Do you think he's inside there right now?"

Molly shook her head. "Not yet. When he comes, you can feel it. Like when a song goes off-key."

Kip rolled over to face her. "That's why you're sleepin' out here, ain't it? You didn't want to be in there with him." He eyed the rank squalor of the stables. "I know it's why I am."

Molly nodded and released a long breath. "You were smarter'n me, though. You knew it was bad almost right away."

"Smart's got nothin' to do with it. I was scared." He swallowed. "I'm still scared." He looked at her face—a paler, sicker version of the sister he loved. He sat up. "I still think we should leave, Molls. Whatever that man's doin' to the folks in that house each night, whatever he's doin' to *you* . . . It ain't good."

She touched her dark hair. "So you did notice?"

Kip nodded. "Hard not to."

"Why didn't you tell me?"

He blinked in the darkness. "I thought you wouldn't listen. And don't say it ain't true, because it is. You looked in a mirror every day for weeks and didn't see nothin'. If your own eyes canna convince you, what chance do I stand?"

Molly looked like she was about to object but instead sighed. She flopped back down, staring up at the rafters for a long moment.

"Sometimes, while I'm sleepin'," she said at last, "I think I can feel him in my room, standin' right over me . . ."

"You canna try an' stop him?"

She shook her head. "It's like I'm trapped inside my dreams, and there's no way out." She clenched her jaw. "And then mornin' comes and everythin' is bright, and I feel safe again." She turned to him, and there were tears in her dark eyes. "I just wish I knew what he was doin' . . . and I wish I knew why."

Kip took a deep breath and placed his hand on hers. "Maybe it's time we found out."

27

Ichor

Molly and Kip spent the next day preparing to spy on the night man—a task that mostly involved steeling their nerves and ignoring their common sense. They still weren't certain how he entered the house each night, and so they decided to wait for him on the lawn. After all the family had gone to bed, Molly met her brother by the woodpile in front of the stables. She brought scarves and hot broth, which they drank in silence as they watched the dark house. "You comfortable?" she asked as Kip adjusted his weight on the logs.

"I could do with a story," he said, rubbing his hands together. "Nothin' scary, though."

Molly shook her head. "That's a tall order. Mother Goose would be scary on a night like this." The truth was, Molly hadn't told a proper story for weeks—not to Kip, not to Penny, not even to herself. She had all but lost the desire. There was only one kind of story that interested her now. She reached into her pocket and removed the most recent letter from their parents. "How about a story from Ma an' Da instead?"

Kip eyed the letter. "What's the point? You already read it once." He swatted the end of his crutch at the tall grass. "Readin' it again won't bring 'em here any faster."

Molly tried to decipher his expression. With each new letter, Kip seemed less and less happy to hear from their parents. She wondered what he would say if he knew where the letters really came from. She put the envelope back into her pocket but kept her hand on it. Just touching the paper made her feel better, made her feel safe.

Molly watched the house. Every window was dark but for her window, which gave off a faint yellow glow. She and Kip had placed a candle on the windowsill. She stared at the steady speck of light, thinking of what it would mean if that flame went out. A part of her didn't want to know what the night man was doing in the house each night. A part of her wanted to forget the whole plan—to crawl back into her warm bed and wake up none the wiser.

Kip sat up. "Do you hear that?"

Molly nodded, her ears prickling. Behind her, the trees had begun to rattle and creak. The grass at their feet rustled as it filled with life. Wind slid through the woods, moving over the lawn, converging on the house. The sky was already dark, but now it went three shades darker. Molly heard shutters clattering, walls groaning. She heard a low moan as the wind whiffled over the chimney tops. She reached out, holding Kip's hand. "Not yet," she said, her eyes fixed on the candle at her window—

The tiny flame flickered and then went out.

"He's in there." She slid down from the woodpile and lit the lantern, which Kip had removed from Galileo's cart. The lantern was heavy, but it had flaps that dampened the glow, allowing them to see without being seen.

Molly and Kip rushed toward the house as quickly as the wind would allow. They reached the front door to find it still closed. Molly dimmed the lamp as low as she could without losing the flame. She removed her boots. The stone stoop was ice against her feet. Kip knelt beside her. His boots were off, and he was busy tying an old pillowcase around the foot of his crutch. "Are you sure we should do this?" he said.

"Not a bit." Molly helped him stand. "Let's go."

She put her hand on the knob and opened the front door. Wind howled inside the foyer—and for a moment she was transported back to that first night with the top hat. She stepped across the threshold, Kip at her side. Leaves swirled around them, spinning and swooping in a gentle, almost beautiful dance. She heard the familiar sound from the back of the house—

THUMP!

THUMP!

THUMP!

Molly grabbed Kip and pulled him down the hall. She peeked around the corner to see the night man appear at the other end of the foyer. He was carrying the same watering can they had seen before, but from the way he held it, she could tell it was empty. She watched his feet leave muddy tracks as he slowly mounted the stairs to the upper rooms.

Molly waited until he was around the corner and then crept after him. She slowly climbed the staircase, her eyes trained on the small pool of lamplight at her feet. She tried her best not to make a sound; she didn't even dare step on a loose board. Kip struggled behind her, keeping one hand on the banister. The cloth around the end of his crutch muffled the sound of his steps somewhat. Molly hoped it would be enough.

She reached the top of the stairs and waited for her brother to catch up. Kip was peering all around him, eyes wide, and she realized that he had never been in this part of the house before. "What's that room there?" he whispered, pointing behind him at the green door, which was slightly ajar. "The one with the lock?"

"Just a broom closet." Molly took his hand and pulled him farther down the passage.

Even with the moonlight and her lamp, it was still hard to see. She kept one hand along the wall to steady herself as she led Kip to the back hall, where the bedrooms were. Doors creaked and clattered as wind moved back and forth through the corridor. From every room, she could hear the voices of the Windsor family, each of them caught in his or her own nightmare.

Molly heard Penny inside her room. "Mummy! Mummy! Mummy!" the girl called out in the darkness.

Molly heard footsteps just ahead. She crouched behind a cabinet along the wall. Kip huddled beside her. A shadow darkened Alistair's doorway, and the night man stepped into the hall. He still had the watering can, only now Molly could hear a light sloshing against the metal sides. He had been filling it. But with *what*?

The night man disappeared inside Master Windsor's room. "Hold this," Molly whispered, giving her lamp to Kip. She crouched low and crept toward the room. Kip stayed right behind her, matching her every step. The door was open, and as Molly approached, she could hear Master Windsor muttering and moaning in his sleep.

Molly peered into the room. Moonlight shone in through the window above Master Windsor's bed. He was thrashing underneath his covers, eyes shut, skin wet with perspiration. "N-n-no!" he pleaded. "D-d-don't hurt them!"

The night man stood over him, watching him toss and turn. He set down his watering can and reached a long hand into his cloak. He removed something gray and limp. A rag. The man pressed the rag against Bertrand's face, gently mopping his brow, his neck, his hands. Molly watched, trying to understand what she was seeing.

The night man took the wet rag and held it over the open mouth of his watering can. He wrung the rag in his pale hands, and silver liquid trickled down, slowly filling the can. When the rag was dry, the man returned to Master Windsor and began again. He repeated this ritual over and over—each time filling his can a little bit more.

Molly tried swallowing, but her throat was too dry. She could feel

Kip right beside her, his breath hot against her neck. She did not know what she was seeing, but she knew she did not want to see it. Even more, she did not want *Kip* to see it. She let go of the door frame and slowly inched backward—

Crisk. She heard a gentle crackling sound as her foot crushed a leaf.

All at once, everything stopped. The house grew silent. The wind ceased. Even the moonlight seemed to disappear. A wave of dread overtook Molly's whole body as she felt something stir in the darkness. The night man stepped through the doorway, his features hidden in shadow.

He moved toward them.

"P–p–please, sir." Molly backed away, bowing her head. "We're sorry. We didn't mean nothin' . . ."

The man took another step toward them, into the light of Kip's lamp. Molly saw his face, and her voice fell silent. The man's beard was a tangle of black roots. His skin was as smooth as bone. His mouth was a crooked scar. His cheeks were hollow and long. And his eyes—

Molly stifled a shriek.

The man's eyes were not eyes at all but two black pits burrowed deep into his skull. He tilted his head, pointing the pits straight at her, watching her with a look of cold curiosity.

Molly stumbled backward, pushing Kip toward the stairs. "Stay away from us!" She groped the top of the cabinet, feeling for something, anything, to ward him off. She took hold of a vase and threw it at his head.

The man, who had moved so slowly before, suddenly snapped to life. He snarled, and a gust of wind rattled down the corridor, knocking her hard against the floor.

"Molls! Get up!" She felt Kip at her arm, trying to pull her up.

She pushed him away. "Kip, run!" Molly rose to her feet, planting herself between her brother and the man. "I won't let you hurt him," she said, her voice trembling. "He ain't done nothin'!"

The man's mouth made the shape of a smile. He let go of his watering can, which fell to the floor with a heavy slosh. He reached a bony hand into his cloak and removed a fistful of dry leaves. Molly watched him crush the leaves into a fine dust and then raise his open hand to his lips.

He blew onto the dust, and it swirled through the air, all around her—

And then the world went dark.

28

ASLEEP

Kip was at the top of the stairs when his sister's body fell. One moment she was standing in front of him; the next she was crumpled on the floor, facedown, not moving.

"Molly!" Kip dropped the lamp and scrambled to her side. He shook her body. "Molls, get up!" His voice sounded faint in his ears, and his stomach was churning. "We have to run!" He turned her over, and her head lolled to one side like a dead weight. He could see specks of leaves stuck to her hair and face. Her eyes were closed, and she looked very pale.

The night man took a step closer, a poisonous grin on his face.

"Molls, you gotta hear me!" Kip shouted, pulling her away from the man. He saw the green closet door was open—if he could just get her inside.

Molly took a sharp breath and clutched his coat. "N-n-no!" she moaned, throwing her head back. "You canna leave us! You canna . . ." She was not talking to Kip but to someone in a dream.

Kip could see her eyes rolling beneath closed lids. Already, tiny beads of sweat were forming across her brow. He glared up at the night man, who was standing over them. "Make her better!" he demanded. "Wake her up!"

The night man raised a hand, and a gust of wind struck Kip, knocking him back from Molly's body. Kip tumbled down the stairs, legs over arms, slamming his shoulders and face against the hard wooden steps. His hand caught hold of the banister rail and stopped his fall. He pulled himself to his knees, wincing. He thought he could taste blood in his mouth. He reached out for Courage but could not find it. His crutch lay at the bottom of the stairs—hopelessly out of reach.

Kip heard Molly moan. He looked up to see the night man kneeling beside her, his back to Kip, the watering can at his side. "You stay away from her!" he screamed.

The man did not even look up. He removed the rag from his cloak and pressed it to Molly's forehead. Kip knew he could not help Molly—his only chance would be to draw the night man away from her. He searched around him for some sort of weapon. The only thing nearby was his lamp, which he had dropped when Molly fell. He grabbed hold of it and threw it at the man, as hard as he could—

Pwhoof!

A blinding burst of light hit Kip's eyes as flames erupted in the darkness. The night man roared as fire swept over his cloak. His arms swirled and thrashed, trying to snuff out the flames. The man staggered to the top of the stairs. He snarled at Kip, his face contorted with rage.

"I said, Stay away from her!" Kip let go of the banister and half ran, half slid down the steps. He hit the foyer floor with a hard crash. He could hear the night man descending the stairs behind him. The whole house shook with the force of his gales. Kip grabbed hold of his crutch and staggered out the open front door. He hobbled across the moonlit lawn, his bare feet sliding on the wet grass. He did not know where he was going; he only knew he had to get the man away from the house, away from Molly. The cloth was still around the end of his crutch, and he tripped several times. Somewhere in the darkness behind him, he could hear the night man stalking the lawn—searching for him.

An angry howl split the air and knocked Kip flat. Apparently the man had spotted him. Kip pulled himself up. He covered his face and staggered toward the woods.

The forest shook and shuddered as wind sliced through branches and bushes. Kip stumbled blindly over the rough ground, shielding his face with one arm. Branches clawed at his clothes and hair. He could hear the night man behind him, getting closer and closer . . .

Kip kept going as fast as he could until he thought his heart would explode. He fell to the ground, trying and failing to catch his breath. Every part of him ached. He looked up and saw that he was at the very edge of the grounds. He could hear the river flowing in the darkness. The ancient garden—whose pale flowers bloomed only at night—shone around him. The wind had stopped. Everything around him was still.

A sudden coldness crept over Kip, like a shadow sliding across his body. He turned around to see the night man standing behind him. The

man didn't look winded or angry. He was just a fact of the surroundings, like the moon and the soil and the trees. Smoke wafted gently
from the edges of his cloak and hat. Kip saw that his hands and face
were unmarked. The flames had slowed him down—but nothing more.

Kip knew what would happen next. The night man would use his
crushed-up leaves to put him to sleep—just like he had done to Molly
and the Windsors. And then he would kneel down and fill his watering
can with . . . what? Sweat? Tears? No, something *deeper*. He would
somehow steal the very *quick* of Kip's being. All to feed the tree.

The man sprang toward him, hands outstretched. But before
he could reach Kip, his body snapped backward, as if restrained by
some invisible tether. The night man snarled, pacing at the edge of
the flowers, his terrible, nothing eyes burning with fury.

Kip scrambled back, dragging himself deeper into the garden,
where the man, for some reason, could not follow. A sharp gust of
wind shook the forest, and then everything was silent.

Kip slowly turned around, blinking into the moonlight. He pulled
himself to his feet, staring at the glowing forest floor. The woods were
calm. Not a leaf stirred. The night man was gone.

Kip's eyes fell on something dark sitting at the edge of the garden,
something the man had left behind. He hobbled toward it and knelt
down to study the object. He picked it up in his trembling hands. It
was small and thin and woven from roots and twigs—

It was a *gift*.

29

To Market

Molly awoke the following morning to find herself in her bedroom, warm sunlight shining in through the window. She was under the covers but still dressed. Her memories of the night before were cobwebby and incomplete. She recalled following the night man into the house but not much after that. She ran a hand through her hair, which was twined with bits of broken leaves. Why couldn't she remember?

She washed and dressed and went upstairs to prepare breakfast, resolving to find Kip the first moment she could. Master Windsor was waiting for her in the kitchen, a small bag in his hands. "Th-th-this is for the market," he said, not even looking her in the eye. "I'm sorry it's not more."

Molly took the bag of coins. She could tell without opening it that it would barely cover food for the week. "You're providin' for your family, sir," she said firmly. "That's never somethin' to be ashamed of."

The man gave a weak smile. "I pray you're right," he replied.

Molly felt certain she knew where the money had come from. It alarmed her to think that the tree's provisions had lately become so paltry. Still, some money was better than none, and she set out for the village with Kip shortly after breakfast. Molly had asked her brother along because he was better with the horse and because she hoped they might be able to talk about what they had seen in the house the night before.

Kip, however, seemed to be in a more pensive mood and spoke very little as they rattled up the valley roads. After an hour of sparse conversation, they pulled onto the main road that ran through what counted as a "village" in Cellar Hollow. It was a small cluster of cramped buildings with thatch-roofed houses and white plaster walls. Smoke trailed up from one or two chimneys, filling the air with a pleasant fragrance that mingled with hot food from the rows of stalls and carts that lined either side of the road.

The good weather seemed to have drawn people from their farms, and the market was uncharacteristically busy that morning. People flowed between the buildings like a shambling brook. Kip parked the wagon alongside some other horses, and Molly climbed down with her basket and bag of coins.

While Molly did not begrudge Bertrand's limited funds, it did make her task more difficult. The villagers knew that Molly worked for Master Windsor, whom they knew to be a wealthy man. Because of this, they seemed unwilling to haggle or bargain, and some of them even quoted higher prices to Molly as she wandered between the stalls. At the rate things were going, she would be lucky to buy enough to make soup, let alone meat.

Molly picked her way through the bustle, brushing against shoulders and pushcarts and locals. She saw a few girls her age who looked to be selling milk and needlepoint pictures. Stray livestock and the occasional small child skittered under her heels. Molly closed her eyes, savoring the smells and sounds. She found it comforting to be close to so many other people, to so much life.

Kip, for his part, did not seem to be enjoying the errand. He hobbled alongside her, eyes fixed on the ground. "You're gonna have to talk sometime," Molly said.

He nodded. "I know. I'm just findin' the words." Slowly, haltingly, he told her what had happened after her collapse. He told her how he had drawn the night man away from her body. How the man had chased him all the way to the moonlit garden at the edge of the sourwoods. And how, when Kip was utterly trapped, the night man had inexplicably disappeared.

"I keep askin' myself why he didn't hurt me," Kip said, staring into the crowd. "He wanted to, I could tell. But when he came at me, somethin' stopped him cold in his tracks. Like he couldn't go no farther." He sighed. "It don't make sense."

"We're well past makin' sense," Molly said, feigning interest in some onions she couldn't afford. For some reason, Kip had been spared by the night man. She was grateful, but she hated the way it placed a rift between them. She peered into a barrel, looking for rotting vegetables she might be able to salvage with a paring knife. "What'd you do after he let you go?"

Kip dipped his fingers into a bin of dried beans. "I came back to the house to help you. But when I got there, it was like none of it'd happened. There was no wind, no leaves—just a few muddy tracks and a broken vase. You were gone, too." He looked up at her, and Molly realized for the first time just how frightened he must have been. "I searched the whole house before I found you, safe in your room, sleepin' soundly under the covers."

Molly shuddered. "Well, not *too* soundly." Even as she said this, she could feel her parents floating up to the surface. She could hear them screaming over the storm. She could taste the salt water. Lately the only way she seemed to be able to keep the dream at bay was to read the letters—over and over again.

Kip cocked his head to one side. "You never told me what your nightmares was about."

Molly gestured to the people around them. "This isn't really the place for it . . ."

Kip took her arm and pulled her away from the stalls, into the mouth of a quiet alley. "Maybe it's important," he said. "Maybe the dreams are a clue of some kind."

Molly clicked her tongue. "If you must know, my dreams are about mountains of dirty laundry and endless hallways to scrub and chamber pots as big as lakes." She smiled. "Find a clue in that, if you'd like."

Kip smiled back but in a hollow way that showed he didn't believe her. Molly felt a wave of guilt wash over her. Why was she lying to him? Why couldn't she just tell him the truth?

She set down her basket. "Kip," she said softly, "I wish I knew the right thing to say. I wish I could tell you we were safe in the stables, safe at that house, but the truth is . . . *I don't know.* I don't know if we should stay and wait for Ma an' Da or run fast as we can away from that place. I'm makin' it up as I go, like a story. Only"—she swallowed—"I'm not sure how this one ends."

For a moment, the village and market melted away and they were standing alone. Molly stared into Kip's wide, bright eyes. She almost thought she could do it—tell him the truth about her nightmares, tell him about the letters and where they came from and what, in her deepest heart, she was afraid to admit that might mean.

"There's somethin' I ain't told you yet," Kip said. He adjusted the grocery sack on his shoulder. "The night man didn't just let me go in the woods. He left somethin' for me. A gift." He reached into the bag and removed a small object made from twigs and leaves.

Molly stared at the gift. It was long and thin and had a small loop at one end. "It's a key," she said.

"Aye." He ran his thumb over it. "But why? And where do you think it goes?"

Molly swallowed, hoping her face did not betray her fear. She recognized the size and shape of the key. It was an exact replica of the key in Mistress Windsor's bedroom, the one that opened the little green door at the top of the stairs. "Kip, you must listen to me: even if you find a lock that fits it, *don't ever use that key.*"

He looked at her. "You know where it goes, don't you?"

"All I know is that any gift from that man is no gift at all." Molly could not say why, but the thought of her brother learning about the tree made her sick. "Give it here." She held out her hand.

"You're lying." Kip inched back from her. "You know, and you're not tellin' me."

Molly snatched the key from his hand and ran past him.

"Give it back!" he cried, struggling to follow.

Molly reached the edge of the road. She threw the key as far as she could into some bushes along a ravine.

"That wasn't yours!" Kip shouted, hobbling closer. He was panting and his voice was choked with anger.

Molly felt a flush of shame—not for throwing away the key but for outrunning him. "Kip, you have to promise me: if that man tries to give you anythin' else, you'll get rid of it—bury it or burn it or throw it in the river."

Kip stared at the bushes, his jaw set.

She bent down, taking hold of his shoulders. *"Promise me."*

A creaking voice sounded behind her. "To demand promises is to invite disappointment."

Molly turned around to see Hester Kettle standing next to a bread stall. She was wearing the same patchwork cloak as before, and her bundle of junk seemed to have doubled in size since they first met. On her face was a look that put Molly in mind of a spider. "Hello, dearie." She stuck out a knobby finger. "You've been avoiding me."

30

A Story Bought, a Story Sold

Molly stood in the market, half wanting to drop her basket and run. What was it about Hester that made her so uncomfortable? "I ain't avoidin' you," she said, stepping in front of Kip. "I just been busy."

"Busy avoiding me, you mean." The woman gave a good-hearted chuckle and moved closer. Her hurdy-gurdy was slung over one shoulder, and it knocked against her side as she walked, releasing an ugly chord with each step. "How many times have you come to market? And not a once did you ask after old Hester Kettle. Why, it's enough to hurt a girl's feelings."

Molly felt fairly certain that it would take more than that to hurt Hester Kettle's feelings—she wasn't even sure people that old *had* feelings. The woman peered into Molly's basket as if it were her own. "Buying groceries, I see." She grabbed a pea pod from the basket and ate it before Molly could stop her.

Molly pulled the basket away. "We're *tryin'* to," she said. "Only folks ain't makin' it easy for us." She snuck an irritated glance at the row of stalls behind them.

Kip chimed in. "Just 'cause our master's rich don't mean we are. Molls here'll be in a good bit o' trouble if she don't come home with a full basket."

The woman nodded, rubbing her earlobe. "Perhaps old Hester can help you there."

Molly gave a smile that she hoped was polite. "Unless you've got a stack o' banknotes in that pack of yours, I doubt it."

"Leave the notes for the bankers," the woman said. "There's more currency in the world than pounds and pennies—especially for a storyteller. You watch and see." She tapped her nose and stepped over to a baker who was selling loaves and rolls. Molly had already tried buying something from this man; even his day-olds had been too expensive. "Ho there, Tolliver," Hester called in the casual tone of an old friend. She gestured to Molly and Kip. "How much are you charging these two pups for a loaf of your best rye?"

The man looked from Hester to Molly. "I told 'em fourpence," he said.

"Fourpence!" She whistled. "That's some fancy bread. There must be flecks of gold in the dough, or maybe it sings as you chew it?"

"It's regular bread," he said, looking a bit more uncomfortable. "And that's the regular price."

"Perhaps it is." She leaned against the stall. "But what if I was to tell you these two here were my kinsmen? What price would you tell them then?"

The man shifted his weight. "Well, then, Hester. I s'pose the price would be tuppence—"

"Tolliver," she said reproachfully.

"—for two!" he stammered. "You didn't let me finish. Tuppence for two loaves—that's what I was gonna say. Honest."

Hester grinned broadly. "That's what I thought." She nodded to Molly, who paid for four loaves and quickly put them in her basket before the man changed his mind. The woman turned back to the baker and leaned close. "Now, Tollie, you run and tell every other farmer and good-for-naught here that these two get the Hester Kettle price and not a pip more . . . and if I hear of any more chiseling, I'll be forced to tell a tale or two about how you spike your flour with ground-up cat bones."

Molly was fairly certain that the business about cat bones was not true. But from the man's face, it seemed that—true or not—the threat was credible. "No need for that, Hester. I'll do as you say." He smiled at Molly and Kip, and when he spoke, his voice had a note of forced kindness. "Any friend of Hester's is a friend of the hollow. If you pair would be kind enough to watch my store, I might not notice if a few of those there biscuits went missing." He hung his apron and started toward the butcher across the way.

Hester watched the man with a satisfied smile. "You heard the fellow," she said, gesturing to the unguarded shelf of biscuits. "Eat your fill." Kip apparently did not need to be told twice; he hobbled past Molly and stuffed a biscuit into his mouth before she could stop him.

Molly hated the idea of owing this woman anything. "You lied to that man," she said, not touching a biscuit. She had half a mind to return the loaves as well.

"And when did I do that?" Hester asked, stuffing a few biscuits into the birdcage strapped to her back. "I might've promised to tell a tale in the future . . . but that's hardly the same thing as a lie."

"You told him we was your kinsmen."

"Why, that bit's true!" She pointed an accusing biscuit at Molly. "I can tell a fellow storyteller when I see one—that makes us kin enough."

"Molls is a storyteller, all right," Kip said through crumbs. "A great one! Whatever folks pay you for stories—I bet they'd pay my sister double!"

Molly felt her cheeks burn. She didn't like Kip talking about her like she was special. Even more, she didn't like him comparing her to this old crone. "There's nothin' so great about me," she said. "I'm just a servant. And you're just a beggar."

Hester shook her head. "Don't confuse what you do with who you are, dearie. Besides, there's no shame in humble work. Why, Aesop himself, the king of storytellers, was a slave his whole life. Never drew a free breath, yet he shaped the world with just three small words: 'There once was.' And where are his great masters now, hmm? Rotting in tombs, if they're lucky. But Aesop—he still lives to this day, dancing on the tip of every tongue that's ever told a tale." She winked at Molly. "Think on that, next time you're scrubbing floors."

Molly had of course heard of Aesop, but she hadn't known anything about him being a slave. She doubted it was true, and even if it was, it didn't change the ugly facts of her own life. "We're grateful for your help with the bread, mum," she said, taking Kip by the shoulder. "But we should get moving before sundown."

"There's plenty of blue left in the sky," the woman said. "Besides, we have business, you and me. You may recall promising me a story about a certain house in the sourwoods?" The woman folded her arms together, perhaps indicating that she was willing to fight for the story, if need be.

Molly hesitated. She could feel Kip watching her, waiting to hear what she said. If it were up to him, he would probably tell the woman everything. Molly, however, did not trust Hester Kettle. Behind the smiles and winks and "dearies" there was an edge to the woman that made her uncomfortable—something dark and crafty that lurked just behind the eyes. What was it Hester *really* wanted?

"Afraid there's not much to tell." Molly shrugged. "It's a big old house. Lots of dust and cobwebs. Lots of chores. Nothin' too strange."

"Nothing *too strange*?" The woman took a step closer. "Tell me: What's the chore, exactly, that makes a young girl's hair shrivel up and her face go pale?"

Molly shifted her weight. She had been careful to tuck her hair under her cap, but apparently she had not been careful enough. She looked back to Kip, who nodded to her, urging her to tell the truth. "I'm just tired," she said, standing tall. "A little sick with fever, maybe. Nothin' more."

The woman sniffed. "I know all about your *fevers*." She glared at Molly, her eyes full of something mean. "It's plain you know something, and it's plainer you refuse to tell it. Very well, I'm not one to grovel. You can keep your story—seems we're less kin than I suspected." She bowed to Kip. "Watch out for *chores*, little man, lest you wind up like your sister." She adjusted the weight of her pack and turned around.

Molly watched the woman move away from them, her collection of junk swinging back and forth with each step. Her relief was mingled with a feeling of regret. Why didn't she want this woman to know about the house and the tree? Why didn't she want to tell her about the night man?

"It ain't fever!" Kip called out.

The woman stopped walking.

"Kip!" Molly hissed.

Kip glared at her. "You promised to tell her, Molls. If you won't do it, I will." He hobbled toward the woman, who was now watching him with keen interest. "There's some kinda spirit who haunts the house at night," he said. "He's makin' everyone sick and pale—just like my sister."

Molly grabbed his arm. "That's enough, Kip!" She wanted to drag him away, to cover his mouth, to make him stop telling this woman things.

Kip pulled away. "And there's a tree—a great big, horrible tree. Every night, the man feeds and cares for it."

"Is that so?" The old woman was watching Kip with a look that Molly could only describe as hunger.

Molly put a hand on her brother's shoulder, but she did not stop him. Kip hopped closer, swallowing. "You know every story there is around these parts. So tell us: Do you know one about a man and a tree?"

The woman looked at Kip and then at Molly. "As a matter of fact, I do."

31

The Legend of the Night Gardener

Claiming that an open market was no place for a proper story, Hester led them both to a tavern at the end of the road. Molly looked up at the wooden sign above the door. It had a carving of a crescent moon dipping below some waves. "The Moon Under Water," Hester said, pushing open the door. "There's no better spot for a pot of ale and good conversation."

Molly stepped inside. The tavern was dark and warm. What little light bled in through the shuttered windows was soaked up by the thick cloud of smoke that floated above the tables—so thick that it hid the rafters. Men and a few women sat in chairs, talking in hushed tones. Every so often, the silence was broken with a startling burst of laughter or a clanking of plates or the sharp scrape of a stool against the wooden floor.

"Ho there, Hester!" one man called. "Come to treat us with a song?"

"Not today, William."

Molly and Kip followed her to an empty table in the corner that seemed to be waiting for them. "Make yourselves comfortable," she said, carefully removing her pack from her shoulders and setting it beside the table. When she was seated, the pack was nearly as high as her head. Kip, who had never been in a tavern, eagerly slid into the corner chair, where, Molly supposed, he would have the best view of the other patrons. This suited Molly just fine because it meant she could better protect him, if trouble came. Trouble did not come, except in the form of a fat barmaid with yellow hair and a broad smile. She set down three mugs of cider, which sloshed as they landed. "On the house," she said.

Hester put her hands to her breast. "Bless you, Franny. I'll be sure to tell folks all about how your mince pies cured a blind man Sunday last."

The woman chuckled. "I wouldn't stop you if you did!" She wiped her hands on her apron and went back to the bar.

Molly watched this exchange, somewhat confused. It seemed like all Hester had to do was threaten to tell a nasty story or promise to tell a good one and folks did whatever she wanted. But if everyone knew that Hester's stories were made up, then why did they pay her any mind?

Molly had had cider once and didn't like the taste. Kip, however, seemed to show a natural affinity. He was nose-deep into his mug before she could blink. "Aren't you a thirsty one?" Hester said, chuckling.

"It tastes like apples!" Kip said, licking the foam from his top lip.

Molly sniffed her own drink. "Rotten ones."

The old woman raised her cup. "To differing opinions: may they ever stay apart." She toasted and then sipped in a manner that could only be described as ladylike.

Molly pushed her drink aside. "You promised us a story."

"Indeed I did." Hester set down her mug and dabbed her lips on the edge of her cloak. "But first there's the question of what kind of story it'll be."

Molly rolled her eyes. The woman had a way of answering questions without answering questions. "What *kind* of story?" she said. "You mean like happy or sad?"

"Stories come in all different kinds." Hester scooted closer, clearly enjoying the subject at hand. "There's *tales*, which are light and fluffy. Good for a smile on a sad day. Then you got *yarns*, which are showy— yarns reveal more about the teller than the story. After that there's *myths*, which are stories made up by whole groups of people. And last of all, there's *legends*." She raised a mysterious eyebrow. "Legends are different from the rest on account no one knows where they start. Folks don't *tell* legends; they *repeat* them. Over and again through history. And the story I have for you"—she sat back on her stool—"why, that one's a legend."

Molly was trying to follow. "So legends are true, then?"

The woman shrugged; again, not an answer. "Who's to say? Truer than the rest, I suppose." She raised a finger. "But you should know: legends are very expensive."

Molly sighed. "We haven't got money, as you're well aware."

The woman waved her off. "I don't want your money. You'll pay Hester the same way everyone does." She gestured to her pack beside her. Molly looked at the jumble of trash and bric-a-brac, realizing for the first time that every object there represented a story. She wondered what sort of story might have been bought with a pair of baby shoes or a tortoise shell or hedging shears.

"If you dinna want money, what do you want?" Molly said.

The woman's eyes drifted to Kip's crutch propped against the wall. "I could always do with a fine walking stick—"

Molly put a hand on her brother's leg. "You canna have that," she said.

The woman chuckled. "I didn't think so. So let's see . . ." She rolled her fingers on the table, screwing up her face in thought. "I couldn't help but notice: ever since I showed up, your brother's had one hand buried in his pocket."

Molly looked down at Kip and saw that he did indeed have one hand in the pocket of his coat. It was balled up in a little fist, as though he were holding something. He shifted, uncomfortable. "My hand's cold," he said.

The woman smiled. "Cold or not. You give me whatever's in there, and we'll call it even."

It was obvious that Kip did not want to do this. Molly leaned to-ward him. "We got no choice," she whispered. The truth was, Molly was grateful that the woman had asked for the contents of Kip's pockets and not her own. In her pocket were the letters from Ma and Da—she would never be able to give those up.

Kip bit his lip. "All right." He pulled his fist from his pocket and placed something small on the table. "It's a wishin' button. Molly gave it to me."

"You don't say." The woman whistled. "Two pups come to me wanting to know about a man and a tree . . . and of all the things they could pay, they give me a button to wish on." She picked it up, holding it between her fingers like a jewel. "I'll take good care of it." She reached over to her pack and removed a short length of string that seemed to have been put there just for this occasion. She carefully laced the string through the buttonhole and then tied it around her neck.

Molly squeezed her brother's hand. She knew it meant something to give up that button, even if it was just make-believe. "We paid your price," she said. "Now let's hear the tale."

"Legend," Kip corrected.

"Indeed," Hester said, leaning close. "We'll call it the Legend of the Night Gardener."

Night Gardener. Just hearing those words sent bumps along Molly's arm. It was as if the woman had given a name to the man in the fog. Molly looked at her brother, who was staring at the woman, eyes wide.

Hester Kettle produced a pipe from her sash and stuffed it with tobacco. She lit the bowl and puffed slowly. Smoke curled up from the end, dissolving into the cloud above them. "Like all legends, it's very old. Goes back further than anyone can tell, before saints and scrolls . . . Might even be the first story there ever was." She raised her brow. "Picture that, if you can."

Molly knew what the woman was doing. She was creating a *mood*. It was something Molly did when she wanted people to really listen. She closed her eyes and tried to imagine what the world might be like before boats and roads and kings and wars. A world fresh and new.

The woman cleared her throat, and when she spoke again her voice had a sort of music to it. "There once was a wise man who lived in a garden. The man had a magic touch about him, and his plot was filled with all manner of strange plants—the like of which hasn't been seen before or since. People called him the Night Gardener, and that was because his garden would only blossom under the light of the full moon."

Molly looked at Kip, who was looking at her. Did this woman somehow know about the flowers in the woods? Was she teasing them? "Did . . . did the flowers glow white?" Kip asked.

"I hadn't heard that," Hester said. "I suppose they might have. Glowing or not, the man loved his garden, and he cared for it year in and year out. He sang to his plants and trimmed their leaves and talked to them as though they were his own children—which they were, in a manner of speaking." She leaned closer. "And then one day there grew a new child: a tree. This tree was different from everything else in the garden. This tree was *alive*."

Molly heard Kip gasp. "Did it have roots that moved?" he said.

Hester puffed at her pipe. "Again, I can't say. The curious thing about this tree was its fruit."

"What was its fruit?" Molly asked despite herself.

"Anything." The woman opened her eyes wide. "The tree would give you whatever you wished for." She shook her head as if she, too, had trouble believing it. "Can you imagine?"

Molly swallowed. She thought of the letters in her dress pocket. "But . . . but the things it gave were real, right?"

"Real as you or me. People came from all around to have their heart's desire granted to them. The poor found riches. The ugly found love. The sick found strength." Molly heard Kip shift in his seat. "And all the tree asked in return was a single drop of your soul—"

"Your soul?" Kip said, clasping his finger.

"Just a drop, mind you. There's folks who'll pay much more than that for much less." She drew on her pipe. "At the end of each day, after all the people had gotten their wishes and gone home, the Night Gardener would make his own wish: 'I've everything a man could want,' he'd say. 'Stars overhead, soil below, and my children around me. All I ask is that it might never end. Just as the blossom turns to seed, I wish that I might never die.' And every time he uttered these words, the tree would always answer the same way:

> *"'Help me grow tall, and you shall receive*
> *All that you wish inside of me.'"*

"Wait." Molly wrinkled her nose. "The tree could *talk*?"

Hester gave her an irritated look. "Legends are not helped by the literal mind. The tree spoke; that's all I know." She relit her pipe, which had gone out. "So the Night Gardener spent his days caring for the tree, and the tree spent its days caring for people. And at the end of every day, when the sun fell from the sky, the Night Gardener would make his wish of the tree, and the tree would answer as it always had:

> "*'Help me grow tall, and you shall receive*
> *All that you wish inside of me.'*

"Years passed, and the tree grew stronger and taller. The other plants in the garden withered and died, but the man did not care. He wanted only to tend his beloved tree.

"And then one day, when the man was very old, he came to the tree one last time. He fell before it, hobbled and weak. 'All I have is gone,' he said. 'My garden is bare. My body is broken. I have given my life to help you grow. In all these years, never once have I tasted your fruit. And now I ask with my very last breath: Will you grant my wish?'

"The tree was now enormous; its branches nearly scratched the sky. And this time, it answered a little differently:

> "*'Now I am tall, so now you'll receive*
> *All that you wish inside of me.'*

"And with that, the tree spread its branches and leaned over with its great, broad trunk. It opened its mouth wide and"—she clapped her hands together—"swallowed the man whole." The old woman sat back in her chair, looking spent. "And that is the Legend of the Night Gardener."

Molly sat for a moment in confused silence. "That canna be all," she said. "What happened to him after that?"

"He died, I suppose. Or he didn't." The woman shrugged. "The legend doesn't tell that part."

Molly felt a flush of anger, the way she did when someone had tricked her. "But it has to! It has to end proper."

"Stories don't *have to* do anything; they just have to be." She leaned forward. "But imagine if it *were* true, hmm?" She stared between them, her eyes shining. "Imagine what a person could do with just a little clipping from a tree like that." She wet her lips. "Why, she'd be queen of the world . . ."

"Or she'd be swallowed whole," Kip said.

Hester rapped her knuckles against the table. "Sharp as ever, this one!" She cackled and peered out across the room. Orange light was bleeding in through the shutter cracks, and Molly realized that it must be nearly sundown. "I'd love to stay here and chat, but then you two would be going home in the dark. And we can't have that."

Kip volunteered to fetch the wagon and suggested that Molly stay behind to help Hester with her pack. Molly helped the old woman gather her things, and the two of them emerged from the tavern. She breathed deep, tasting the fresh air of the late afternoon.

"I'm sorry if my story wasn't to your liking." Hester adjusted her pack, teetering slightly. "Perhaps you can make up an ending that suits your fancy."

"Seems like cheatin'," Molly said. She was staring at the button hanging from the woman's neck.

Hester touched the button. "Funny things, wishes. You can't hold 'em in your hand, and yet just one could unmake the world." She looked up at Molly. "I can imagine that a person who knew where to get wishes might think it was smart to keep it a secret . . ." The woman had the same hungry look in her eyes as before.

Molly took a step back, wishing that Kip would be faster with the cart. "There's no use talkin' about it," she said. "It's all just made-up lies, anyway."

Hester gave a light chuckle. "You asked me for a story; now you call it a lie." She folded her arms. "So tell me, then: What marks the difference between the two?"

Agitated as she was, Molly couldn't help but consider the question. It was something she had asked herself in one form or another many times in her life. Still, Molly could tell the difference between the two as easily as she could tell hot from cold—a lie put a sting in her throat that made the words catch. It had been some time, however, since she had felt that sting. "A lie hurts people," she finally answered. "A story helps 'em."

"True enough! But helps them *do what*?" She wagged a finger. "That's the real question . . ." The old woman swung her hurdy-gurdy off her shoulder. "I'll leave you with that." She gave a curtsy and started down the road, playing as she walked.

Molly thought the song sounded familiar, but she couldn't tell where she had heard it before. She shivered, putting her hands into her pockets. Her fingers touched the letters from Ma and Da.

From Ma an' Da, she thought to herself, *or from the tree?*

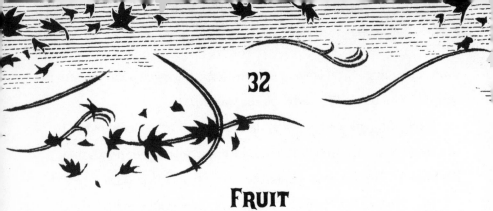

32

FRUIT

Whennen Kip reached his sister outside the tavern, she looked annoyed. "What took you so long?" she muttered, climbing onto the bench of the wagon.

"I got turned around," he said, wiping mud from his knee. He couldn't tell her the real reason it had taken him so long to return with the cart. Not yet.

The ride back to the sourwoods was quiet. Kip held the reins and watched the road. The whole way, he could feel Molly beside him, staring into the shadows. "Kip?" she said after a long silence. "What do you think about stories?"

Kip could tell from her tone that she wanted a serious answer. He shrugged. "I like your stories. A lot more than old Hester's, that's for sure."

She caught his eye. "So you dinna believe those things she said . . . about the Night Gardener?"

"How can I?" Kip scratched the back of his neck. "The way I figure: if that tree at the Windsors' was really the same one as in the story, then it'd have magic fruit—and we ain't had no wishes granted lately." He grinned. "Unless you been holdin' out?"

"Nay." Molly looked away. "I haven't."

Kip had meant that as a joke, but his sister was not smiling. He eyed her in the fading light, his fist clenched tight at his side.

When they finally reached the house, it was dark. Molly, who was late for making supper, went straight in with the food from the market. Kip went to the stables to feed Galileo. He brushed the horse, biding his time, keeping one eye on the house. On the second floor, just beside the tree, was a small window he had never noticed before. He saw light as someone slipped into the room from what must have been the upstairs hall. He studied the person's shadow, wondering who it might be. He was looking for red hair, but then he reminded himself: Molly's hair wasn't red anymore.

Kip waited a good hour before approaching the front door of the house. He wanted to be certain that Molly and the family wouldn't see him. He reached the stoop and paused. He looked down at his hand, at the treasure he had been carrying ever since he'd left the market—

The night man's key.

This was the real reason that he had taken so long in returning with the wagon. Kip closed his fingers around its earthy twines. Molly had forbidden him from using the key. He knew she would be furious to see he had it now. But after hearing Hester's story about the Night Gardener and the tree, he had to know.

Kip took a breath and opened the front door.

The house was warm inside, much warmer than the stables. It smelled better, too. Kip crept into the foyer, trying not to make a sound. He wished he had thought to put the pillowcase around the end of his crutch to muffle his steps. He could hear the family somewhere in the back of the house, eating supper—the sharp rapping of forks against plates. Kip closed his eyes and tried to ignore the smell of meat pies. He carefully shut the door behind him and then hobbled upstairs.

The first time Kip had seen the little green door at the top of the stairs, he had asked his sister what it was. Molly had told him that it was a closet. Perhaps she was just repeating what the Windsors had told her. Either way, Kip knew better. He knew that people didn't put locks on closet doors.

When Kip reached the top of the staircase, his heart was pounding. He gripped his crutch and hobbled to the green door. He held up the key, clutched tight in his sweating hand. When Molly had seen the key in the market, she had looked afraid. What possible terrors might be awaiting him behind this door? With a final glance over his shoulder, he slid the key into the lock—

It fit perfectly.

He turned the key and heard the sound of a bolt sliding away from the jamb. The strain was apparently too great for the root-made key; it came apart in his fingers, crumbling into dust. It didn't matter. The gift had worked.

Kip pushed open the door and stepped into the room.

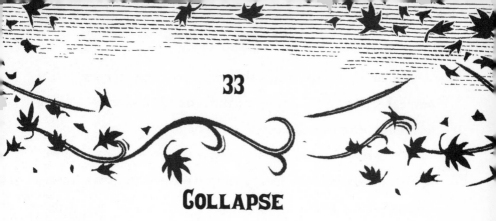

33

COLLAPSE

Molly carefully pulled the tea cart into the yard. Cups and saucers rattled as it rolled over cobblestones and mud. "Your tea is ready, mum."

Mistress Windsor was out behind the house, admiring her garden. The garden was hers because she owned the land that it sat upon. But really, it belonged to Kip. He was the one who had spent all spring weeding and tilling and planting and pruning. Where there had been decay and ruin, there was now abundant life. Flowers of all different colors ran along the winding stone footpath—stones that Molly had helped him carry from the bank of the river. Above the path were hanging baskets that Kip had made from wire, now overflowing with ivy and begonias. There were moss-covered stumps and even a small pond. It was not a proper English garden, perhaps, but it was something.

Molly cast an eye across the lawn. She could see her brother chopping firewood—something he did when he wanted to think. Ever since their trip to the village two days before, Kip had been distant toward her. She pushed a flood of worries from her mind, not wanting to dwell on what thoughts might be troubling him.

Molly brought the cart alongside Mistress Windsor, who was seated in a wrought iron chaise longue. It was a hot morning, but the woman had two blankets wrapped around her shoulders nonetheless. "Tell your brother the pond needs skimming," she said, adjusting the ring encircling her finger.

"Yes, mum." Molly poured tea into a cup.

"And the ivy is beginning to choke the hedges."

"Yes, mum." Molly added two lumps of sugar and stirred until the white grains had dissolved into nothing. She offered the tea to her mistress, who took it in her pale hands. The teacup clattered violently against its saucer as Constance brought it to her lips. Molly tried not to stare, but she could not look away. The woman seemed almost translucent in the sunlight. Tiny blue veins shone just beneath the skin of her neck. Her once-shining hair was wispy and thin, like a mess of black cobwebs. Her mouth had turned as dark as her eyes. Molly had never seen a dead person before, but she knew she was looking at death.

Mistress Windsor must have marked the concern on Molly's face, for she pulled herself upright and set aside her cup and saucer. "Is something the matter?"

"No, mum." Molly turned her cart around. "I was lost in my thoughts."

Constance caught Molly's arm in her cold hand. "And what thoughts would those be?"

Molly could not tell if this was a plea or a challenge. She stared at the ring on the woman's emaciated finger. "I was just thinkin' of somethin' you said when me and Kip first came here. You talked about a 'reasonable fear of illness'—those were your very words."

Constance let go of her arm. "You have a prodigious memory."

Molly took a shaky breath. "If this house is makin' you sick, then why do you stay?"

Constance creased her lips. "I could ask you the same thing . . . but I already know the answer." Her dark gaze drifted to Molly's side. "Those letters you keep in your pocket—"

Molly started. "You know about the letters?"

Constance waved off her alarm. "Not their precise contents, mind you. I've seen you poring over them when you think you're alone. But, of course, no one's ever alone in this house, not truly." She glanced toward the branches towering over the roof. "I remain here for the same reason you do. I would no sooner leave this place than you would burn those letters."

Molly put a protective hand over her apron pocket. "Never . . ."

Constance smiled. "Exactly. Without the tree, without its gifts, we would be completely unmoored." She sat back in her chair. This time, when she took her teacup, she used both hands so it would not shake. "I should think that a touch of fever is a small price to pay for such a bounty." She sipped. "Wouldn't you agree?"

"Yes, mum."

The conversation was over. Molly curtsied and returned to the house. She closed the kitchen door behind her, feeling an icy knot of dread in her stomach. She slid her hand into her pocket and removed the stack of envelopes from the tree. Each one was stained with salt water and addressed in the same fragile hand. It was her mother's handwriting. She knew it was. And yet . . . what if it wasn't? What if the words inside these letters were not written by her parents but written by some magic of the tree—a tree that fed off people and needed to keep them close?

She removed one of the letters from its envelope. Like every other letter in the stack, it ended the same way: with Ma and Da promising that they would come soon and then giving Molly one final instruc‐tion: *stay put*. Molly said the words aloud, and this time she did not hear Ma's voice in her head. Instead, she heard a distant, more hollow voice. A voice like the wind.

Molly did not even know what she was doing as she approached the stove. She crouched down and opened the iron door to the oven. Hot air swept over her face. The embers inside were still red. Molly ran her fingers over the stack of letters. Her bottom lip shook as she tried to form the words that might help her let go. "Good-bye," she said, sliding the envelopes into the stove.

Molly blinked through tears as fire licked up the side of the paper, consuming the letters . . .

"No!" She snatched the envelopes back from the oven, burning her hand. She smothered the flames in her apron. The envelopes were singed on one end, but they had been saved. She had saved them. Molly closed her eyes, clutching them against her breast.

"I'm sorry . . ." She sobbed. "I'm sorry . . ." But she did not even know whom she was talking to.

Crash!

Molly heard a noise outside. She hurriedly tucked the letters back into her pocket. "Is that you, mum?" she called, opening the door.

There was no reply.

Molly ran toward the garden. "Mum?" A shattered teacup lay on the ground. The cart was overturned. Mistress Windsor lay on the gravel, not moving.

Molly grabbed hold of the woman and shook her. "What's happened?" Constance was ice-cold to the touch. Her eyes were turned up in her head. Her dark lips were parted, and from them Molly could feel no breath.

"Kip! Master Windsor!" she cried. "Someone help!"

34

Leeches and Lizards

Molly stepped into Mistress Windsor's bedroom. "Doctor, I've brought more water." She held up a sort of wineskin made from India rubber. It was filled with boiling water that made it almost too hot to hold.

"At her feet, girl," the doctor said.

Constance Windsor lay in bed, tossing her head back and forth, muttering under her breath. Molly went to the end of the bed, which was piled high with nearly a dozen blankets. She pulled the blankets back to reveal Constance's bare feet. Molly felt uncomfortable handling them. They were macilent, clammy, and far too cold. She slid the bag of hot water beneath the feet and retucked the blankets under the mattress.

"Oh, Connie . . . my sweet poor Connie." Master Windsor stood by the far wall, wringing his hands. His hair was disheveled, and his face was gray with stubble. It had been two days since his wife had collapsed in the garden. In all that time, he had not left her side.

Doctor Crouch took a measurement of the patient's head with a pincer tool. "Seems normal enough . . . ," he muttered, consulting a chart on the bedside table. He wore gold spectacles on the very end of his nose, which forced him to tilt his whole head to look at people—not that he ever bothered looking at Molly. He opened his black leather bag and removed a sort of copper funnel, the small end of which he put into his ear. He held the other end over Mistress Windsor's chest and listened for a few seconds. "Hrmmmm . . . very peculiar . . ."

Bertrand stepped forward. "Wh-wh-what is it?"

The doctor removed a little book from his vest and, consulting his pocket watch, made a notation. He spoke as he wrote. "Heart rate and eye movement lead me to believe that your wife is not asleep. Rather, she is caught in a sort of ether state—something *between* sleeping and waking. Call it suspended somnambulism." He made a pleased face. "Yes, that's just the name for it!" He quickly scribbled another note to himself, chuckling. "Crouch, old boy . . . just wait until the academy hears of this . . ."

"Surely there's a cure," Bertrand said in a tone befitting a question.

Doctor Crouch finished writing. "Bed rest. And not just for her. The mysterious fever I witnessed in your family before has clearly accelerated. I fear it will only be a matter of time until the rest of you succumb."

Molly cleared her throat. "You're not gonna try leeches, sir?" This was what healers had always done in Molly's village back home. They were supposed to draw poison from the blood.

"Leeches?" The man snorted. "Does this woman look like she has fluids to spare? Next I suppose you'll tell me to ply her with nightshade or bathe her in quicksilver. My girl, we are on the cusp of a *modern age*—and with it comes modern medicine." He dug a fat hand through his bag and removed a small bottle. "Take this laudanum, for example. Wonderful stuff! I have a few drops in my tea each morning to calm the nerves."

Molly felt her cheeks burn. The man had a way of talking that made her feel stupid. "I'll go check on supper," she said. She lowered her head and retreated to the hall. Alistair and Penny were huddled outside the door.

"Is Mummy all right?" Penny asked, craning her neck to see into the room.

"Of course not," muttered Alistair, his mouth stuffed with peppermints. "That's why Father called the doctor, dummy."

"Hush, both of you," Molly said. She stroked Penny's hair. "Your mum'll be fine. Doctor Crouch is the best in England—maybe the world. Why, I heard that when Napoleon got his head chopped off, it was the good doctor who stitched it back on."

"Napoleon was poisoned," Alistair corrected. "And that was thirty years ago."

Molly eyed the bag of sweets in his plump hand. "Perhaps you've had enough of those," she said.

Alistair glared at her, chewing like a cow. "You're probably right." He spit out a huge glob of sticky peppermint goo. It landed on the floor with a wet plop. He smiled. "You should clean that up. Someone might slip."

Before Molly could respond, a door slammed behind her. Master Windsor rushed from his wife's room, fists clenched. He marched right past Molly and the children, who had to leap aside to avoid being knocked over.

"Where's he going in such a rush?" Alistair muttered, wiping sticky slobber from his chin.

Molly did not answer; instead she led them both to their bedrooms and instructed them to wash up for supper. When the children were gone, she went to the front hall. Molly knew where Master Windsor had gone. She had seen the key in his hand.

Just as she suspected, the green door at the top of the stairs was open. It sounded like Master Windsor pacing inside. She could hear his strained voice—something between a shout and a whisper. "*I said*, Make her well!" he demanded. "You're not listening—I need a *cure*! Ointments! Medicines! Anything!"

Molly peered into the room. Master Windsor was facing the tree. Sovereigns, shillings, and pennies spilled from the knothole in front of him. The man charged forward and plunged his arm into the hole, digging beneath the coins. "Enough money! I want"—he pounded his fist against the tree trunk—*"out!"*

He slumped to the floor, burying his face in his hands. "I want out . . ." He uttered a moan, his body heaving with tight sobs.

Molly watched, unable to look away. She had seen men cry before but never like this. Bertrand Windsor sounded like a lost child, and perhaps he was just that.

She took a careful step into the room. "Master Windsor?"

"Molly!" Bertrand sprang to his feet, wiping tears from his eyes, awkwardly trying to put himself between Molly and the knothole. "I was just t-t-talking to myself about . . . affairs regarding . . ."

"It's all right, sir," she said, sparing him the indignity of going on. "I know about the tree."

His alarm crumbled into something resembling defeat. "I s-s-suppose it was only a matter of time." He sniffled. "I was never much good at keeping secrets."

Molly knew she was meant to leave, to pretend she hadn't seen her master in this state. But she knew equally well that she was no normal maid. She was no longer "the help." She was part of the Windsors' story now. She removed a handkerchief from her pocket and offered it to him. "You look like you could use it."

"Th-th-thank you," he said, wiping his nose. He ran a hand over his pale, unshaven chin. "I must be a dreadful sight."

Molly pushed her dark hair from her face. "We all are." She offered a kind smile. "You're doin' everythin' you can for your wife."

Bertrand nodded, looking down. He creased the handkerchief over and again on itself, as if he could fold it into nothing. For a moment, Molly thought he had forgotten she was there. "It . . . it wasn't supposed to be like this," he said finally. "I had plans to make something of myself, to prove myself to her—"

Molly inched nearer. "Mistress Windsor told me about how hard you tried to make her comfortable."

"Is that how she put it?" He made a bitter face. "Connie insisted she didn't care about 'being comfortable'—but I knew that she did. She deserved more than what a clerk could provide. And I was determined to give it to her. If I couldn't earn the money through honest work, I would do it through speculation."

Molly knew that "speculation" was a sort of gambling men did with imaginary money. Money they did not always have. She stared at the man cowering before her. How many times had she silently defended him—imagined him the victim of a cruel and unloving wife? But now, as Molly thought of Constance unconscious in her bed, she knew who the real victim was. "You mighta done wrong, sir. But you did it for right reasons," she said, trying to hide the judgment from her voice.

"But I *didn't* do it . . . That's the problem. Markets turned, investments went sour. I had to borrow more and more just to keep creditors at bay. The banks seized my accounts, our home, everything!"

"That's when you came here? To the place where you grew up?"

"I first thought of selling the land," he said. "But when I returned to this house . . . and I saw the door—I suddenly remembered everything: how my father's studies brought us here, how he built a house around the tree to keep its secret, and how one night he and my mother . . ." He shook his head, warding off some horrible memory.

"What happened to 'em?" Molly said softly.

He smiled like he hadn't heard her. "When I opened this door,

I found something else." He held up a single coin. "My wish." He clenched his fist around the coin, his expression turning to bitterness. "I thought it could save us. You must understand: we had nowhere else to go."

Molly did understand. She remembered being alone on the streets with Kip. She had been willing to do anything to get him away from that—including bringing him to a house that her every instinct told her was not safe. She folded her arms, warding off a shudder. How well the tree had known just what Master Windsor had needed. Just what *she* had needed. They had, both of them, come to the tree in desperation. But had they just traded one evil for another?

"No matter what I do, things only get worse," he said absently. "The debt, the loans . . . It's like an anaconda, coiled around me, squeezing tighter and tighter."

Molly stared at a thin branch protruding from the wall—it was indeed snakelike. "We dinna got snakes in Ireland," she said, a thought forming. "A good saint chased 'em off long ago."

Bertrand nodded, looking a little confused. "I'd heard that."

"What we do got is lizards." She peered out the window, remembering. "Lizards aren't snakes, but they can still bite. Worse, they're bad luck in a garden. So folks have an old trick for gettin' rid of 'em. What you do is wait till just before sundown, when the air's cool but the lizards ain't yet gone into their holes. You take a red-hot rock from the fire and set it in the middle of your garden. The lizards—why, they hate the cold, and they'll come runnin' straight for that rock and curl up right on top o' it. Come mornin', you'll wake to find 'em still on that rock, their bodies cooked alive." She turned back. "You see: the rock saves 'em from chill only to kill 'em in its own way."

Down the hallway, Molly heard a faint moan. She took a step toward Master Windsor and placed a hand on his shoulder. "Sir. What your wife needs isn't jewels or money or even medicine." She nodded toward the open door. "She needs the same thing as that lizard—to get out of the cold."

She fixed her eyes on him, hoping the meaning of her story might sink in.

"You're right," he said. "You're right." But Molly still wasn't sure he had understood her. Bertrand bent down and collected the remaining coins from the floor. He stuffed the money into his pockets. "F-f-for the doctor," he said apologetically. He lowered his head and retreated into the hall.

Molly felt a flood of emotions eddying inside of her—an overwhelming mixture of regret and shame. These were not just things she felt about Master Windsor; they were things she felt about herself.

A light lapping of water broke the silence, and Molly caught the familiar smell of salt air.

She turned around and saw that the knothole was no longer empty. It was filled with dark water. And floating on the surface was a new letter with her name on it. Molly took a step closer, seeing the careful script written in her mother's loving hand. It bobbed up and down, waiting for her . . .

35

A Spirited Debate

The mood at supper was grim. Even Alistair, who usually spent his meals happily taunting Penny, was silent. However, when Molly appeared in the hall with Kip behind her, he spoke up. "What's *he* doing here?"

"N-n-now, Alistair," Bertrand said. "With all the chaos in the house lately, I could hardly expect Molly to prepare a separate meal for herself and her brother. He'll eat with us tonight." He smiled at Molly. "No need to stand on ceremony."

Molly led her brother to an empty seat beside Penny. "It's very kind of you, sir." She nudged Kip with her foot.

"Very kind," he repeated, though his attention seemed to be on the platter of steaming mutton on the sideboard, purchased courtesy of Hester's special discount.

"Quite right!" declared Doctor Crouch, tucking a serviette into his collar, indifferent to the mood of the family. "I've always said the only real difference between an Englishman and the most savage foreigner is their place of birth . . . That and brain size, of course."

"Just ignore Alistair," Penny whispered, scooting her chair closer to Kip. "He has a stomachache from eating too many chocolates."

Molly rested Kip's crutch against the wall and set to serving the table. Since Mistress Windsor was too sick for travel, it had been decided that Doctor Crouch would remain at the house for a few days to monitor her condition. This meant more work for Molly, who had to manage a guest while still playing nursemaid to her mistress. It was a miracle that she had been able to pull off even a simple roast.

Molly served mutton to everyone around the table. She noticed that Kip looked a little ashen—perhaps ill at ease about being inside the house—and made sure to give him an extra-big piece with plenty of fat around the edges. Master Windsor, usually talkative during meals, was apparently feeling more somber tonight. Instead, the silence was filled by Doctor Crouch, who droned on in an almost ceaseless monologue on the finer points of his profession.

"The thing that troubles me most," he said, already on his second helping, "is how many of my esteemed colleagues are still taken in by superstition and nonsense." He was one of those people whose speech could not be stopped by something so trivial as a full mouth. "Why, just recently, the academy announced it would host a symposium on the existence of the spiritual plane—can you imagine such a thing?" He rapped his wineglass, and Molly rushed to fill it. "I simply cannot understand—a little more, my dear—how in this modern age, forward-thinking men get hoodwinked into believing the unbelievable. Psychics and mediums? More like swindlers and mountebanks."

Kip had apparently been listening more closely than the others. "So you dinna believe in spirits?" he said from his plate.

Doctor Crouch glanced up, looking equal parts amused and annoyed. "I believe in the natural world and empirical facts, my boy. Superstition is merely the reaction of a weak mind confronted with what it cannot fathom. Primitive man found spirits in every blade of grass and bush. Take that unusually large tree in front of your house, for example—"

Penny perked up. "Oh, it's a *magic* tree."

"P–p–preposterous!" Master Windsor cut her off. He smiled at the doctor. "I don't know where she would get such an idea . . ."

"But the child proves my point!" Doctor Crouch rejoined. "In a less enlightened age, people would call the tree magic and make up a story. It would likely receive the same treatment as Homer's lotus blossoms or the proverbial garden of paradise—which, coincidentally, archaeologists now place in the outer regions of Persia—hardly paradise, if you ask me."

"Not all stories are made up," Kip said.

Molly was unnerved to see that he was looking not at the doctor but at her. She shot him a glare, warning him to watch his manners.

"Of course stories are made up, my boy—otherwise, they'd be called 'facts.' We in the modern age should know better than to believe in such flimflam. Returning to our *magic* tree: clearly the surrounding soil provides a unique balance of nutrients that perfectly suits its nutritional needs." He popped a slice of roast in his mouth. "Much as this mutton suits mine!"

Kip seemed undeterred. "What about good an' evil?" he said. "Are they just made up, too?"

Doctor Crouch gave an amused chuckle. "It seems we have a little philosopher among us!" He put down his knife and fork and folded his hands over his belly. "Young sir, please don't think me unreasonable—indeed, I am a slave to reason. The curious mind investigates all possibilities. I only ask for scientific rigor. If you say, 'The spirit world exists,' I say, 'Show me your proof.' And if one *could* produce such proof? Why, he would find his name emblazoned alongside the greatest minds in history—Euclid, Plato, Copernicus . . ." He stared above the table, his eyes shining at the thought of achieving such immortal glory.

Bertrand clapped his hands together. "All right, then," he cried, apparently keen to change the subject. "Who knows any good corkers?"

The remainder of the meal was unremarkable. Kip finished eating and retired to the stables to tend to Galileo. Molly cleared the table and set to preparing Doctor Crouch's room for the night. She made up the sheets, eyeing the portable medicine chest he had brought with him from town. It was filled with a vast array of notebooks and jars and shining scientific instruments—a traveling laboratory. She stared at the strange tools, wondering how they worked. Surely such marvelous equipment would be able to cure Mistress Windsor's sickness. She wondered if they could do more . . .

Molly dropped her work and rushed to Mistress Windsor's room. She found Doctor Crouch at the bedside. He had a special glass tube called a thermometer inside Constance's mouth. He took it out and examined some numbers at the end. "Well, that's not right," he muttered, frustrated, and put the glass back in her mouth.

"Any luck with the patient?" Molly said from the hall.

The doctor sighed. "I'm afraid not. *Crouch Fever* seems to be incurable." It took Molly a moment to realize that he had taken the liberty of naming Mistress Windsor's illness after himself. "I've tried everything I can think of, with no success."

"You've not tried *everything*," Molly said. "I been thinkin' about what you said at supper. 'The curious mind investigates all possibilities.'" The man showed visible pride at the idea of hearing himself quoted thus. "Well, what if it's some kind of magic that's done this?"

"Ah, I see." Doctor Crouch stood, a patronizing smile on his face. "Irish, yes? I forget that yours are a credulous people—prone to superstition." He patted her on the shoulder. "It was not my aim to confuse your little mind with speculations about the natural world—"

"I seen one," Molly said. "A real live spirit."

His smile froze into something less patient. "You mean you *thought* you saw one." He snapped his fingers. "Perhaps delusions are another symptom of the disease?"

"It's no delusion." Molly shook her head. "He comes every night to the house, goes room to room. And that's what's makin' us sick. You ever heard of anythin' like that in your studies?"

The man stroked his chin, engaging despite himself. "There are, of course, creatures that can carry disease. I am reminded of the Black Death in the Middle Ages, but those were rats"—he gave a disingenuous smile—"not spirits."

Molly bit her tongue, reminding herself that it did no good to argue with a person whose mind was set. "Spirit or not," she said, "this creature is real. And it's like nothin' you've ever seen."

His face perked up. "An undiscovered species?"

It seemed Molly had lit on something. "*Very* undiscovered," she said. "I'll introduce you. Tonight. And then you'll have the key to savin' the mistress." She fixed her eyes on his. "To discover Crouch Fever is one thing, but what about *curing* it? The Queen herself would probably knight you. And you'd live on forever, your name next to them other smart men you talked about, blazed in history."

"*Emblazoned*," he corrected softly. "Emblazoned in history . . ." The man stared beyond her, his small eyes darting back and forth, as if imagining the possibility.

"It's the greatest men who took the greatest chances." Molly spoke with a lilt. "It's your duty as a man o' science to at least try."

Doctor Crouch screwed up his chin. "Perhaps I *could* look into it—if only to cure you of your delusions."

"By all means, prove me wrong. I ask just one thing." She stepped closer. "If it turns out I am right and the spirit *is* real—will you catch him and take him with you?"

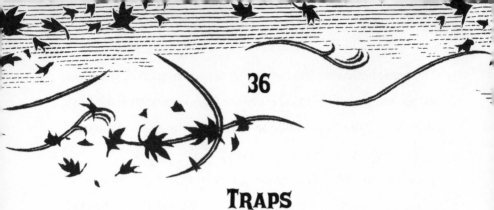

36

TRAPS

Kip dragged his rake back, pulling dead leaves from the Gardener's hole. "But what good can a doctor do?"

He glanced at Molly who was sitting beneath the tree on an overturned bucket. "Doctors know all sorts of special science tricks." On her lap lay a tattered old net that had been left in Galileo's cart, which she was now mending. "He's probably got ways to trap the Gardener with a mirror or stuff it in a bottle."

Kip wiped his brow. "I dinna think that's how science works." He had spoken to the doctor twice now and did not share his sister's high opinion. Doctor Crouch was the sort who needed to be right about everything. You could tell him his head was on fire, and he'd tell you why you were wrong, even as he burned. "Besides"—he hopped closer—"you told me he dinna even believe you. He just thinks it's some kinda animal."

"We don't need him to *believe* us," she said. "We just need him to help."

"What are you two talking about?" Penny called, leaping up from behind a hill. "And what's that net for?" She was occupying herself with a game that seemed to involve jumping over the grassy mounds. Kip had thought it looked like a fun thing to do—not that he would ever be able to do it.

"Go back to playin'," Kip said. He hopped toward Molly, his voice low. "I think it's a mistake what we're doin' here. I think we should keep as far from that Gardener as slugs from salt."

Molly laughed. "Slugs! Just what every girl wants to be called." Kip didn't smile, which seemed to annoy her. "Kip, I know it's tall odds, but if this works, the Gardener'll be gone. We'll be safe."

"An' if it don't work," he said, "he'll be mad and we'll be . . ." He shook his head, unsure of what, exactly, might happen. He knew in his bones that it would be bad. Bad like what had happened to Master Windsor's parents all those years back.

"I hear you whispering over there." Penny took a running jump over a hill. "Are you talking about the night man?"

Kip and Molly both snapped, "No!" This, at least, they seemed to agree on.

Penny made a sour face and went back to her game. Kip leaned on his crutch, massaging his left leg. It was throbbing at the knee—throbbing everywhere, really. His mind went to the story that Hester had told them in the village. He thought of the house and the tree and what he had found in the room with the little green door and wondered, once again, how much Molly truly knew about this place. He watched her tie two pieces of rope together, going over and then through, the way their father had taught them. "It's been a while since we heard from Ma an' Da," he said. "You think they're all right?"

Molly's hands slowed. "I'm sure they're fine." She untied her knot and started over.

Kip hopped closer, watching her expression. Something was obviously wrong. "Maybe you could read us an old letter, just to pass the time?"

Molly shook her head, not looking up. "I dinna got 'em with me. They were gettin' cumbrous in my apron, so I put 'em somewhere safe." She held up the net. "Besides, we got work to do. Doctor's orders."

Kip felt his throat tighten. "Doctor's orders," he muttered. Why couldn't Molly just be honest with him and say she was scared of the Gardener? Why did she hide behind smiles and stories? But Kip knew why. It was because she thought he was too small, too frail. And wasn't he? He watched Penny jumping between the hills with abandon. What he would give to be whole like that. What he would give to swim and jump and run and play like a normal boy.

Kip gripped his rake and went back to work. Doctor Crouch had instructed him to clear the area around the tree for their trap. Ever since his ordeal with the roots, Kip had been careful not to walk too close to the tree or the hole. Until now, the hole had remained undisturbed beneath a blanket of leaves. He cleared the bottom and was surprised to see that it wasn't any deeper than before—he had several nights since heard the Night Gardener digging in the darkness, but the hole looked untouched.

Kip hobbled away from the hole to clear a pile of leaves nearby. He balanced himself on one leg and gripped the rake with both hands. "Any last words?" he said. He brought the rake down like an executioner. The iron tongs sliced right through the pile and kept going. Kip had been expecting to hit hard dirt, and when he did not, the surprise caught him off-balance. He fell to the ground, landing hard on his shoulder. "I'm fine," he called to Molly before she could offer help.

Kip stood, breathing hard. His shoulder was throbbing, and it hurt to hold the rake in that hand. He hopped closer to the spot and, using just one hand, raked back the edge of the pile. Where he should have found dirt or grass, he saw only more leaves. Kip flipped his rake around and pushed the long handle into the spot. It sank deep into the leaves—

Another hole.

"I think you should see this," he called to Molly. "And watch your step."

Kip and his sister spent the next half hour clearing the area around the tree. What had started as two holes had now become six, all in a row. They were of similar size but for length, which ran from short to long. The hole closest to the house was about the size of a grown man; the hole at the other end was about the size of a little girl.

A breeze stirred the hairs along Kip's neck. He looked back over his shoulder at the lawn where Penny was playing. Little green hills rose and fell as far as he could see, each of them about the length of a body. "Molls, I dinna think those are just hills . . . ," he said, staring at the rolling mounds. More than he could count.

He felt Molly's hand wrap around his own. Her skin was clammy with perspiration. "This whole place . . . ," she whispered. "It's one giant graveyard."

"Nay." Kip swallowed, peering back at the tree. "It's one giant trap."

"What's all that behind you?" called Penny, who had seen them looking in her direction. She skipped toward them. "Are you making a fort?"

"Stay back!" Kip called. He hopped in front of the smallest grave, blocking her path.

"Penny," Molly said, her voice sweet but tense, "could you go back inside and check on your mum's hot water? And tell the doctor we're almost finished—he'll know what that means."

Penny stared at them for a moment, no doubt suspecting that she was being left out of something very interesting. "Fine," she said and marched toward the house.

"That was close," Kip said when the girl had finally disappeared through the front door. He looked up at his sister, who was still staring at the expanse of graves.

"You were right," she said. "I shouldn't 'a brought us here."

Kip stared at her pale face. Her once-green eyes were now almost black. He wanted to tell her that he understood, that he knew why she hadn't listened to him. He winced, feeling an ache in his left leg.

"C'mon," he said, turning around. He brought up some phlegm from his throat and spit into the grave at his feet, the one meant for him. "We got a monster to catch."

37

Camera Obscura

It was nearly dark by the time Molly finished setting the net. It was large, nearly twenty feet across. She hammered a wooden peg into the earth, fixing the net in place directly below the tree. "All finished, Doctor," she called, struggling to her feet.

Doctor Crouch reclined on the stoop, enjoying the last sips of his tea. While he made no secret of his doubts regarding Molly's story, he nevertheless seemed to have thrown himself into the experiment with commendable spirit. He had spent the whole of the afternoon collecting supplies in the village and now looked completely different from the genteel physician who had attended Mistress Windsor's bedside. His girth was hidden behind a leather apron similar to what a butcher might wear. Hanging from his shoulders was a jumble of fishing rods, bear traps, sketchbooks, telescopes, and a few things the purpose of which Molly couldn't begin to fathom. On his head was a hat with a sort of lantern attached as well as a pair of goggles with thick black lenses.

"I shall be the judge of that!" The man set his tea down and pulled

himself upright. He walked to the net, which Molly and Kip had secured with wooden pegs placed at regular intervals around the edges.
"Excellent work—and those extra holes are a clever touch."

Molly exchanged a look with her brother. They had decided not
to tell him what the "holes" really were, for fear of frightening him.

The doctor returned to his tea, calling behind him, "Now cover
it up with leaves."

Kip groaned. "More raking?"

Doctor Crouch either did not hear him or did not care. He had
already explained to them that he was not disposed toward "manual
labor." Molly picked up a rake and handed another one to Kip. "Least
this way, we dinna have to look at our own graves."

The final part of the trap was a long rope, which connected to the
net. Molly was instructed to loop the rope over a large overhanging
branch from the tree. The branch was very high, and it took her several
tries to toss it over the top. When she had succeeded, she gave it to
Kip, who was waiting at the "counterweight"—that being the doctor's
fancy word for Galileo's wagon.

"Tie it tight, my boy!" Doctor Crouch instructed.

Molly stood over Kip, watching him secure the rope to the back
of the wagon. He said nothing, but it was clear from his manner that
he did not want to be doing this.

"Are you feelin' all right?" she said.

"Why wouldn't I be?" he said, his voice sharp.

In recent days, Kip had been quieter and slower to smile. It felt like every question that came from his mouth was some sort of test that she was destined to fail. Every so often, she noticed him massaging the hip of his bad leg, a strained look on his face. Molly supposed that he had always felt pain, but only recently was he letting it show.

Kip cinched the knot tight and hopped past Molly. "Doctor, we're all set!"

The only thing left now was to wait. Molly, Kip, and the doctor all huddled behind the wagon, which concealed them from view. Doctor Crouch hummed to himself, tending to his arsenal of expensive equipment—all of which the children were strictly forbidden from touching. He had allowed himself a chair from the garden but insisted that the children crouch on the grass "to keep them alert." Molly pulled her coat close, reminding herself that however uncomfortable she was, Kip was more so. As the night wore on, Galileo became increasingly tense, pulling against his bit. It was Kip's job to keep a hand on the horse and prevent him from moving. "Gal's mighty keen to get away from this tree," he said, struggling with the reins. "Maybe we should let 'im."

Even in the darkness, Doctor Crouch's irritation was clear. "Perhaps we should leave the plan making to more evolved minds, hmm?"

"My brother didn't mean nothin', sir," Molly said. "We're grateful for what you're doin'."

"As well you should be," Crouch said, sounding a bit hurt. "It is no ordinary doctor who would condescend to test your hypothesis. Lucky for you, I am far from ordinary."

"You can say that twice," Kip muttered.

Even in the cold, Molly felt a hot flush of irritation. Why was Kip so negative about everything? Why couldn't he just trust her? But then, what reason had she given him to trust her? "Doctor," she said sweetly, "perhaps you can tell us a bit more about your plan. I'm sure it's a thing of brilliance."

"I wouldn't go that far, child . . ." He gave a laugh that was probably meant to communicate humility. "According to your own reports, the creature appears near this tree each night—from which I can only conclude that it is some sort of burrowing mammal—perhaps a weasel or badger."

"It's an awfully big badger," Kip said. Molly gave him an elbow to the ribs and a look to match.

Crouch seemed not to hear him. "When the creature appears—*if* the creature appears—I shall give the sign for you two to start the horse running. He will pull the rope, and our trap will be sprung, at which time, I shall run forward and capture the creature!"

"Capture him how?" Molly said tactfully. "A net won't hold him forever. You'll need to lock him up."

"Or kill him," Kip added.

"I shall do one better," the doctor exclaimed. "I shall freeze it forever in time." He gestured proudly to a device perched atop a tripod. It looked like a pair of billows attached to a bread box, wearing a cape. A variety of straps and cords dangled from the back, one of which seemed to contain a button.

Molly studied the strange apparatus. "What is that thing?"

The man chuckled. "This 'thing' is a *camera obscura*. I had planned to document some local fauna, but you've potentially led me to something far more promising." He excitedly removed something that looked like a dustpan from his bag, which he affixed to the top of the box and filled with some white powder. "This is a magnesium flash. I ordered it from France just last month. When I pull the lever on this handle"—he showed her a small trigger—"it will ignite the powder— creating enough light to capture the subject's likeness on one of these plates." He lifted the cloth in back and removed a sheet of tin, about the size of a postcard. "A perfect photographic specimen."

Molly looked at Kip, a dread realization creeping over her. "Its *likeness*?" she said. "You said you'd trap him and take him with you."

"And I am . . . in a manner of speaking!"

Molly stared at the tree, at the trap, at her brother. "We need more than manners!" she snapped. "We need it to *go away*."

She felt Kip's hand on her sleeve. "Molly?" he whispered.

Molly stood up, glaring at the doctor. "You lied to us. You made a promise that you would help, but you just want to get your name in some fancy books."

"You observed as much yourself when enlisting me," Doctor Crouch said patiently. "Chin up. If this creature does appear, there will doubtless follow a legion of eager researchers in my wake. Surely one of them will manage to help you."

"Molly?" Kip repeated, louder.

"We need help now!" she shouted.

Doctor Crouch stood. "Don't let's get hysterical. Perhaps I should prescribe you something . . ."

"Molly!"

Molly turned around. "What is it?" she snapped.

Kip pointed toward the tree. "Someone's comin'," he said.

Molly and Doctor Crouch both ducked down, peering around the side of the wagon. "The spirit's very tall, cloaked all in black," she whispered. Through the gray fog, she could see a shadow winding its way over and through the hills. It moved uncertainly, furtively, creeping and then stopping.

"Good heavens," Doctor Crouch said, grabbing his camera. His hands were shaking. "That's a lot bigger than a badger . . ."

"Told you," Kip said.

Molly studied the figure. It seemed different from the Gardener, shorter and less sure of its steps. As it moved, it rattled. There was something strange yet familiar about the sound. The figure crept onto the leaf-covered ground surrounding the tree. It paced back and forth. In its hand was something long and sharp. "Doctor," Molly whispered, "I dinna think—"

"Shhh!" the man hissed. "On my mark."

"But Doctor . . ."

"Now!"

Molly didn't move.

"I said, *Now!*" the man shouted. He pushed past her and struck

Galileo's backside with the broad of his hand. The horse reared up and sprinted off—pulling the wagon and the rope with it. Molly heard a shriek of surprise as the net swept up from the ground, catching its prey in the air.

There came a blinding flash of light. Molly fell back as sparks spewed from the doctor's camera and instantly turned to smoke. She covered her mouth, coughing, feeling her way through the cloud. "I've got you," she said to Kip, who had been knocked over in the confusion.

Doctor Crouch was already at the net, hopping from side to side like a lucky prospector. "I've done it!" he shouted. "I've done it!"

Molly blinked, her eyes still adjusting. The net dangled from the giant branch, the ropes groaning with the weight of its quarry, which twisted and rattled in protest.

Crouch held his camera in front of him like a weapon. "Back, beast!"

The net slowly turned around, and Molly saw a weathered face crowned by white hair and two fiendish eyes. "It's you!" she said.

Hester Kettle gave a wry, toothless smile. "You were expecting someone else?"

38

SHEARS

What are you doin' here?" Molly demanded.

Hester dangled before them, her arms and legs jutting out of the net at odd angles. "Why, just hanging about." She gave a sideways smile as she rocked past.

"Just as I thought!" Doctor Crouch thrust a finger in the air. "Your spirit is nothing more than a disease-ridden vagrant."

"Storyteller, if it pleases," Hester said.

"Contagious, no doubt. She's probably given Crouch Fever to half the valley." Doctor Crouch traded his camera for a large syringe from his belt and removed a cork from the end of the needle. "Now, children—hold the woman down while I collect a sample of her blood!"

"Save your time," Molly said. "She's not what's makin' us sick."

The doctor hesitated, needle poised. "Are you quite certain? Because were I to *imagine* a source of Crouch Fever, it might look something like that."

Hester batted her eyelashes. "You're too kind, sir."

Molly grabbed the net, turning Hester to face her. "You didn't answer my question. What are you doin' here?"

The old woman hemmed and hawed. "Well, luv, it's hard to say . . ."

Molly folded her arms. "Try."

"She's come for the tree." Kip stepped beside Molly. "Just look at what she's carryin'." He indicated the sharp thing clasped in the woman's hand. In the light of Doctor Crouch's lamp, Molly could see that it was a pair of old shears. "She was gonna take a cutting of the tree," he said. "Snip off a little bit so she could plant her own."

Molly looked back at Hester. "That true?"

Hester sighed. "True or not, it's clear you're set on believing it." She eyed the branch overhead, which was sagging perilously. "Perhaps you might let me down so we can hash it out like good neighbors."

Much as Molly would have liked to let Hester dangle, she knew that if the branch snapped, their trap would be ruined. She nodded to Kip, who hobbled to Galileo and set to coaxing him back toward the house. The net jerked up and down as the horse fought against its reins. "Easy with that horsey," Hester called. "You wouldn't want to drop an old woman on her head."

"Wouldn't we?" Molly stepped back as the net slowly worked its way to the ground.

The doctor, who had evidently gotten his hopes up about finding a cure, was clearly out of sorts. He removed the tin plate from his camera and tossed it aside. "My dear woman, do you realize that you've just interrupted—I daresay *ruined*—an extremely important experiment?" He swatted a leaf from the air in front of him. "I am on the cusp of a discovery that could change my career. Have you anything to say for yourself?"

Hester looked as if she were about to oblige but stopped short. A hollow moaning filled the darkness. She widened her eyes, looking past the doctor toward the house. Her expression was a mixture of terror and fascination. "As luck might have it"—she swallowed, raising a trembling finger—"you still might get your chance."

An icy gust of wind rattled the leaves around them. Galileo snorted, frantically pulling at his reins. The net swayed perilously from side to side, and the tree groaned overhead. Molly shivered, slowly turning around—

The Night Gardener was watching them.

39

THE BROKEN BOUGH

Molly stared at the Gardener, who was standing at the edge of the drive, the open front door behind him, the shovel and watering can in his hands. Even in the shadows, his skin shone with a silver light. He did not move but cocked his head, looking between them with patient curiosity.

"Like a story come to life . . . ," Hester murmured breathlessly.

"Keep still," Molly whispered. "Don't nobody move or shout. He's just here for the tree. He won't hurt us none." She tried not to think about whether or not this was in fact true. She definitely tried not to think about the open graves at her feet.

Doctor Crouch grabbed his camera box and inched toward the Night Gardener. "I just need one photograph . . ."

"Doctor, no!" Molly reached for his arm, but she was too slow. Crouch was already on the other side of the tree. He uncorked a bottle from his belt and dumped some powder into the flash tray.

Hester leaned toward Molly. "You sure he won't hurt us, luv?"

Molly swallowed. "I'm not sure of anythin' anymore."

Doctor Crouch was now only a few feet from the drive. The Night Gardener had not moved, but Molly could hear a low sough of warning.

"Crouch, old boy, say hello to history." The doctor inched closer, like a man hypnotized. The spirit cocked his head, his black, black eyes fixed on the doctor. Dead leaves circled around him like a barrier. Doctor Crouch slowly aimed his camera at the Night Gardener—

Whoosh!

The leaves attacked, knocking the doctor back. He shouted as a gust of wind ripped the camera from his hands. The wooden box sailed through the darkness, flying straight past Molly's head and smashing against the side of the house.

"So much for his experiment!" Hester called, her net swaying in the wind.

"Run, you fools!" Doctor Crouch was sprinting straight toward them, a look of bloodless terror on his face. "Out of my way!" He shoved Molly aside, nearly knocking her into one of the open graves.

"Step aside, boy!" he bellowed. "I'm commandeering this wagon!" He was fighting with Kip for control of the reins.

Kip, however, would not give up. "Let go, you fat gob!"

Galileo snorted, pulling against his harness. The wagon rolled forward and back. Molly heard a loud clatter as Hester's net swung wildly to one side and slammed against the side of the house. She heard more shouting from the wagon, and the net slid high into the air. "Perhaps you might give your brother a hand," Hester called down, the humor drained from her voice.

Molly looked back at the Night Gardener, who now had the shovel in his hand, raised like a weapon.

Molly looked to the wagon and saw that Doctor Crouch, who had knocked Kip to the ground, was now pulling himself onto the bench. She sprang to her feet and ran toward him. "The trap! We have to lower the net!" She grabbed hold of his apron—

"Unhand me!" The doctor struck Molly hard across the cheek. She gripped the side of the wagon, gasping. She could taste blood in her mouth, and her entire face throbbed with a pain she had never felt before. She tried to stand up, but her legs were too weak. Doctor Crouch stared down at her. "Don't look at me like that," he said, taking the reins. "It's survival of the fittest."

"You don't touch my sister!" Kip grabbed his leg, pulling him down from the bench. The man hit the ground beside them, the reins still in his hand. Galileo neighed, rearing up on two legs. Molly heard a sharp creaking sound as Hester's net swayed from the tree and then—

Crack!

The branch snapped clean from the trunk. Hester cried out as her net plummeted to the earth. She hit the ground with a backbreaking crash, pinned beneath the branch.

Molly heard a windy snarl. The Night Gardener staggered forward, stumbling to his knees. He dropped his shovel and watering can, which spilled uselessly onto the grass.

Doctor Crouch watched beside Molly. "Wh-wh-what's happening to it?"

The Night Gardener was doubled over, writhing in pain. Leaves darted over his head, slashing this way and that in a flurry of confused rage. Molly looked up at the tree. Black sap covered the place where the branch had been torn off, like blood from a wound. "I dinna think he liked that," she said.

The Night Gardener planted his hands on the ground and slowly, painfully, brought himself to his feet. He teetered from side to side, his weight unsteady. He saw the broken branch atop Hester's body. He released a roar that shook the very ground.

Doctor Crouch forgot about the horse and scrambled to his feet. "It was all their idea!" he cried out. "It's them you want!" He started running as fast as he could in the opposite direction.

The Night Gardener pointed his skeletal hands toward the stables. Molly heard a sharp wrenching sound as a gust ripped the wide stable door clean off its hinges. The Night Gardener snapped his arms in the direction of the doctor, who was halfway to the bridge. The giant door soared across the lawn, spinning toward its target—

"Don't look!" Molly grabbed Kip, covering his eyes. There was no scream—only a sharp crashing sound. She looked across the lawn; where the doctor had been there was now only a door with two unmoving feet sticking out from beneath it.

She stared back at the Night Gardener, who wore on his face a look of icy satisfaction. "You killed him . . ." Her voice was barely a whisper. "Killed him in cold blood right in front of us . . ."

The spirit tipped his hat as if accepting a compliment. He stepped to the place where Hester lay. The old woman turned over, groaning under the weight of the branch. "You pups best run," she croaked. A shimmer of blood trickled from her mouth.

Kip grabbed Molly's arm. "I can get the horse, but that rope's still tied to her—if we run, it'll kill her."

Molly scanned the moonlit ground, searching for something, anything that might protect them. She remembered what Kip had told her before, that the Night Gardener didn't like fire. She needed a torch or lamp or even a match—

Then she saw it.

Lying among the splintered bits of the doctor's camera was the metal flash pan. "Cut the rope from the wagon!" she called. "I'll do the rest." She scrambled across the dirt, nearly tumbling into one of the graves. She grabbed the flash. Inside the pan was a small amount of white powder. Molly hoped it would be enough.

The Gardener had removed the branch from on top of Hester's body and set it beside the trunk. He held out a hand, and his shovel flew into it.

Molly charged at the man, holding the flash in front of her. "Over here!" She pulled the trigger, and a burst of fire erupted in her hands.

The Night Gardener staggered backward, thrashing his arms as flames swept over his body.

Molly coughed, shielding her face from the smoke. She scrambled to Hester's side. "We're gettin' you outta here," she said. She grabbed

Hester's shears and cut the net away from her body. The woman groaned in pain as Molly hoisted her up on her shoulder. Molly half carried, half dragged the woman to the wagon. Kip was there, waiting with the gate down.

The Gardener roared behind Molly. She looked over her shoulder to see him staggering toward them, his body smoldering in the moonlight. The flames had burned away his cloak, and Molly gasped to see the man's leg; it was twisted in on itself, the bone splintered at the knee. Black sap ran thick down his trousers and boot, staining the grass as he moved.

"Get in front!" Molly shouted, holding Hester's body. "I've got her!"

Kip scrambled through the bed of the wagon and grabbed the reins. Molly braced her shoulder against Hester's weight and, with a strained cry, lifted the woman onto the cart. "Go!" She scrambled in after her.

Kip snapped the reins, and they bolted ahead. Molly gripped the side rails as they raced over the hills toward the gravel drive. *Not hills*, she thought, *graves*.

She could see the Gardener coming after them. Even with his broken leg, he was inhumanly fast.

"Hold tight!" Kip yelled as the wagon hit the drive and shot forward.

The Gardener—still right behind them—raised his hand, and a

gust of wind brought Hester's shears into his open palm. He flung them at the wagon—*thwunk!*—Molly rolled to one side as the blades sank into the wood behind her, quivering like an arrow.

"Faster!" she shouted at Kip as they rattled onto the wooden bridge.

The Gardener reached out a bony hand, snatching her leg. Molly screamed, kicking herself free. She heard a sharp howl and saw the Gardener's body jerk backward. It fell to the bridge with a crash. Molly nearly fell with him as Kip turned onto the road on the far side of the river. She clung to the side of the wagon, eyes fixed on the Gardener. He snarled, pacing back and forth along the far end of the bridge— furious but, it seemed, unable to cross over.

Molly, Kip, and Hester rattled up the path and around the bend. She could hear the Gardener's howls echoing behind them.

PART THREE
DEPARTURES

40

The Last Story

They rode for what felt like hours. The sky above was limpid and black; it shone with pinprick stars that did little to light their path. Molly sat beside Hester, holding her hand. The old woman's fingers were stiff and sticky with blood. She hardly moved, only sitting up occasionally to release a rattling cough. "You're all right," Molly whispered, stroking her hair. "You'll be all right."

Hester swallowed. "I know enough to know that's not true." She smiled and then coughed again. Molly wiped fresh blood from the edges of her mouth. She tried not to let the old woman see the worry on her face. A bloody cough meant she was bleeding on the inside.

The wagon rounded a narrow bend, turning away from the river and toward the village. "Stop the cart . . . ," Hester murmured, raising her hand.

"We're takin' you to the village," Molly said. "We'll find you a warm bed and hot meal and—"

Hester coughed. "You'll be hauling a corpse by the time you get there," she said. "This'll do."

Molly rapped against the side of the wagon. "Pull over," she called.

Kip nodded and steered to the side of the path. Molly watched as he grabbed his crutch and slid down from the bench, his face a picture of stony resolve. In the faint moonlight, he almost looked like Da. Molly wondered when he had become so grown up. She gently lowered herself off the wagon. Her whole body was sore and bruised. It hurt to stand. She looked at the woods around her—they were in a small clearing where the path broke into three parts. "The crossroads . . . ," she said. "It's here we first met you."

Hester propped herself up on one elbow, peering around. "So it is." Even now, even in pain, she had a coy glint in her eye.

Molly and Kip helped the old woman off the back of the wagon. She was still wearing her pack of junk. It dangled from her shoulders, a mess of splinters and shards. In the moonlight, it was hard to tell where the pack ended and Hester's body began.

"I'll find some firewood," Kip said.

"There'll be plenty of time for that after, dearie." Hester grimaced, doubling over in pain. "Help me get this thing off," she said.

Molly and Kip gingerly removed the pack from her shoulders and set it on the ground. Without it, the woman looked absurdly small. Hester stared at the pile of wreckage and gave a wry chuckle. "No need to search for firewood; you got all you need right here." She pulled her briar pipe from the pack. The stem dangled from the bowl, snapped off but for a few fibers. "So much for old friends." She tossed the pipe back into the pile.

Hester nodded at a rotting stump and limped toward it. Molly rushed to her side and helped her sit. "Thank you, luv." She groaned, gripping Molly's hand tight.

Molly knew she should have been angry at Hester, should have yelled at her for ruining their trap. But right now, she only wanted the old woman to live. She brushed a strand of silver hair from her wrinkled brow. "Where does it hurt?"

"Where *don't* it hurt? That's the fairer question." Hester chuckled, and her chuckle turned to pain. She hunched over, her eyes clenched tight.

Molly watched her coughing and felt a swell of nausea. "This is all my fault," she said. "If that net hadn't been there—"

"Hush, you." The old woman waved her off. "It wasn't any net or fall or even phantom Night Gardener. It was curiosity that killed Hester Kettle, plain as that." She stared into the trees, shaking her head. "Oh, I knew it was dangerous—why do you think I stayed away all these years? But in the end, I just *had* to go. Had to see it with my own eyes. And I'll tell you right now: it was worth it." She gave a sort of vague smile, her eyes fixed on some invisible plane. "What's a storyteller but someone who asks folks to believe in impossible things? And for one perfect moment, I saw something impossible. And that's enough for me."

Kip had tied Galileo's reins to a branch and joined his sister and the old woman. "But you didn't just go there to *see* the tree," he said, his voice tight. "You wanted a piece of your own. You wanted a wish— same as everyone."

Molly looked at him, dread rising. "How do you know about wishes?"

Kip ignored her and turned back to Hester. "So let's hear it: What was your big wish?"

"Kip, not now . . . ," Molly said.

"He's fine." The old woman bobbed her head. "It's foolish, really. Do you remember all those pretty things I said about Aesop?"

"You called him the king o' storytellers," Molly said.

Hester knotted her fingers together. "I suppose I wanted to be the queen." She peered up at the dark sky, her eyes bright. "I wanted the world to remember me for the stories I told."

Molly heard this and felt a pain within, for she knew what it was to see a story vanish even as she told it. "You could just write 'em down," she said. "Make a book."

"A book!" Hester laughed. "Can you imagine it? Me hunched over a little desk, quill in hand, putting down all those fancy scratches on paper?" She shook her head. "Truth is, I never learned my letters."

"I can write," Molly said. "I could teach you. We could start right now."

The old woman shook her head. "Afraid there's no time for that . . . or much else, for that matter." She groaned, pulling herself to her feet. "Though, there is time for one last thing." She limped to her pack. "Most folks don't value a good story, and they pay accordingly. But every once in a while, something a little more special comes my way . . ." She plunged her arm right into the heart of the pack, feeling her way past pots and birdcages and lightning rods. "Here it is," she said, standing up. "Been carrying this for goodness knows how long. Don't think I'll get around to it now."

She handed Molly a small oilskin bundle wrapped tight with twine. Molly turned the package over in her hands. "What is it?"

"Something special. I never had much use for it, not being the settling-down type, but you two? I've a feeling it might be just what you're after." Molly started to unwrap the bundle, but the woman stopped her. "There'll be time aplenty to open that later." She coughed into her fist. "Once I depart."

Molly looked up from the gift. She knew what the woman meant by "depart." "You're not gonna die, Hester." Her voice was shaking. "You're gonna live and tell stories. You're gonna be the *queen* of stories, remember?" She did not know why, but she could not bear the thought of a world without Hester Kettle in it.

The old woman patted Molly's hand. "That's a heavy crown for this old brow." She turned back to her pack. "Well, lookee here!" She lifted her hurdy-gurdy from the wreckage. Two strings were broken and it had a giant hole in the body. She plucked one of the remaining strings, which obliged with a faint tone. "Let it never be said that Hester Kettle wasn't a lucky woman." She slung the instrument over her shoulder. "Much as it pains me, I'd best be moving on."

Kip hopped to Molly's side. "Where're you goin'?"

Hester took a deep breath, facing the black woods. "It's time for old Hester to tell one more story. It's one I've been working on for a long time. Maybe my whole life. Call it 'The Last Story.'"

The phrase put a chill through Molly. "What's it about?"

"Apologies, luv." She sounded genuinely sorry. "This one's for me and me alone. That's the way it goes with Last Stories."

Molly wanted to tell her that she could stay, but she knew the truth—there were some places you could only go alone. She blinked, her eyes burning with tears. "I bet it'll be a real grand one."

The old woman smiled kindly. "It ends well enough."

Molly looked at her. In the blurred moonlight, she could almost see Hester as a young girl with yellow hair and plump cheeks and scraped knees. Molly would have liked being friends with such a person. "I've a feelin' someday," she said, "when I tell my own Last Story, it might have an old woman with a pack on her shoulders in it."

Hester raised an eyebrow. "Wouldn't that be a thing?" She bowed her gray head in a half curtsy. "You pups take care." She swung her instrument from her shoulder and turned the crank. A low, sonorous melody filled the air, echoing through the darkness. With that, the manikin woman turned and hobbled slowly into the trees, humming to herself secret things that no soul would ever hear.

Molly held Kip's hand in her own. They stood together in silence, listening as Hester Kettle's song receded farther and farther into the night.

And then it was gone, and the woods were silent.

41

ALONE IN THE DARK

Molly and Kip picked over Hester's discarded pack, salvaging what food they could. They found dried beef and nuts and berries and even some cheese—enough to last them several days on the road. The rest, they burned.

Molly stared into the flames, watching the last of Hester Kettle's life smolder into nothing. Hester Kettle, who only a few hours before had been alive. She closed her eyes, trying to imagine the woman's weathered features. Already her face was slipping from Molly's memory—a shifting landscape of eyes and nose and mouth and hair that refused to fix itself into a living thing. "I never seen a person die before," she said. "Tonight I saw two."

"Good riddance to the doctor, I say." Kip stabbed the end of his crutch in the fire. "He left us to die out there."

Molly wanted to chastise him, to tell him it was wrong to say something like that, but she stopped herself. What right did she have to tell him anything? "I saw it happen," she said. "Saw the door come down on him like a house. He couldn't even scream. One minute he's running, and the next he's not."

"Just be thankful it wasn't us," Kip said, though he didn't sound thankful. "So what's next? Back to the orphanage?"

"Never. We'll go to another town and find work. Someplace safe. Maybe a nice cemetery? Or a coven?" She tried to smile, but her heart wasn't in it.

"Maybe you could tell stories like Hester," Kip said.

"Aye, maybe," she said. There was a time when Molly would have enjoyed the idea of roaming the world, telling tales to strangers. But that was before tonight. Before she knew what the world was really like. What could a story possibly do in the face of a thing like the Night Gardener? Hester had told stories her whole life, and what did it get her? She looked at the oilskin packet that the woman had left them. She couldn't bring herself to unwrap it.

Kip prodded the flames. "Fire may burn bright, but it makes the world darker. Can't hardly see a thing out there." He shivered, eyeing the shadows. "I keep thinkin' I can hear him out in the trees."

"The Night Gardener?" Molly shook her head. "I been goin' over what happened on that bridge. He was in the cart, right behind us, but when you hit the road, he fell back—like somethin' stopped him. And remember when he was after you in the woods? Maybe he didn't hurt you because he couldn't reach. So instead he gave you that key, to lure you back in."

Kip shifted his weight. "So you think he's tied to the tree, like a leash?"

"I think it's deeper than that. I think they're *connected*. You saw what happened when that branch broke. He howled like his own leg had snapped clean off. He's a slave to that tree, and the only way for him to go on livin' is to keep it alive."

"I hardly call that livin'." Kip pulled his coat tight. "But that's how the tree works, ain't it? It gives you what you wish for but not in a way that makes things better. I suppose that's the difference between what you want and what you need."

Molly nodded. "Maybe that's what Hester really meant when she said it takes your soul." She thought about Master Windsor's money. She thought about Constance's ring and Penny's stories and Alistair's candy. She thought about the letters from her parents. She had been given what she wanted. But what did she *need*?

Kip, as if reading her thoughts, spoke. "What should we do about Ma an' Da? If they're comin' to the house, shouldn't we warn them?"

Molly opened her mouth to agree, but the words caught in her throat.

He looked up at her. "Molls? You all right?"

Molly stared into the darkness. She swallowed. "Kip . . . there's somethin' I been meanin' to tell you. Somethin' I *need* to tell you." She finally met his eye. "It's about the letters."

Her brother resumed poking the fire. "It's all right," he said. "I think I know where you got 'em from." He leaned to one side and dug a hand into his pocket. He removed a small tin. It was roughly the size of a biscuit. "Same place I got this."

Molly didn't understand. She scooted closer and took the tin. It was cold to the touch and smelled like tree sap. A paper label ran across the front:

DOCTOR ROOTLEY'S WONDER–BALM

"It'll cure what ails you!"

Below the words was a picture of children dancing and running and singing. She looked at a drawing of one little boy leaping into the air, his crutches thrown above him.

"Everythin' I wished for," Kip said, taking the tin back.

Molly felt dread grip her stomach. "How long have you known?"

"Since that night in the village. I wanted to tell you before . . . but I was afraid."

Molly looked at his leg, which looked as it always did—thin and turned the wrong way. His crutch rested on the log beside him. "You didn't open it?" she said.

"No. I wanted to. So bad." He swallowed, touching the label. "But then I thought: Even if it works, what happens when I run out? I'd go back for more. And more after that. It'd never be enough."

"Aye," Molly said, and she knew he was right. She remembered even now the longing to read another letter and another after that.

"Tell me somethin' . . ." He was looking at her now. "Why was the tree givin' you letters from Ma an' Da?"

Molly looked down at her skirt and ran her fingers over the muddy, frayed fabric. "Sounds like you already know," she said.

"I need to hear you say it."

Molly clenched her jaw, recalling the things she had fought so hard to banish from her mind. Somewhere in the darkness, she could hear the river flowing between black trees. "Every time I hear that river, it brings me right back to the sea." She could hear them now, screaming over the crash of waves. She swallowed. "You dinna remember when we left Ireland. By the time we reached port, you was sick with fever."

Kip hung his head.

"It's not your fault. Lots o' folks were gettin' sick. And that boat didn't help none. It was shameful the way they packed us in—kept us locked belowdecks like animals—barely any food or water. I s'pose we *were* animals to them." She clenched her fists, remembering. "The second night, it was all four of us huddled in one little bunk. There was a storm. The boat was rockin' so violent, folks were slidin' right off their beds. We could hear the rain outside. Wind and thunder shook the whole sea. Black water started comin' in through portholes; the crew was runnin' and shoutin' on the deck. We called for 'em to let us out of the hold, but nobody listened. That whole time, Ma kept you in her arms, singin' to you softly, the way she did when we was little."

Molly blinked into the flames, hearing her mother's voice. "Finally there was a huge crack, like the spine of the earth breaking in two. Water started pourin' in from the deck above, fillin' up around our ankles. Da and some other men broke through the door and everybody ran to the deck. I helped Ma carry you up. One of the masts had snapped right in half. White sheets was all ripped to rags. The rain was comin' sideways. Waves big as mountains all around. The crew was gone—they'd deserted us, left us to die."

Kip was holding his crutch. "There weren't no lifeboats?"

"Aye, there was one left—with enough room for maybe twenty. People fought like beasts to get into it. But Da, he fought harder. We reached the boat just before they was gonna cut it loose. The men said there was only room for two." Molly looked away from Kip. Her heart was pounding in her ears. It was hard to breathe. It was harder to speak. She took a slow breath. "Ma an' Da put you in my arms and put me on the boat. I screamed at 'em not to, but they wouldn't hear me. Ma pulled me close. 'Take care o' him,' she said. 'He's yours now.' She let go, and then . . ." She blinked, tears spilling from her eyes. "And then they were gone."

Molly crumpled, her face in her hands. The tears she had been storing inside her for so long broke free. The sobs took hold of her entire body. If Kip spoke, or moved, she did not hear it. She swallowed, wiping her face. "I meant to tell you, I swear. But when we landed and you woke up and you asked where Ma an' Da was . . ." She shook her head as a new wave of tears came. "I couldn't do it. I couldn't *say* the words." She pressed her lips together. "And . . . so I told you a story."

"You didn't tell a story," Kip said softly. "You lied." Even in the orange light of the fire, his face looked pale.

"I know there's nothin' I can do to fix this." Molly reached toward him, but he pulled away. "I was scared. I wanted it to be true. I wanted to think of them out there in the world, havin' adventures. And part o' me thought it *could* be true. Their ship was lost, aye, but maybe they got away."

"They didn't," Kip said; he sounded firm.

Molly nodded. "I know, I know. And I was gonna tell you the truth, but then . . . I found the tree. And I found the letters—writ in Ma's own hand—and I thought . . . *What if they were real?* What if a miracle had happened, and Ma an' Da were still out there? If somehow they survived? It would mean my lie wasn't a lie at all. It would mean we weren't alone. I dinna expect you to forgive me—not now, maybe not ever. But I need you to understand that I was tryin' to protect you . . . I was tryin' to do right."

Kip released a heavy breath. "How many folks buried round that tree thought they was doin' right?"

Molly did not answer. She couldn't answer. Her brother glared at her and lowered his head. "I wanna hate you. I wanna kick and scream at you for lyin' to me. But the lie wasn't really for me—that was *your* wish. I had somethin' else in my heart. Somethin' I longed for even more than Ma an' Da." He clasped the tin in his hands, and when he looked back at Molly, his eyes were shimmering with tears. "So what kinda person does that make me?"

Molly grabbed hold of him, pulling him to her. "It makes you a regular person. No more, no less." She felt his arms clasp tight around her ribs. She pressed her face into his messy red hair. They held each other for a long moment, arms tight, faces buried. It was a different sort of embrace. There was no coddling: it was strength upon strength—Kip held her up as she held him up.

"I think I figured it out." She sniffed, looking up at the stars. "Hester asked me what the difference between a story and a lie was. At the time, I told her that a story helps folks. 'Helps 'em do what?' she asked. Well, I think I know the answer. A story helps folks face the world, even when it frightens 'em. And a lie does the opposite. It helps you hide."

She felt Kip's arms loosen. "S'pose that's all the tree does, really?" He pulled back to look at her. "It helps you lie to yourself and pretend the world ain't there." He reached for the medicine, which was resting on the log beside him. He gave a wistful smile, perhaps for a moment imagining himself whole, and then tossed the tin into the fire.

Sparks flew up into the darkness as the tin began to crackle and hiss. His dream, burning into nothing. Molly stared at him, watching as he stoically stirred the charred remains with his crutch. "Kip, you're the bravest person I ever met."

Kip wiped his nose and stared into the fire. "You know what I wish for?"

"No." Molly shook her head. "No more wishes."

He turned toward her. "I wish that Ma an' Da could see us right now."

"Oh!" Molly laughed, wiping her eyes. "They'd be horrified."

"Nay." Kip shook his head, smiling. "They'd be *so proud*. Especially of you." Molly looked away, not wanting to cry again. "And do you know what they'd say to us?"

Molly pressed her lips together. "Tell me."

"They'd say, 'Kip, Molls: we love you dearly, and we want you both to live a good, full life'"—he stared out at the woods—"'but there's a whole family at that house that needs saving.'"

Molly looked at him. In the warm glow, she could almost see the lines of her father's profile. Even more, she knew Kip was right. Escaping the Night Gardener meant deserting the Windsors. She thought of Constance, her skin pale, body wasting away. She thought of the graves. She thought of Penny.

Kip caught her eye. "Those folks are in trouble, Molls. Someone needs to go back to warn 'em before it's too late. And we're all they got." He nodded toward the wagon. "Well . . . us and Galileo."

Molly took a deep breath. She longed with everything in her to leave this valley and never return. But she knew that running solved nothing: they had to go back. She squeezed his hand tight. "Let's hope that's enough."

RETURN TO THE SOURWOODS

Kip and his sister decided to wait until daybreak before return-ing to Windsor Manor. They had only ever seen the Gardener appear at night, and they hoped that the light would protect them. After a few fitful hours by the fire, they awoke with the first rays of dawn and set out on the wagon. They rode into the valley without speaking—silence to match the silence. Kip clutched the reins, going over the plan they had discussed the night prior. He would collect their things from the stables and—if he could be found—give Doctor Crouch a proper burial. Molly, meanwhile, would go into the house and make one final attempt at convincing Master Windsor to leave with his family. It wasn't much of a plan, but at least they could say they tried.

The job seemed simple enough, but when they rounded the final bend and Kip saw the house, he felt his entire body tense. "You sure it's smart to go back there?" he said.

"I'm sure it's not." Molly reached down and squeezed his hand. "But there's what's *smart* and what's *right*. And Ma an' Da would want us to do what's right."

"Hold your breath," Kip said, and they rolled over the bridge. He eyed the river beneath them. He remembered his first time crossing this rotting bridge, the unnameable dread he had felt upon seeing the manor and grounds. It seemed like years ago, when, in fact, it had been only a little over a month. When they reached the other side, he stopped the cart.

"What're you doin'?" Molly said as he climbed down from the bench.

"There's somethin' I want to look at." An idea was coming to him. Maybe there was a chance to do more than just warn the family. He slid Courage out from beneath his seat and fit it under his arm. "I won't be long."

"You'd better not be," she said, taking the reins. He saw her nervously glance toward the river. "You be careful near that water."

Kip smiled. "You be careful near that tree." He eyed the sun over the sourwoods. "Mornin's half over. If we want the family out by sundown, you'd best get movin'."

Molly nodded, snapped the reins, and continued toward the house. Kip watched her shrink into the distance: a tangle of wild hair atop a slender frame. She looked so different now, less like his big sister and more like a grown person—not a stranger, exactly, but like someone he knew only in passing, someone with thoughts and joys and pains that were hidden to him. His gaze shifted to the tree. It rose up like a tower in the harsh morning light, offering welcome shade on a hot day. And, scattered around it, a bed of comfortable leaves to lie upon. He shook his head, thinking about what was waiting beneath those leaves. "Watch your step, Molls," he said under his breath.

Kip turned around, resting his weight on his crutch. When Da gave it to him, the crosspiece had been taller than Kip's head. Now it was an effort to keep the crutch from slipping out from under his arm. Still, it was his Courage, and he felt better simply for having it with him. He looked at the bridge that separated the island from the main road—maybe this bridge was the key to stopping the tree?

Kip had seen what the Gardener was capable of and had no intention of fighting him. But if he could somehow make the bridge collapse, then at least other people wouldn't be able to cross over. Maybe the tree would die on its own, from a lack of fresh victims? It was at least worth a try.

Kip moved onto the bridge, keeping one hand on the thick rope, looking for weak spots in the wood. It was an ancient structure, and he felt continual surprise that it hadn't fallen into the river ages ago. He hoped this meant that it wouldn't take much to chop it down. The boards were slick with dew and mildew, and he nearly slipped a few times as he hopped from plank to plank. He stopped a few feet from the main road, where he thought the bridge might be weakest. He set down his crutch and gingerly got to his knees. The sound of rushing water filled his ears as he leaned over the edge, peering at the beams beneath. Thick black tendrils consumed the undercarriage; the roots extended all the way from the island and ended just before the road.

"So *that's* why this bridge ain't fallen down yet," he muttered, almost impressed. "The tree don't want it to."

Kip stared at the roots, something else sticking in his mind. He remembered their flight in the wagon: the Night Gardener had chased them to the end of the bridge and then stopped at this very spot, as if pulled backward by some outside force. He remembered that night he was spared in the garden, when the same thing happened. "Of course!" he said, sitting up. "He can only go as far as the roots!"

"*Who* can?" said a voice in his ear.

Kip turned around to see Alistair standing a little bit behind him. The sound of the river must have covered his approach. His face was as pale as ever, but there was a red puffiness around his eyes that made it look as if he'd been crying. He was holding Kip's crutch in two hands like a broad sword.

Kip slowly pulled himself to his feet. "Good mornin'," he said, trying to keep his voice casual.

"I'd hardly call it morning. It's nearly lunch." Alistair waved the crutch like a magic wand. "Where were *you*?"

It took everything in Kip not to grab for the crutch. If Alistair knew he was bothered, then things would only get worse. He clenched his fist tight, trying not to let his irritation show. "We went for a drive."

"A drive?" Alistair's expression soured. "My mother's sick, and you go off on a *drive*?" He wagged the crutch like an accusing finger. "I can tell you're lying. You've done something rotten. The doctor's missing—Father's having a right row. I'm going to tell him it's you two that frightened him off."

"He was frightened, all right. But it wasn't us that done it." Kip looked behind Alistair. In the middle of the lawn he could see the shape of the fallen stable door—but no sign of the doctor beneath it.

"You do know something! I'll have you sacked."

Kip could not hide the smile that crept up on his mouth. "Won't do much good—'cause we quit."

Alistair stepped back like he'd been struck. "You *what*?"

"Molly's in there right now, tellin' your father. We're runnin' away. And if you was half as smart as you pretend to be, you'd do the same."

Alistair put the crutch over his shoulder, gripping it like a mallet. "And why is that?"

Kip bit his lip. "I know you think that tree's a good thing, but it ain't."

Alistair's face tensed. "You don't know anything about the tree."

Kip hopped closer. "I know it put your father in debt with those men from town. I know it made your ma sick." He could not resist himself. "I know it made you fat."

Alistair narrowed his eyes. He raised the crutch above Kip's head. For a moment, Kip thought he was going to strike him, but then Alistair swung his arm out to the side, letting the crutch dangle over the edge of the bridge. "Say that again."

Kip hopped closer, feeling a clutch of panic. "Please, don't. I'm sorry—"

Alistair opened his hand, and the crutch fell from his grasp. "Oops."

Kip heard a splash in the river below. His heart plunged with it. He stumbled past Alistair, who was laughing, and peered over the edge. Courage was gone.

Alistair moved behind him. "Good luck *runnin' away* now." He said the words with a mocking brogue.

Kip teetered to one side, his stomach reeling. That crutch was the only thing he still had from his da and now it was gone. He closed his eyes, forcing back tears. He could not let Alistair see him cry. He breathed slowly through clenched teeth. "That was a horrible thing you done."

Alistair crossed his arms. "Are you going to hit me? Tell me you hate me?"

Kip gripped the edge of the bridge, his body trembling with rage and shame. "I don't hate you." He pulled himself upright and hopped toward Alistair on his one good leg. "I feel sorry for you."

Alistair responded as though he'd been struck. "Why do people keep saying that?" he said quietly.

Kip hopped closer still. "'Cause it's true." The pain was excruciating, but he kept his gaze steady. He wasn't looking just at Alistair but at every boy who had ever taunted and chased him—and he was determined not to let them win. "Your ma's inside that house, halfway to dead, and that's a painful thing. But worse: she'll go to her grave thinkin' she's mother to a selfish, mean-headed bully who never did a kind thing for no one. . . and she'll be right."

What little color remained had drained from Alistair's face. His jaw was set and trembling. Kip thought Alistair might shove him or swear or even throw him off the bridge. But he didn't care. He turned around and, wincing with every step, headed out to the lawn. Alistair did not come after him.

When Kip reached the stables, he glanced back toward the bridge. Alistair was still there, watching him.

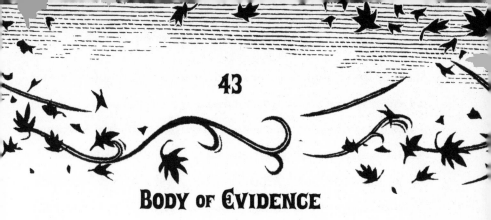

Body of Evidence

43

Before Molly talked to Master Windsor, there was one thing she wanted to do. She crept downstairs to her old bedroom and closed the door behind her. It had been less than a week since she had last been inside this room, and yet it appeared to her a foreign place. She looked at the ugly black roots pushing through the ceiling and walls and shuddered, thinking of how she had once slept soundly in that bed. *Not too soundly*, she reminded herself.

She walked to the wardrobe and opened the doors. Below empty pegs sat the old sea chest she had brought with her from home. She raised the lid with her foot, as one might lift a rock with a snake underneath. The trunk was now empty, save the small bundle of letters from her parents. Just seeing them made her heart beat faster. She did not have an exact plan as to what to do with the letters, but she knew she couldn't leave them at the house. The idea of some other person coming upon them and reading them was too much to bear.

She knelt and picked up the letters, and even now—even knowing that they were not real—she felt a longing to read them one last time.

She held the envelopes to her nose, savoring the saltwater air. Her parents may have been gone, but a part of them still lived inside the letters, their voices woven into each word. She stuffed the envelopes into her pocket and went upstairs to find Master Windsor.

Bertrand was, as she expected, sitting vigil at his wife's bedside. Since the collapse, he had spent hours this way, clutching Constance's hand, quietly reciting stories of their early marriage—courtship follies and wedding day jitters and the thrill of early parenthood. Molly noticed that when he told these stories—when he was dwelling on a happier past—he did not seem to stutter as much.

"Master Windsor?" Molly said softly.

If she startled him, he did not show it. "The prodigal maid returns." He spoke without looking up. "I feared you'd run off with the doctor." His voice had the drained quality of someone too exhausted to fight.

Molly shifted her weight. She wished she had more time to think about what to say. "The fact is, sir, my brother and me canna work here no more. I think you know why. I've come for our things, and then we're movin' on."

His face twitched. "You're . . . you're *leaving us*?"

"This house is a bad place, sir. Havin' grown up here, you know that better than anyone." She gave him a meaningful look.

"Y-y-you can't quit." He stood, pushing his chair back from the bed. "My family needs you."

"It's already done, sir. And it's for your family that I'm up here talkin' to you now." She took a step closer, fixing her eyes on his. "You should come with us, all of you. Tonight."

"Impossible!" He paced in front of her. "Connie is ill. M-m-my associates are coming tomorrow, and I still cannot pay them—"

"So leave before they get here."

"You're not listening!" he snapped. "I need to stay *here*, with the tree. If I can j-j-just get enough from it . . ." He held up the key to the green door, clutching it in his hand.

Molly could see that Master Windsor was deaf to mere arguments. He needed proof. She rushed forward and snatched the key from his grasp.

"G-g-give that back!"

Molly was already halfway down the hallway. "You'll get it back, sir. But before you do, there's somethin' you need to see." She marched downstairs, a protesting Master Windsor in tow.

Kip was waiting for them outside, rake in hand, standing next to a pile of leaves. He was balanced on his right leg, and Molly wondered why he wasn't using his crutch. "Did you find him?" she said.

"Aye." Kip hopped back, revealing the cleared grave. "But it ain't pretty."

Molly led Master Windsor to the edge of the hole, which was no longer empty. Doctor Crouch's corpse lay crammed into the narrow trench. His face was bloodless, his eyes wide open in a look of abject terror. A mesh of thin roots covered his entire body, swallowing him.

"G-g-good heavens . . ." Bertrand looked like he might be sick.

Molly knew better than to prod him or speak in any way. She waited. After a long moment, he turned to her. "Did . . . did he suffer?"

"It was fast. He didn't even have time to call out."

"You should thank him," Kip said. "That grave was meant for you."

Molly shot her brother a look. This was no time for malice. She took a step closer to Master Windsor, meeting his eye. "The doctor was murdered, sir. In cold blood. And I think you know what it was that done it."

Master Windsor did not answer, but she could see in his face that he did know. "This is bad," he said. "This is very, very bad . . ." He stepped back from the grave, wringing his pale hands. "Doctor Crouch was an important man—a gentleman. He will be missed. There could be an inquiry, an investigation, even prison . . ."

"There's more at stake than prison, sir." She nodded to Kip. "Show him the rest."

Kip proceeded to rake the leaves from the remaining holes. Bertrand watched but said nothing. Finally Kip reached the last of the graves, the smallest one. Bertrand stared at it, one hand over his mouth. "It's Penny's size . . . ," he whispered.

"There's one for each of us, sir. The tree's waitin' until we're too sick to move, too sick to fight back—and from the look of you and your family, that won't be long."

"No, no, no . . ." Master Windsor shook his head from side to side like a child in denial. "It doesn't make s-s-sense." He turned toward the tree. "It's not the way it works. The doctor must have *done* something. He must have provoked it or threatened it or . . ." His voice fell silent as he saw the giant branch that had broken from the trunk. "Who did this?" he said, his voice colder.

"It was an accident." Kip leaned on his rake. "The doctor was helpin' us make a trap and—"

Bertrand spun around. "He *what*?" A new panic flushed his face. "If you hurt the tree—if you even *talk* of hurting it—"

"Then what?" Molly cut him off. "We end up like Crouch? Quick or slow, it's the same end for every person who comes here." She could feel her blood rising, her heart pounding in her ears. "I know you think your tree's a miracle, sir, but that same tree puts bodies in the ground." She gestured toward the hills covering the lawn.

Bertrand turned around, staring at the graves, his lips parted. Molly could not tell from his expression if he had known before that moment what lay beneath those hills. She watched his shining gaze dart from mound to mound, as if searching for something. She suddenly realized that not all of the bodies in the ground were strangers. Not to him at least. "Your ma an' da," she said. "They're out there, aren't they?"

"I never saw it." He shook his head, at a loss. "On the night when . . . when it happened, I was in my room. I remember hearing my parents arguing in the hall. My father had changed his mind about the tree. He thought it was making us sick somehow. He wanted to cut it down or poison it—I don't remember. What I do remember is the storm." He set his jaw. "There was no rain or thunder. Only wind. It shook the entire house, like it was inside the walls. I could hear my father shouting downstairs and this inhuman sound—like someone, or some*thing*, was down there with him. My mother came into my room. Her eyes . . . she was *so frightened*. She pulled me from bed and told me to run. Run and never come back. I was young, I didn't know what to do . . ." His voice was shaking but not with fear. "She helped me climb through the window, and I fell to the ground. I called to her to jump, but she was gone." He stared into the empty air, his dark eyes shining.

Molly at once recognized the horror on his face. It was the expression she had worn when her parents pushed her onto the lifeboat and disappeared. It was the shame of someone who had survived. She cleared her throat. "If you hadn't a' run, you'd be buried there with 'em," she said. "Your ma, she wanted you to *live*. To eat and sleep and breathe and laugh. To meet your wife. To have your children. Runnin's not a bad thing, sir, so long as you're runnin' toward somethin' good."

Bertrand's face crumpled. He sank to the lawn, his head in his hands. "We can't leave. This house is all I have left. There's no money, no credit, nothing. And Connie—she's too sick to travel . . ."

Molly stepped closer. "The creature that buried your folks is comin' back, sir. Tonight. It's time to choose." She held out the old key. "You can take this, go back in the house, and wait for your miracle . . . or you can come with us and live."

44

FLIGHT

Molly opened the door to Penny's bedroom. "Are you finished, miss?"

"Finished? I've only just started!" Penny sat on the floor of her room, an open suitcase before her. It was overflowing with stuffed animals and toys and blocks. She held up two dolls, one in each hand. "I can't decide which one to keep." She looked between them and then threw them both to the floor, exasperated. "Why are we even leaving?"

"Your father thinks it's best. And I'm inclined to agree." Molly wandered through the room, collecting an assortment of clothes for the girl's journey, which she placed over one arm. She passed over the most beautiful dresses—instead taking clothes that could stand the most wear. She did not know where Master Windsor and his family would end up living, but it would likely be no place for frills.

Molly knelt down next to Penny and began repacking the suitcase.

"But what if I don't want to leave?" Penny asked.

Molly removed most of the toys, to make room for Penny's clothes. "I thought you hated it here, miss."

"I do hate it! Only . . . there's some things I don't want to leave behind."

Molly removed a stuffed bear to find a stack of *Princess Penny* books. The gilded pages shone bright even in the shadows. "Things like these?"

The girl nodded. She touched the topmost book, picking at its corner. The cover was adorned with a bright picture of the princess battling an ogre who looked surprisingly like Alistair. Molly put a hand on the girl's shoulder, looking her straight in the eye. "Miss Penny, there's better stories in the world than these."

The girl looked like she might cry. "Like your stories?"

Molly winked. "On a good day." She gently removed the books from the suitcase and set them on the floor. "Besides, the dolls might want somethin' to read." She closed the case, latched it tight, and led Penny into the hall.

The rest of the house was in a state of complete disarray. Since deciding to leave, Master Windsor had become a man of pure action—perhaps fearing that if he didn't leave quickly, he might lose his nerve. He had spent the last few hours rushing from room to room, collecting what essentials they might be able to fit on their carriage. A reluctant Alistair trailed behind him, helping when necessary.

Molly went outside to check on her brother, who had been given the job of preparing the wagon for their journey. She found him in the drive, hoisting a large metal canister onto the bed of the wagon. There were several other canisters, all of them different, some of which she recognized from the kitchen. "What's all this?" she said.

Kip wiped his hands on his trousers. "Lamp oil, axle grease, turpentine, lard, even a bit o' brandy."

"You planning to cook somethin'?"

"Sort of." He steadied himself on the wagon, trying to keep off his bad leg. Molly looked around for his crutch but once again could not see it. "I know we canna hurt the tree, but I think we can make it harder to reach. If we take down the bridge, it'll be a long time before anyone comes near here again. The wood's too thick to cut down, but I think there's a better way." He tapped a canister. "Soon as we're across that bridge with the family, I'll pour every drop of oil on the beams and light the whole thing up."

Molly looked at the rows of rusted canisters. "You sure this isn't just about makin' a giant explosion?" she said.

Kip grinned. "That, too."

By late afternoon, the family was packed and ready to go. Bags and trunks lined the foyer. The last step was Mistress Windsor. Constance had regained consciousness but was still too weak to move on her own.

Molly entered the bedroom with Master Windsor and Alistair to find Constance clutching her breast, panic on her face. "Bertrand!" She sat up. "My ring!"

Master Windsor rushed to her, clutching her hand. "No, my love. No more rings." He stroked her brittle hair. "We're getting you out of here. We're going someplace safe."

Molly saw Alistair out of the corner of her eye. He was watching his parents, and his usually scornful look had given way to something more complicated. He bit the inside of his cheek, as if calculating some difficult sum. Molly glanced out the window. The red sun hung just above the crest of the valley. She put a gentle hand on Bertrand's shoulder. "It's nearly sundown."

Master Windsor let go of his wife and stood. The bed frame was too wide to fit through the doorway, and so they decided to carry Mistress Windsor separately from her mattress, which would have to be turned on one side. He carefully lifted her into his arms, while Molly and Alistair dragged the heavy feather mattress out into the hall.

Master Windsor walked behind them, whispering to his wife as one might whisper to a child. By the time they reached the foyer, she seemed to have fallen unconscious once more. Bertrand gingerly lowered her onto the mattress, which Molly and Alistair had placed in front of the stairs. Molly helped Bertrand wrap blankets around his wife's frame. "If she doesn't make it . . . ," he said, touching her sleeping face.

Molly heard the sound of a horse approaching on the drive. "That'll be Kip with the wagon."

Bertrand stood up, a suitcase in his hand. He lingered in the middle of the foyer, his eyes drifting from the walls to the windows to the ceiling—one final look at the house he had grown up in.

"I don't think I'll miss it," he said.

"You'd be surprised," Molly said. But then she added, "That still don't mean you should stay."

Bertrand walked to the front door, took the handle, and opened it—

"Evenin', guvnor!"

Bertrand let out a small shriek of alarm, dropping his suitcase. Molly looked up to see two men propped against the doorway—one improbably tall, the other unusually squat—both reeking with the unmistakable odor of the city. Mister Fig and Mister Stubbs stepped into the house, eyeing the shocked family.

Stubbs grinned. "Goin' somewhere?"

45

Unwelcome Guests

Molly lay on the foyer floor. Her feet and hands were tied with coarse rope, which cut like sandpaper against her skin. She struggled against the binds, trying to find a loose spot to slip her hand through, but none would reveal itself. The room around her was now a wasteland of overturned suitcases and torn curtains and broken furniture.

"Molly, I'm scared," said a voice in her ear. It was Penny, tied up like the rest of them. Her glasses had fallen off her face and were lying on the floor.

"Hush, love." Molly forced a smile. "You'll be fine." A sort of cascading crash hit her ears. It sounded as if one of the men were pulling books down from the shelves in the study. Unlike on their previous visit, Fig and Stubbs had wasted no time with threats and ultimatums. They had tied up the family almost immediately and begun ransacking the house.

"Sounds like they're having fun," Kip muttered from her other side. He had, at first, tried to hide in the stables, but Fig had found him and put him next to Molly. This, at least, allowed them to talk openly without startling the others.

"We have to get outta here," Molly whispered, too quietly for Penny to hear. "When that sun goes down, the Night Gardener'll be here. And somethin' tells me he'll still be angry." She craned her neck, looking through the open front door. The sun over the trees was a boiling red—the last gasps of daylight quickly draining from the sky.

"So much for our simple plan," Kip said.

Fig and Stubbs wandered back into the foyer with a casual, almost friendly air. Long splinters and bits of cushion fluff clung to their shabby coats. Fig had the Windsor portrait in his hands, holes punched into the canvas. "Lookit this, Stubbs!" He pushed his head through a hole above Constance's body. "Ain't I pretty?" he said, making kissing sounds.

"Well—that does it for the study," Stubbs said, wiping his hands. "Next stop: the bedrooms." He looked at Master Windsor, who had blood on his face from where they had struck him. "'Less you just want to save us the trouble?"

"I already t-t-told you, I have nothing!" Bertrand sputtered.

Stubbs cocked his head to one side. "An' I *tuh-tuh-told* you: a man don't leave his house without squirrelin' away a few earthly possessions."

Fig pulled something from Constance's open trunk. "How's these for earthly possessions?" He waved a pair of stockings over his head.

"This wasn't our agreement," Bertrand said. "You weren't supposed to be here until tomorrow!"

"Well, that's the thing," Stubbs said, scratching his head. "When you been in this business long as me and Fig, you learn a few things. Like how folks tend to disappear right when they're expectin' you. So we like to pop in a day or two early." He propped a foot on one of the suitcases. "Which, I think you'll agree, is a wise precaution."

The grandfather clock, which had been opened but not overturned, rang seven times. Bertrand exchanged a look with Molly to show that he, too, understood the importance of getting out of the house before nightfall. He turned back to the men, putting on a smile that might have passed for charm in another circumstance. "My good sirs. I owe you both an apology. You've come all the way out here, and I've been incredibly rude. Take everything—furniture, clothes, the whole house. Only please: *Let us go.*"

Stubbs stood over him, his belly protruding from his coat. "You're awful eager to go ridin' out in the dusky fog." He drew a handkerchief from his vest, and Molly caught a glimpse of the large knife at his belt. "You know, Fig," he said, polishing his monocle, "I heard that some rich folks sew money right into their clothes—to hide it from robbers and brigands and the like."

Fig stood up, joining his stout companion. "Now that you mention it, I think I heard that, too."

"Well, then," Stubbs said, replacing his monocle, "perhaps this merits a more *thorough* search." He drew the knife from his belt and handed it to Fig as one might pass a brush to a painter.

Fig took the knife, flipping it casually in his large hand. He paced the length of the room, pointing the blade at each person as he passed. "Duck . . . duck . . . duck . . . *goose*."

He had stopped at Constance. The woman, who was only barely conscious, stared at the man towering over her. "B-B-Bertie?"

"No!" Master Windsor pulled against his binds. "Not her! She's ill!"

"Then she won't put up a fight," Fig said, kneeling. With a flourish he removed the blanket from over her body and cut a slice along the side of her mattress—feathers spilled onto the floor. "Tell me when I'm gettin' warm," he said and thrust a hand inside her mattress, searching for hidden valuables. Constance recoiled, closing her eyes.

Bertrand thrashed like a madman. "Get away from her!" he screamed.

"Temper, temper!" Stubbs swung a boot, hitting him square in the face.

Bertrand's head snapped back, and when Molly saw his face again, there was blood coming from his nose. "Please . . . ," he whimpered.

Molly studied the expressions of the two men, at once gleeful and grim. They looked like they would be more than happy to do this all night. And Molly did not have all night. She searched the floor for a bit of broken glass or a stray nail—anything that she might use to cut the rope. She again noticed the blade tucked into the back of Fig's belt. If she could just distract him, she might be able to get it. She closed her eyes and dug deep within to find the part of herself that could, just possibly, save them. When she opened her eyes again, they shone with a spark of determination.

"Had enough?" Stubbs said, striking Bertrand again. "'Cause I could go all night."

"Hit him all you want," Molly called over the din. "He ain't gonna tell you a thing. These rich folks'd rather die than lose a penny to those beneath 'em."

Silence fell over the room and she felt every person look at her.

"You want to take his place?" Stubbs said, turning.

Molly raised a coy brow, as if to imply she might enjoy such attentions. "You and me ain't like the Windsors," she said, a hint of song in her voice. "I could tell it the first time we met. We wasn't born with silver spoons in our mouths. We gotta take what we can, however we can, and hang the rest." At this, Stubbs gave an involuntary nod. Molly fought back a smile—it was working. "Take me with you, and I'll show you the money myself. How does that sound?"

Stubbs screwed up his mouth, clearly at war with his instincts. "What would a little maid know about secret loot?"

Molly tilted her head back, a defiant smirk on her face. "Servants know everythin' about a house—especially the secrets. This here's my fifth maid's job. I work long enough to get the lay o' things and then cut loose with all the cash I can carry. Now I'm thinkin' it's time I got myself some business partners—maybe take up work cleanin' a bank in the city?"

"Molls, what're you doin'?" Kip hissed.

Molly ignored him and continued. "The Windsors never cared about me, an' I don't care about them." She tried not to imagine the look on Penny's face as she said this. "The way I see it, you two are the comeuppance they got comin'."

Stubbs grinned, as if the idea of being the arm of cosmic justice appealed to him.

"There's a little key in Master Windsor's waistcoat," she said. "It unlocks the closet at the top of the stairs. Inside there is everythin' you could ever want." She held Stubbs's gaze in her own. "Everythin' you *deserve*." She cast out this last word like a fishhook on the sea.

Stubbs blinked at her, half-hypnotized. The monocle had slipped from his eye and was dangling from a chain on his lapel. He swallowed and nodded to Fig. "Might as well check his coat, eh?"

Fig left Constance and searched Bertrand. "Looks like she was telling the truth," he said, pulling a key from his pocket.

"You'll come with us, pet." Stubbs grabbed Molly's arm, pulling her up to her feet. "And if it turns out you're lying . . . it'll be cadavers we search next."

"You gonna carry me up?" she said, indicating her bound ankles. Stubbs rolled his eyes and nodded to Fig to cut her feet free. Molly felt a rush of circulation as the rope fell from her legs. She watched closely as Fig slid the knife back into his belt—only a few inches away from her hands.

The two men led Molly up the staircase. She truly did not know what would be waiting for them inside the room, but she hoped it would be enough to distract them at least for a moment.

When they reached the top of the stairs, Stubbs took the key and slid it into the lock. "After you." He tipped his hat and swung the door wide.

Molly took a breath and stepped into the room.

46

TRUST

Kip watched his sister disappear behind the green door, the two thugs right behind her. The door swung shut with a violent slam. He didn't know why she was showing those men the tree room, but he could tell from her face that she had a plan—it was the same look she got when telling a story.

"Did she mean those things?" Penny said. "About not caring for us?"

"My sister cares more than you'll ever know." Kip smiled at her, trying to ignore the pain shooting up his left side. When the men had tied him up, they had been especially rough on his leg. "We just have to trust her."

Master Windsor had managed to move next to his wife and was now holding her hand, whispering things in a calming tone. "I hope you're right," he said. "Because the moment those two learn about that tree—what it does—there'll be nothing to stop them from killing us all."

Kip looked at the quickly darkening sky outside. "Even if they don't, when the Night Gardener gets here, we'll all be done for."

"What do you think they're all doing up there?" Alistair said, adjusting his weight. "Why is it so quiet?"

Kip stared at the closed door. "I don't know. Maybe the tree's not workin' because there's three of 'em inside—"

He was cut off by the sound of screams.

Kip could not tell at first if they were screams of pain or joy. Then the door burst open, and the fat one appeared at the top of the stairs, clutching little sheets of white paper. "Promissory notes!" he shouted, raining them down over the banister. "Hundreds of 'em!" He jabbed a finger in Master Windsor's direction. "Broke indeed, you old cad!" He gave a whoop of joy and ran back into the room.

"What's promissory notes?" Kip said.

Alistair stared at the papers scattered across the floor. "It's money." He peered at the nearest crumpled sheet. "A *lot* of money."

"I want to see." Penny scooted herself toward one of the fallen slips of paper—

"Don't touch it, either of you!" The command came from Master Windsor. "We're done taking things from the tree."

Kip listened to the men whooping and laughing like children inside the room. Whatever his sister was planning, she had better do it fast.

The two men appeared on the stairs, arms overflowing with more money. They were nearly skipping as they raced outside, a trail of notes in their wake.

Kip watched through the open front door as they stuffed the notes into the cart and ran back into the foyer, breathless with exhilaration. The fat one grabbed an overturned trunk and emptied its contents on the floor. "Last one upstairs is a rotten egg!" They thundered up the staircase, pushing and shoving to get to the room first.

Kip watched the tall one taking the stairs three at a time. A smile crept across his face. "Molly, you little sneak."

"I don't see how this is funny," Master Windsor said.

"Then you weren't lookin' close enough." Kip nodded toward the room. "His knife was missin'."

COMEUPPANCE

Molly wrapped her fingers around the handle of the stolen knife, pressing the blade up against her ropes. She knew she would have to act carefully. The rope was thick, and she could only make the smallest sawing motions without being detected. Fig and Stubbs ran around her, raking heaps of paper out of the knothole, to fill a trunk they had brought from downstairs.

"Is that the last of it?" Fig said when the knothole had been emptied.

"Can't see the bottom." Stubbs reached an arm into the hole, plumbing its depths. "I reckon there might be more down in there, but I can't reach . . ."

Molly ignored them, concentrating on cutting the rope. Even with a weapon, she knew she couldn't overpower the men. But if she could just get to the hall with her hands free, she might be able to lock them inside the room—giving her enough time to free everyone and make a run for the main road.

Fig clapped his hands together. "I got an idea!" He said this with the excitement of someone for whom an *idea* was a very rare thing. "I'll be right back." He ran out the door and thumped downstairs.

Stubbs, meanwhile, busied himself with collecting stray notes from the floor. What couldn't fit inside the trunk, he stuffed into his own pockets. "Soon as we've gotten the last scraps outta this here tree, we'll be off," he said by way of conversation. "Though not before puttin' old Windsor and the rest out to pasture."

Molly felt her heart lurch. "You . . . you're gonna kill 'em?"

He shrugged. "Can't be helped, I'm afraid. We wouldn't want anyone telling tales about our . . . good fortune." He shoved a fistful of notes into the waist of his trousers. "I know we promised to take you with us, pet, but I'm afraid the plans have changed. No room for a third person on the cart, you understand."

The door swung open. "Look what I found in the stables!" It was Fig, and he was holding something in both hands.

Molly's entire body went cold. "What's that?" she said.

"What's it look like? An axe!" He hefted the blade in his hand. "We can hack open the hole and crawl right inside!"

Molly watched as he stomped toward the tree, axe raised over his head. "N–n–no! Listen to me!" she cried. "You canna hurt the tree! If you hurt the tree—"

Whack!

The axe head sank deep into the wood surrounding the knothole.

Fig jerked the blade free. Black sap ran down the trunk, as thick as molasses.

Molly heard a low wind rising over the grounds. The whole house creaked as the air slid through cracks in the walls. "You have to stop— *now*!" she said. "You don't know what you're doin'!"

"Oh, don't I?" Fig raised the axe over his head and brought it down again—

This time the axe did not strike the wood.

Instead, it was stopped just above the tree by a pale, thin hand.

A hand connected to an arm clothed in tattered black rags.

An arm stretching out from deep inside the tree.

Fig let go of the handle. The axe remained where it was, held in place by the spectral hand.

"Wh-wh-what is it?" Stubbs said, inching behind Fig.

"Somethin' wicked," Molly said. She sawed furiously at the final strands of rope—almost free.

Wind howled through the room, dragging crumpled notes into the air. Fig and Stubbs were now holding each other. "Maybe we should run," said Stubbs.

Fig nodded. "Maybe so."

But neither man ran. They were transfixed by the thing before them, unable to move, unable to look away.

They watched as a second hand gripped the rim of the knothole. Slowly, impossibly, the Night Gardener pulled his winding torso out of the tree—and unfolded himself until he was standing before them.

He teetered for a moment, as if remembering how to stand. A thick smear of black liquid ran down the side of his neck. He studied the axe still clutched in his hand, still dripping with sap.

Molly did not need to stay and see what would happen. The moment she felt her knife break through the final strands of her rope, she was on her feet. She scrambled out the door, grabbing the handle.

"No, wait!" Stubbs cried, running after her.

Molly slammed the door in his face. She broke the key off in the lock. The man pounded against the other side of the door. "Open up! Open up!" A burst of wind shook the door. She heard a violent crash and then screaming. Molly raced down the staircase, knife in hand, the cries ringing out behind her.

"Molly!" Penny shouted.

Molly reached the bottom of the stairs, nearly tumbling over herself, "I told you she'd come!" Kip said as Molly cut him loose.

Another violent gust of wind shook the house, and Molly thought she heard something heavy hit the floor. "That door canna hold long. We have to run. He'll be after us next."

Kip massaged his freed wrists. "I have an idea. Stay here and help the family. I can slow him down long enough for everyone else to get away." He gripped the wall behind him, trying and failing to stand. "I ain't much good at runnin' right now . . . I may need help."

"I'll help you," said a quiet voice behind them.

Molly and Kip turned to see Alistair. "You?" she said, unable to hide her surprise.

The Windsors were all looking at Alistair now, but Alistair kept his eyes on Kip. "It's my fault you've got no crutch." He lowered his head. "It's only right that I go with you."

Constance sat up, clutching her husband's hands to her breast. "Bertie, you can't let him. Tell him he can't go . . ."

The house shook again. Molly heard one final, bloody scream, and then the room upstairs went silent.

Fig and Stubbs were gone.

Molly ran to Alistair's side and cut the ropes around his ankles and hands. "You dinna have to do this," she said.

"I know." He stood tall. "But I want to." He went to Kip and threaded one arm under Kip's shoulder.

There was another burst of wind, and the green door flew off its hinges, crashing down the stairs and landing in front of the family.

Bertrand gasped, clutching his wife's hand. "It's him . . ."

"The night man," Penny whispered.

The whole family watched in horror as the Gardener stepped into the hall. He stood at the top of the stairs, the axe still in his hand. His cloak was slick with something wet and dark. Molly did not think it was sap.

Alistair backed toward the open front door, Kip supported by his shoulder. "You said he doesn't like it when you hurt the tree?" Alistair said.

"Aye," Molly answered.

Alistair grabbed hold of a thick branch growing through the wall beside him. "Then he'll hate this." He pulled down on the branch with his full weight. The limb snapped, breaking away from the wall.

The Gardener flinched, dropping the axe. He howled in pain, clutching his hand to his chest.

"Catch as catch can!" Alistair cried as he and Kip disappeared out the front door.

HIDE-AND-GO-SEEK

Kip staggered down the gravel drive, his arm over Alistair's shoulder, trying to keep apace. "We need to draw him to the woods on the far side of the island," he said. "We'll be safe there." He knew a place where the tree's roots had not yet grown—a place where the Night Gardener couldn't reach them. They only had to get there alive.

A furious howling swept down the drive, nearly knocking him over.

"He's too fast," Kip said, gasping. "We'll never outrun him."

"We don't need to." Alistair veered off the driveway onto the lawn. He let go of Kip, who collapsed to the grass. "I'll meet you at the woods," he said and dropped to his knees. Kip watched him disappear behind a nearby hill. Once in the shadows, he was completely hidden from view.

The sky overhead was lit by a harvest moon, which shone bright over the lawn. Kip lay flat on the ground, marshaling his wits. He tried to remember the hours they had spent playing on the lawn. *It's just like hide-and-go-seek*, he told himself. Only he knew it wasn't. This time, getting caught didn't make you "it"—getting caught made you dead. He closed his eyes, wishing desperately that he had something to hold. Wishing that he had Courage.

Kip heard a howling behind him. He peered over the top of the hill. The Gardener stood in front of the house, searching the grounds. Kip pressed his body to the grass, making himself as flat as possible. Slowly he raised up on one elbow and pulled his body a few inches forward. He did this over and over again until he was one hill closer to his destination.

The crawling hurt—not just his bad leg, but his whole body. He thought of Molly and the Windsors. If he didn't reach the woods, they were lost. Kip kept an ear to the air, trying to tell the Night Gardener's location by the sound of the wind.

A shadow slid over his body, and he felt a shiver in the air. He looked up to see the Gardener beside him, his lightless eyes scanning the tree line. Kip stared up at him, afraid to move, afraid to breathe—

Pok!

A rock struck the Night Gardener's back. He snarled, turning away from Kip.

"Over here!" shouted a voice. Alistair appeared from behind a nearby hill. He blew a raspberry and then disappeared into the grass. The Gardener stormed after him, a cyclone of leaves in his wake.

Kip could hear the Gardener searching the lawn where Alistair had been. He grabbed a rock next to him, pulled himself upright, and threw the rock as hard as he could—

Pok!

It was a perfect shot. The Night Gardener's hat tumbled from his head. Kip let out a triumphant laugh and then dropped down. By the time the Gardener reached the spot, Kip was already gone.

Pok!

    Pok!

        Pok!

            Pok!

The two boys slowly worked their way along the lawn, throwing rocks as they went. The Gardener raced from hill to hill, enraged, confused. Kip grinned, feeling a thrill that was altogether new to him. He and Alistair were working as a team—doing something that neither of them could have accomplished alone.

Kip saw a row of moonlit trees just ahead. Somehow, impossibly, he had made it! He heard a snarling sound as a gust of wind knocked him backward. He rolled over to see the Gardener racing toward him, his clothes tattered, a halo of angry leaves swirling around him. "Alistair?" Kip called, trying and failing to pick himself up.

Kip saw movement from the corner of his eye. "Run!" Alistair shouted, grabbing hold of his arm. Kip felt his body jerk across the ground as the two of them staggered into the woods.

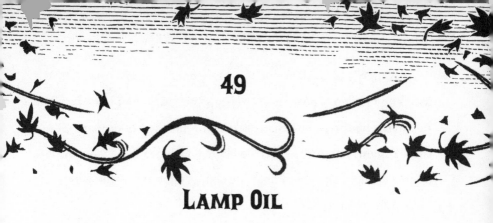

49

LAMP OIL

Wind slithered in a circle around the house, sending leaves high into the air. Fig and Stubbs's horse had run off in the storm, but Galileo was still there, waiting for instructions. "As loyal as you are stubborn," Molly said, patting his flank. The horse gave a nervous snort, raking the gravel with his hoof.

Molly went back inside to fetch Penny. The girl was not injured, but she was frightened, and she gripped Molly tightly about the neck. Molly lifted her over the side of the wagon. "Watch your feet," she said, setting the girl onto the wooden bed.

Penny scrambled to her knees and gripped Molly's hand. "Will Kip and Alistair be safe from the night man?"

Molly stared into her face, wishing she knew how to answer. She wanted to tell her a story to make her feel better, to make her brave. But there were some things that stories couldn't do. "The truth is, Miss Penny, I dinna know." She patted the girl's hand. "But I wouldn't worry just yet. Brothers are sneaky."

Penny nodded sagely. "That's true."

An angry gust of air swept past Molly and struck the wagon, nearly toppling Galileo. "Easy, boy," Molly said, grabbing his tackle. She pulled the hair from her eyes, looking toward the woods. Kip was out there somewhere. And so was the Night Gardener. For a moment, she almost thought she could hear his shouts echoing on the wind. She hoped desperately that she was wrong.

"I have you, my love. Just a few more steps . . ." Master Windsor appeared in the doorway, holding Constance in his arms. The woman was clinging to his neck, her head on his chest. Her eyes were open and her body heaved with shallow, pained breaths. "I have you," Bertrand whispered. "I have you."

Molly pushed aside the canisters of oil to make room in the bed of the wagon. "Sorry, mum. It's hardly a coach and four." Master Windsor laid his wife down as one might lay a paper boat on the water.

Molly shut the gate. "We'll get 'em both to safety, sir, and then wait by the road for Kip and Alistair." She indicated for him to climb aboard.

Bertrand nodded, but he did not move. His eyes were fixed on the woods—a black mass crested by moonlight. "That *thing* is after them . . . ," he said.

"They'll be fine," she said as much to herself as to Bertrand. "Kip's outrun the Gardener before. He knows a special place where the monster canna follow."

"But they might not *reach* the safe place," Bertrand snapped. "Your brother's lame. Alistair is just a boy . . ." He ran a shaking hand through his hair, no doubt imagining his only son alone in the darkness. Or was he imagining his parents on a night like this all those years before?

A hollow roar shook the valley. "It's no use thinkin' about it, sir. Kip and Alistair bought us some time, and we best take it. They're on their own now."

Bertrand fixed his eyes on her. "But what if we could *help* them? You said the only way to stop this Night Gardener is to kill the tree . . ."

Molly shook her head. "I don't know for sure."

Bertrand reached over the side and seized one of the oil canisters from the bed. "So let's kill the tree and find out."

50

MOONLIGHT

U p that way!" Kip called, pointing toward a patch of light in the distance. He and Alistair raced through the moonlit woods, black branches all around them. They were running toward the ancient garden at the edge of the island—the place the Night Gardener could not reach. "If we can just make it to that patch o' light, we'll be safe."

"We'll make it." Alistair adjusted his grip around Kip's side, putting more of Kip's weight onto his own body. Kip glanced up at the boy, whose face was set with determination.

The Gardener's howl rang out behind them, and wind struck Kip's back, knocking him to the ground. Kip cried out as pain wrenched through his side. Branches rattled as the Night Gardener appeared to burst from the shadows behind them. He was not walking slowly as he usually did—he was running, his face lit white by the moon.

"Come on!" Alistair grabbed Kip, pulling him up from the ground. They staggered over rocks and roots. So long as they could still see the glowing light, they had a hope of survival. Kip thought of his sister back at the house. She and the others should be on the wagon by now—almost safe. Kip doubled his speed, his eyes fixed on the shining garden—now less than a hundred feet away.

The wind stopped around them, and Kip could tell their pursuer had slowed his pace. He glanced back to see the Gardener standing with both hands outstretched. The man uttered a low, inhuman moan as he worked the air like a weaver at his loom.

"Why'd he stop?" Alistair said, gasping for breath.

The Night Gardener's call grew louder. A chill slid up Kip's spine as he felt the wind change, coming alive. Cold mist lifted from the ground, shivering the treetops as it rose higher and higher into the air.

Kip peered up through the moonlit branches. "The sky," he said. "It's changin'..."

The mist swirled and condensed above the treetops, forming an impenetrable fog that blocked out the stars and covered the moon. Kip looked back at the Night Gardener. In the fading light, he caught a final image of the man's face, contorted in a tight smile—

And then the woods went dark.

"We gotta keep movin'—now!" Kip grabbed Alistair's arm, but when he turned towards the garden, he saw nothing but a wall of darkness.

"Which way?" Alistair said, panicked.

Kip scanned the shadows, looking for light to guide them, looking for safety.

The moon had been blotted out.

And with it, their only hope.

51

THE HERO AND THE DAMSEL

Molly was wary of Master Windsor's idea—many people had tried to cut the tree down, and none had succeeded before the Night Gardener could stop them. But she and Master Windsor had something faster than an axe or a saw—thanks to Kip, they had enough oil to set the world ablaze.

Master Windsor set to preparing the tree while Molly led the wagon to safety. She had asked Penny to sit up on the bench with her so that the girl could see how driving worked. When she reached the road at the far end of the bridge, she stopped. "It's your turn now, Miss Penny." She handed the reins to the girl, who clutched the leather straps with white-knuckled intensity. "Now, if somethin' happens— if the fire gets too big or the night man shows up—I want you to snap these reins as hard as you can." She made a motion. "Just like that."

Penny nodded.

"You keep snappin' till your arms feel like they're gonna fall off— and not a moment before. Can I trust you to do that?"

Penny placed a hand to her heart. "Mummy is my damsel. I will protect her with my very life."

Molly made an impressed face. "Who's the hero now?" She squeezed Penny's hands—*Not good-bye*, she told herself—and climbed down from the bench.

"Thank you," said a thin voice in her ear. "For what you've done." It was Mistress Windsor. She was sitting up, a blanket wrapped tight around her frail shoulders.

Molly shook her head. "Don't thank me, mum. It's Kip and Alistair who done the brave thing."

"Not that." Constance smiled gently. "For what you've done to *him*." She stared out across the bridge toward the house. In the distance, Molly could see Bertrand in front of the tree, emptying a large canister of oil over the black roots. His coat was off, and his sleeves were rolled up. "For the first time in a long time . . . I feel as though I have my husband back." In the dim light, Molly could almost picture a different Bertrand Windsor—strong, determined, the man Constance had fallen in love with all those years before. A howl shuttered through the forest, and heavy clouds slid over the moon, leaving them in darkness.

"Let's make sure he sticks around." Molly took a box of matches from the wagon and ran back to the house. When she reached the tree, Bertrand was shaking the final drops from a canister. He threw the empty container onto the lawn.

"That's the last one," he said, wiping his hands.

"Then it's time." She handed him the box of matches and a stone from the drive.

Bertrand opened the box and removed a single match. "My hands are shaking," he said.

Molly stared up at the tree, its black branches spreading out like a poison across the moonless sky. "They should be."

Bertrand took a deep breath. He drew his match against the stone. It burst to life. He held the tiny flame over the roots—

And let the match fall.

52

COURAGE

Kip and Alistair clung to each other, staggering through complete darkness. The two of them were lost beyond all hope. Kip couldn't even tell where the house was anymore. The Gardener's windy voice hissed in his ear. Now that the moon had vanished, they had no way to find safe ground. Every direction they ran, it seemed like the Night Gardener was waiting for them. Branches rattled around them, clawing at their clothes and face. "I dinna know where to go!" Kip said, panting.

They heard a hiss of wind and leapt backward, changing direction once more. "Why won't he show himself?" Alistair said, his voice choked with fear.

"He's havin' fun with us," Kip said. He craned his neck, searching for some clue of where to run next. His heart pounded in his ears. "That way!" he said, spotting some light between the trees. He and Alistair ran as fast as they could over rocks and bramble. They broke through into a clearing—

"Wait!" Alistair cried, pulling Kip back.

Kip looked down, realizing only now that he had very nearly run them off the edge of a cliff. He stared at the river rushing beneath him—black and cold.

Kip heard a twig snap. He turned around to see the Night Gardener standing behind them, a grim smile on his face. He had led them to the edge of the water. "We're cornered," he said. "It's him or the river."

The Gardener took another step closer. He was standing right over them now, a look of amusement in his bottomless eyes. Kip adjusted his footing, feeling the soil crumble away beneath his boots.

The Gardener had scarcely moved when a thundering roar shook the night. He snarled, staggering backward. He swatted at his clothes, collapsing to the ground. Kip could see tiny flames licking at the bottoms of his feet. The flames climbed up his cloak, slowly spreading. Wind howled around the Gardener—but the flames would not go out.

"What . . . what's happening to him?" Alistair said. "Why is he burning?"

Kip looked past the Night Gardener toward the house. In the distance he could see a faint orange glow rising up to the sky. "It ain't him that's burnin'," he said. "It's the tree—they're trying to kill it!"

The Night Gardener spun around, howling in the direction of the house.

Alistair grabbed Kip's arm. "If he gets there before they're done, he'll bury them all. We have to stop him!"

Kip swallowed, barely able to stand. He needed to buy his sister more time. He searched the darkness for a weapon—something to swing or throw—anything that might stop the Night Gardener.

Over the roar of flames, Kip could hear the black river rushing behind him. He pushed past Alistair and grabbed hold of the man's burning cloak. "We know you don't like fire—let's see what you think o' water." He charged for the edge of the cliff, sending himself—and the Night Gardener—into the river below.

The Conflagration

The house crackled and roared like a giant's funeral pyre. Molly shielded her face from the heat, watching with Master Windsor. Windows shattered and bricks crumbled as the flames engulfed the entire house, spewing black smoke into the air. But even as the fire roared, the tree remained unharmed. Icy wind whipped through its branches, beating back the flames as quickly as they could spread.

"It's not working," Master Windsor shouted above the din.

Molly flinched as something crashed down inside the house, sending sparks and flaming debris out the front door. "It's no good," she said. "That fire could burn for days and nothin'd happen to the tree."

She glanced back at the forest, which was alive with thrashing wind. She wondered where Kip was and why he hadn't yet returned. Bertrand rested a hand on her shoulder. "We have to run," he said. "We tried, but there's no more time."

Molly glared at the tree. There *had* to be a weak spot somewhere—a soft underbelly, a chink in the armor—some way to hurt the tree. Her eyes fell on the tiny window on the second floor. "I think I know what to do," she said. She broke from Master Windsor and ran toward the flaming house, matchbox clutched in her hand.

Close up, the fire was even more awesome. It blinded her eyes and sucked the air from her lungs. She felt Bertrand grab her arm. "I'm not letting you go in there alone!" he shouted.

"I'm not asking permission. You got a family that needs a father."

She was right, and Bertrand knew it. "If the Gardener comes back," he said, "I'll slow him down."

Molly turned and sprinted through the front door. Flames covered the walls inside, creeping along the rafters and floorboards. A veil of black smoke blurred the air, stinging her eyes. She covered her mouth and picked her way over a fallen beam to the staircase. She sprinted up the steps, jumping over spots where the runner had caught fire.

Molly reached the top of the stairs and ran through the open doorway. The heat was less intense there, and she could breathe without coughing. Compared to the rest of the house, the room seemed almost calm. The floor was thick with the ashes of burned banknotes. Little embers swirled gently through the air like snowflakes. In one corner, Molly saw two shapes that might have been the late Misters Fig and Stubbs, now corpses. She turned away, fixing her eyes on the knothole. It waited for her like an open gullet.

Molly clutched the matchbox in her sweating hand. She opened it and removed a single match. "Open wide." She struck the match and brought it to the open mouth—

Phoof!

A sharp breath of air knocked the match from her fingers. It fell to the floor, disappearing into the ashes.

Molly took a second match and struck it—

Phoof!

Another gust of wind, this one stronger.

She peered outside through the shattered window. The Night Gardener emerged from the edge of the woods, staggering, his tattered cloak hanging from his body like a wet skin. The light from the fire reflected off his dripping face, making him look red, angry.

The Gardener waved a hand, and a gust of wind shook the house. Molly grabbed the wall to keep from falling. She heard a crashing downstairs and a scream of pain. She rushed into the hall and saw Master Windsor sprawled on the foyer floor. He staggered to his feet, wiping blood from his face. "Whatever you're doing up there," he shouted over the roaring flames, "I suggest you do it quickly!" He grabbed the axe lying beside him and charged back outside.

Molly searched the hallway for something bigger than a match— something the tree couldn't blow out. She grabbed hold of a banister rail that was burning on one end like a torch. She ripped it from the floor and ran back into the room—

PHOOF!

This time the air hit her like a wave, knocking her hard against the wall. She shrieked, throwing the extinguished torch at the trunk. It was useless—the tree would allow nothing to pass.

Smoke filled the room, stinging her eyes. Molly stared at the tree, tears running down her cheeks. She had tried to kill a monster, and the monster had won. A black ember floated past her—the final remains of a banknote. She smiled bitterly, thinking how quickly dreams could be reduced to nothing. The little scrap spun and swooped and then disappeared into the knothole. Molly sat forward, blinking—

The banknote had gone *into* the knothole.

"Not a banknote," she whispered. "A *gift*." All at once she understood. The only things the tree would take in were *its own gifts*.

Flames swelled around Molly as wind coursed through the house. She heard a crashing sound from downstairs and a furious roar. The Night Gardener was coming.

Molly scrambled to her knees, searching through the rubble for another banknote. But as she raked her fingers through the char, she could find nothing. She shrieked again, throwing black ashes at the wall. The banknotes were gone—just like all the tree's gifts.

And that was when Molly remembered.

There was one thing remaining.

She slid a hand into her pocket. Her heartbeat quickened. Nestled safely between the folds of fabric, she could feel them waiting for her—

The letters.

54

ASHES

S moke billowed in from the hall, stinging Molly's eyes. She pulled the stack of worn envelopes from her pocket and stared at the word written across the top envelope—

Molly

She held the letters close, tears spilling down her cheeks.

The walls around her were consumed with flames. Molly touched the letters to the fire, and they caught almost at once. The paper crackled and curled as the flames spread. She raised the burning envelopes in her trembling hands and walked toward the tree. "Good-bye," she said and dropped them into the knothole. The letters disappeared into the black abyss—

Falling...
Falling...
Falling...

Molly heard a cracking noise as the fire took hold somewhere deep inside the tree. The sound grew louder. Orange light flickered in the hollow darkness, growing brighter and brighter until hot flames burst from the knothole, consuming the tree.

She heard a wheezing breath in her ear and turned to see the Night Gardener in the hall. His pale skin was charred and cracked. His hat was gone, and from his tattered clothes wafted a thin trail of black smoke. He hissed at Molly, his lips pulled back in a hateful rictus.

She was trapped inside the room, flames on every side. She inched back from the man. The Night Gardener lunged at her—

Snap!

He howled as his foot broke off from his leg. He clung to the doorway, still staring at her, his eyes two smoldering embers of rage. Smoke now billowed out from his clothes, his mouth, his every pore. He pulled himself upright and took another step—

Snap!

He fell as his other leg broke off at the knee, turning to ash. He hissed, dragging his body toward her. He reached out a trembling hand.

Snap!

His fingers crumbled into fine dust, peppering the floor. With a final wheezing sound, the Gardener collapsed into a pile of ash.

Molly clutched her hands to her racing heart, staring at the remains of the Night Gardener.

They had fought the monster.

And they had won.

It took Molly a moment to realize that the house was coming down around her. She leapt back as part of the ceiling fell through in a shower of sparks. She coughed, covering her face, and ran to the shattered window. She hoisted herself up on the frame and clambered onto the roof.

Outside, the flames were even wilder. They roared like an ocean in her ears. She looked out over the eaves—the ground below seemed to twist and waffle in the blistering heat. Somewhere in the distance, she thought she could hear Bertrand shouting her name. And more distant still, she thought she could hear her parents.

Through the quivering heat, she saw Master Windsor dragging his wife's mattress across the lawn, feathers trailing behind him. He brought it below the house. Just below Molly's feet. She took aim and jumped—

Molly hit the mattress with a hard crash. She rolled onto the grass, clutching her ankle, which felt sprained. A faint voice sounded in her ear. She opened her eyes to see Bertrand kneeling over her. He took her by the shoulders and pulled her upright. Master Windsor dragged her across the lawn, shouting something that sounded like "The house! The house!"

Suddenly she heard a tremendous ripping sound. She looked back to see the tree and house collapsing in a giant explosion of flames. Molly stared at the mountain of fire, tears filling her eyes. "It's over," she said, her voice hoarse.

Master Windsor held her shoulders. "It's over!"

They held each other, hugging with everything in them.

Already the flames had begun to die down, the roar replaced by a low, crackling murmur. It was above this sound that Molly heard a new voice.

"Papa! Molly! Hurry!" Molly looked toward the road.

Penny was running toward them, waving her arms.

Molly clung to Master Windsor, both rushing to meet the girl.

"What is it?" Bertrand said.

"It's your brother!" Penny stepped to one side, and beyond her Molly saw a heavy figure moving toward them. Alistair, his face and clothes dripping wet, and clutched in his arms was Kip.

"Kip!" Molly let go of Master Windsor and stumbled toward them.

Alistair fell to his knees and lay Kip's body on the ground. "I'm sorry," he said, gasping. "He jumped in the river . . . He saved us . . ."

Molly stared at her brother who was limp and unmoving. His mouth was open, but Molly could hear no breath. A cry crept up through her chest and came out as a whimper. "No," she said. "No, no, no, no, no . . . Not Kip. Not him."

She took his dripping body, pulling him to her chest. "You canna do this," she whispered, a desperate, tuneless keen. "You canna die . . . Not you . . . Not you . . ." Molly could sense people standing around her, but she could not see them. She did not care. All she cared about was Kip. She buried her face in his wet hair and closed her eyes. She tried to find words, something she could say, something to bring him back. And in the darkness, the words came to her—

There . . . once . . . was . . .

Molly swallowed, and she spoke the words aloud. "There once was . . . a little boy named Kip." She swallowed again, forcing back tears. "He was a very special little boy, like none other. He had red hair like his father, and green eyes like his mother, and a fightin' spirit like the devil himself. But most of all . . . he had a sister who loved him more than anythin' in the whole world." She pressed her lips together. "But one day, that sister made a mistake . . . And she didn't care for him like he needed, like he deserved. And she didn't tell him the truth." She closed her eyes, unable to go on. "I'm sorry," she whispered into his ear and then released him. "I'm sorry."

Kip lay motionless, his face lit bright against the flames. His body shuddered. He coughed, his head lurching forward, gulping for air. Water spewed from his mouth, spilling over his chin and neck.

Molly leapt back, startled. "Kip!" She hunched over him, afraid to touch him, afraid that what she was seeing might not be real.

Kip gasped, shivering, blinking into the firelight. He swallowed, catching his breath. "Wha . . . ?" His eyes met Molly's, and a faint smile crept across his lips. "What happened next?"

55

WHAT HAPPENED NEXT

The flames died down just before dawn. Where the house and tree had once stood, there was now only a mountain of black ashes that smoldered gently in the dewy light of early morning. Already the life of the valley had begun to encroach upon the long-decaying island, and all around her, Molly could hear birds and insects chirping and buzzing.

The fire had been bright enough to attract attention from the village. And with the morning light came a few brave locals, who marveled at what they saw. Even without knowing the truth about the tree, it was plain to anyone who set foot in this place that the sourwoods were cursed no more. Word spread quickly within Cellar Hollow, and soon men and women were appearing on the long-neglected road—to see the burned remains, perhaps, but also to leave baskets of food and blankets and clothes for the Windsors.

The gifts were welcome, for the great fire had consumed every last piece of the Windsors' former lives—everything, that is, *but* their lives. And for that, they were all of them grateful.

Molly walked along the dew-kissed lawn, enjoying the warm, charcoal air. The smell of new beginnings. She smiled, watching Penny and Alistair play among the hills.

"Look!" Alistair shouted, pointing at what might have been a grasshopper or butterfly. "The fairy's getting away!"

"I've got it! I've got it! I've got it!" Penny shrieked, hands swiping the air.

Molly knew that Alistair was too old to chase insects, let alone fairies. He was making believe for his sister's benefit, and it was working: Penny leapt between hills with an almost manic glee—her cheeks flushed with color. Some might have thought it disrespectful for children to play among the dead, but Molly knew differently. She knew that among those hills lay Penny and Alistair's own grandparents. Molly could almost picture them, resting underground—listening happily as the children of their child laughed and ran overhead.

Constance approached Molly's side. The woman still looked thin from her sickness, but she was standing on her own. "Listen to them play," she said, her voice touched with awe. "It's like music." She looked at Molly, her eyes creased as she smiled. "We have you to thank for that."

Molly shifted her feet. "I'm just the help, mum."

Constance laughed—the first real laugh Molly had heard from her in all their time together. She took a deep, hungry breath, surveying the world around her. "Things are going to be different this time. Better."

"I'm glad to hear it," Molly said. "I suppose you're movin' back to town?"

The woman shook her head. "We're staying here. Some people from the village have offered to let us stay with them until we can re-build a home. Bertrand had a bit of insurance on the house. It won't be much money, but it will be enough." She turned to Molly. "We might even have room for a few more . . . not as servants, you understand. As family." She took Molly's hand, and Molly was surprised by the warmth coursing through the woman's fingers.

Molly felt tears spring to her eyes. "Mum, I . . . I dinna know what to say." A part of her wanted to say yes, to live forever in this new place. But she knew it wouldn't be right. The Windsors needed time to rebuild themselves—time to be a family. And some things, Molly knew, had to be done alone. "It's kind of you, mum, it is. But Kip and me belong somewhere else . . . and it's my job to find that place."

The woman smiled, and Molly could see that she understood.

"Look who I found!" called a voice from the trees. Molly turned to see Master Windsor emerge from the woods, Galileo in tow. The horse, who had run off in the fire, was covered in brambles and burrs and specks of mud.

Master Windsor caught up to them, a little out of breath but smil-ing all the same. "I found him in the woods by the riverbed. He was munching on these." He drew a bouquet of flowers from behind his back and offered them to his wife. They were not magic glowing night flowers but plain spring wildflowers—and they were lovely.

Constance took the bouquet, pressing it to her nose. "Oh, Bertrand..." She clutched them to her chest as if these flowers were more precious than all the diamonds in the world.

Molly looked between them and started to feel as if she maybe shouldn't be there. And she was right—no sooner had she led Galileo away than Master Windsor pulled his wife close and kissed her, right there in broad daylight!

Molly walked the horse to her brother, who was standing at the remains of the house. Steam rose from the warm embers as they crackled in the early light. "It's almost beautiful," Molly said, standing behind him.

Kip nodded but did not move. "I keep thinkin' about all of it. About the tree, these graves, the Gardener—"

"He canna hurt us."

"I know, I just . . ." Kip shook his head. "He was once a regular gardener, like me. Them flowers in the woods, he planted 'em, cared for 'em. Then the tree came along, and he cared for that, too. What was his crime? Makin' a wish? Wantin' something that couldn't be?" Kip blinked his eyes. "That's no different than me. So why did I deserve to live?"

Molly put a hand on his shoulder. "We'll never know. And maybe that's best. It's a bad tale that has all the answers."

Kip hopped back, looking at her. "I suppose there's one difference between him an' me. He didn't have *you* protectin' him. Ma an' Da done right to trust you."

Molly pulled her mouth tight, not wanting to cry. "Just you wait. There's time for me to kill us both yet." She mussed his hair and led him toward the wagon. She was surprised to feel his hand on her arm, using her for support as they went.

The Windsors assembled on the drive to see Molly and Kip off. Master Windsor had loaded up the back of the wagon with several baskets of food—telling Molly that it was far more than his family could want. He also gave them blankets and some clothes. Molly accepted the offerings with a polite nod.

"But *why* do you have to leave?" Penny said as they loaded up the last of their things. Her face was pinched and prickled with red, her fists clenched—an imitation of anger.

Molly knelt down. "Oh, Miss Penny." She stroked the girl's hair. Her wiry black strands were softer and touched with an auburn hue that almost glowed in the sunlight. "You're old enough to look after yourself now. Besides, Kip an' me got our own road ahead of us. I promise, though, you've not seen the last of me."

"Will you . . . ?" The girl took an enormous, trembling breath. "Will you visit often?"

"I canna say." Molly smiled. "But when I do, I expect you'll give me a good and proper tucking-in. Fair?" She crossed her heart to show she was serious.

Penny did the same. "Fair." She wrapped her arms around Molly's neck, squeezing her with surprising strength.

There were more hugs and good-byes and a good share of tears.

Molly even saw Alistair shyly approach the wagon and offer Kip a crudely formed branch, which he had shaped into a crutch—a new Courage. She was pleased to see Kip take it and shake his hand. At last, Molly and Kip climbed onto the bench of the wagon and, with a flick of the reins, Kip steered them across the bridge and up into the valley.

56

STORYTELLER AT THE CROSSROADS

Molly and her brother rode in silence for some time, each of them mulling over all they had seen and experienced, and what they were leaving behind. When they reached the crossroads, Kip pulled the reins, stopping the wagon. "Where to?" he said.

Molly squinted against the sun. The road spread out before them in three directions, all of them glowing with dew and steam. "I got no idea." She slid a hand into her coat pocket. A smile played on the corners of her mouth.

"What is it?" Kip said.

Molly pulled her hand out, showing Kip the oilskin parcel that Hester had left them. It was very light and fit easily in the palm of her hand. "She said it was somethin' special. Somethin' we might want."

Kip leaned close. "You think we should open it?"

"I think the time might be right." Molly carefully removed the twine. She unfurled the oilskin, holding her hand underneath to catch whatever was inside. But nothing came out. "The skin's empty," she said, feeling a twinge of disappointment.

"No, it ain't." Kip took the skin from her and turned it over. He spread it out on the bench between them, smoothing out the creases. The inside of the skin was marked with faded blue lines that ran together to make roads and rivers and mountains and seas.

"It's a map," Molly whispered.

"And look!" Kip pointed to a place in the topmost corner where the land had been marked with a red dot. "Do you think it's a buried treasure?"

Molly shook her head. She ran her fingers over the skin, tracing the roads. She recalled Hester's words. She had said she wasn't the "settling-down" type. "I think . . . I think it's a home!"

"How do you know that?"

Molly shrugged. She thought of the look in the woman's eye as she handed Molly this final offering. "I just have a feelin'." Molly smiled.

"A home, eh?" Kip took the map, staring at the twisting little roads. "It looks like an awfully long way," he said. "We've little food and less money."

Molly peered into the trees. Somewhere in the distance, she thought she could hear the faint honeybee drone of an old hurdy-gurdy. "I bet there's more than a few folks willing to swap room and board for a good story." She winked at Kip. "And I know a whopper."

Kip took the reins, urging Galileo onto the middle path. The wagon rocked and rattled as it rolled over the muddy road. "I hear there's dragons in some lake up north." he said. "Maybe we can stop on the way?"

"Oh, they're a sight to behold!" Molly put an arm around her brother. "If we're lucky, maybe the flyin' ones will be out for summer!"

Molly and her brother swapped stories as their little wagon carried them out of the valley and into the warm light of the new day.

Author's Note

Writing this story was a story in and of itself. Nine years and countless drafts stand between the original idea and the book you now hold. I would be remiss in not mentioning some of the books, facts, and people who helped me along the way.

The first and greatest inspiration was *Something Wicked This Way Comes* by Ray Bradbury. My father read this book aloud to me when I was eleven years old, and it scared me silly. Indeed, it was during a *Something Wicked*—inspired nightmare that I caught my first glimpse of the Night Gardener. I have since always imagined that the Gardener's haunting visage lurked just beneath the surface of Mr. G. M. Dark's smile.

Another crucial work was *The Sketch-Book of Geoffrey Crayon, Gent.* by Washington Irving. This book long ago taught me the rare pleasure of stories that contain both horror and humor. It includes many famous episodes, chief among them "The Legend of Sleepy Hollow" and "Rip Van Winkle." At some point while writing *The Night Gardener*, I became lost in the gloom of the Windsors' plight, and in desperation

I went back to Irving. It was there I rediscovered a character I had all but forgotten: the roving story collector Geoffrey Crayon. Behind every tale hides Irving's kind, mysterious storyteller, who guides readers safely through the darkest valleys; it was while reading this character that I first heard the voice of Hester Kettle, asking an important question about the difference between a story and a lie.

Two other favorite works helped me to better understand Molly and Kip. The first was *The Secret Garden* by Frances Hodgson Burnett, whose characters are seeded into every page. An even greater inspiration was "Courage" by J. M. Barrie. "Courage" is not a book but a speech delivered to the students of the University of St. Andrews in 1922. It is as brilliant and stirring as anything you might expect from the man who wrote *Peter Pan*. "Courage" is about a walking stick, a storyteller named M'Connachie, and what it means to fight for peace. Most important, it is about what young people are to do in a world in which adults have failed to care for them. These are by no means the only works that inspired *The Night Gardener*, but they are the ones without which I could not have written my story.

History played a role in *The Night Gardener* as well. Being married to a Victorian scholar, I spend a lot of my time learning interesting facts about the nineteenth century—and by interesting I mean *horrifying*. Chief among them is the Great Famine in Ireland. The famine (or "The Great Hunger," as it was often called) brought untold devastation to the people of Ireland. Between 1845 and 1852, an estimated one million men, women, and children died from starvation and disease. The problem was not a lack of food but the fact that the good food grown in Ireland was shipped to England, leaving only blighted potatoes behind for the farmers and their families.

Molly's family and hundreds of thousands like it were forced to flee the country in search of work and food, first journeying to England and later to North America. The exact number of those who left Ireland is unknown, as few ships kept passenger lists. What is known is that these ships were very dangerous. One in five people who boarded a ship bound for America died at sea from disease or starvation—which led to these vessels being called "coffin ships." These were not the only dangers. In 1850 alone, over a dozen ships were destroyed in storms that tore through the Atlantic Ocean and the Irish Sea. Those who did manage to reach their destination were—like Molly and Kip—often greeted with derision and scorn.

While Ireland continued to suffer into the 1850s, England began to enjoy remarkable prosperity. The expansion of empire, development of the middle class, and spread of industrialization created tremendous wealth in the Victorian era. There were, of course, many people left behind. Poverty among the lowest classes was devastating, especially in the cities, which were overrun with beggars. Even those in the middle class were not safe—more than a few men like Bertrand Windsor found themselves in debtors' prison or worse.

The Victorian era was perhaps the last point in Western history when magic and science were allowed to coexist. As the world's understanding of science and the natural world grew, so, too, did a fascination with magic, spirits, and fairy stories. In 1882, English scientists banded together to form the Society for Psychical Research, a group dedicated to investigating the paranormal. Great rational minds, like philosopher William James (brother of *Turn of the Screw* author Henry James) and Sir Arthur Conan Doyle, dedicated their later careers to the investigation of ghosts and spirits. One can only imagine what Doctor Crouch would have thought of all this! It was while learning about these early ghost hunters as a boy that I first developed a desire to tell a ghost story of my own.

Beyond these sources, I have been helped in much more tangible ways by numerous friends and colleagues: Sally Alexander, Jim Armstrong, Katherine Ayres, Chad Beckerman, Tamar Brazis, Caroline Carlson, Liam Flanagan, Markus Hoffman, Doris Hutton, Lynne Missen, Joseph Regal, Thomas Sweterlitsch, Kate Weiss, Jason Wells, John Wheeler, and, above all, Mary Elizabeth Burke. To these people I say, *Thank you.* Your support is more than I could wish for.

✦ ABOUT THE AUTHOR ✦

JONATHAN AUXIER teaches creative writing and children's literature. He is the author of *Peter Nimble and His Fantastic Eyes* and *Sophie Quire and the Last Storyguard*. He lives in Pittsburgh with his family. Visit him online at www.TheScop.com.

READER'S GUIDE
DISCUSSION QUESTIONS

1 Molly and Kip meet Hester Kettle and learn that the old woman is a storyteller. Molly is intrigued by this line of work, as she thinks of herself as quite a talented storyteller. She has told stories to get her brother out of an orphanage. She has told stories to get a free horse. Is it OK to tell stories, if the goal is to make someone feel better about a bad situation? What do you think the difference is between a story and a lie?

2 Kip's father named his crutch "Courage," explaining that all good tools deserve a title. Why do you think he gave it this name? Think of a "tool" you use every day (pencil, pen, notebook, backpack, phone, game controller, etc.) and give it an appropriate name. Why did you choose this name?

3 Alistair is a rotten sort of character for most of the story. He's rude and horrible to many of the people around him, but he saves his worst behavior for his little sister, Penny, and then Kip. Why do you think he directs his spite toward them? Why does he change his behavior at the end of the book?

4 After Master Windsor gets himself into deep trouble with Stubbs and Fig, the children see him removing items from the dining room and taking jewels from his wife. One thing he takes is Mistress Windsor's ring. Mistress Windsor is later seen by Molly leaving the room with the green door wearing that same ring. Why is the ring so special to her? Why does she constantly replace it, even though it holds no real monetary value?

5 When Molly finally comes face to face with the knothole in the room with the green door, she hears gentle wave sounds and notices that the knothole is full of seawater and smells of home. The tree knows her heart's desire. What would you hear inside the knothole? Molly was given a letter by the tree. What gift might you find from the tree?

6 Alistair uses his gift from the tree for sweets, which seems insignificant compared with the tree's other gifts. Why do you think Alistair receives sweets? Is his heart's desire truly for candy or for something more meaningful?

7 When Kip and Molly run into Hester Kettle at the market, they complain about the difficulty they're having finding a decent deal. Hester offers to help them get a better price at the market stalls. How does she get the vendors to give her a better deal? Is this fair?

8 Bertrand was haunted by memories of his family and the Windsor manor, yet he still brought his family to live there. Why did he choose to return? Do you think he understood the risk and possible danger he was putting his family in by moving them from town back to his family house? Why might he have been willing to take such a risk?

9 The Night Gardener seems to have once been a simple gardener doing his job, just like Kip. He started out needing little, asking the tree only for time to continue tending his beloved blossoms. What thoughts do you have about the original gardener? Was he driven toward evil, or did evil find him?

10 Why does Dr. Crouch ridicule Molly and Kip for being Irish? Can you think of times in the story when the differences between being English and being Irish appear? Can you think of people who are similarly mocked for how they look or talk?

11 The entire Windsor household, along with Molly, falls sick with a peculiar illness—their skin goes pale and hair goes dark. Yet Kip remains strong. Why do you think he never gets sick?

SUGGESTED ACTIVITIES

1 A major theme in *The Night Gardener* is "A good story can save the day." Try to imagine a difficult situation you could find yourself in where telling a story might get you out of trouble.

2 Try giving a well-known story a new ending. Or perhaps you'd like to make up a story with a friend, adding sentences back and forth so that it's a collaboration full of mystery and surprise. Have fun telling tales!

3 Reread the paragraphs describing the physical appearance of the Night Man on pages 186–87. Use your imagination to draw the face of the Night Man based on this description. Let him haunt your dreams as you fall asleep tonight!

BONUS MATERIAL CREATED BY J. MICHAEL HUTCHINSON